Patricia Wagoner

The Unexpected Awakening

Inherent Dynamics, Inc.

To my husband and daughter, Jerry and Erica. They are the cornerstones of my life. Their unconditional love, support, and understanding have sustained me throughout the years, filling my heart and soul each and every day. Without them, this work would never have been created.

Acknowledgments

I am deeply grateful to the rest of my family and friends who enrich my life in immeasurable ways. Special thanks to those who read my manuscript and offered invaluable feedback and assistance.

I also want to express my appreciation to Ben Neal for designing my book cover, and to Dulcie Taylor for allowing the use of her lyrics of the song *Love Like Yours and Mine* from her album, Mirrors and Windows.

Patricia Wagoner

Patricia Wagoner

The Unexpected
Awakening

ONE

It was the fourth day straight that she had noticed the same man watching her. His appearance wasn't unique – medium height, lean athletic build, and dark brown hair neatly trimmed. But his ice-blue eyes and penetrating expression sent an unusual sensation down her spine. It seemed like she knew him, but she was certain she had never seen him prior to the cruise. She took her husband's hand as he rested on the deck chair next to her.

"Is something wrong Christine?"

She rolled onto her stomach, the sun hot on her back. "No." She handed him her suntan lotion.

Michael turned on his side and rubbed the lotion into her skin. "Are you sure? You seem tense."

"I'm sure." She forced a reassuring smile but deep inside she could not shake the feeling that overcame her.

He finished rubbing the lotion into her back. "I think I have had enough sun for one afternoon." He sat up in his deck chair, placed the cap back on the suntan lotion, and stretched his arms. "I'm going to shower and head to the casino for a little while before dinner tonight. Care to join me?"

She turned, shielding her eyes from the sun. "No thanks, I think I'll catch a few more rays." She put her head back down on her towel. "If I change my mind, I'll come looking for you at the black jack tables."

"Fair enough." Michael stroked her back one last time before rising from the chair and grabbing his beach towel. He leaned down and kissed her on her cheek. "See you later."

She drifted off to sleep and later awakened to the same unnerving feeling as before.

Startled, she jumped at the sound of a deep male voice sporting a British accent.

"So you decided to take your chances with me?"

She sat up and glanced at the man towering over her. She reached for her beach towel and wrapped it around her shoulders. "I don't know what you are talking about." She leaned down and began placing her sandals on her feet, avoiding eye contact.

"Of course you do." A smile etched its way across the stranger's face. "You've been watching me these last few days as much as I've been watching you."

A spark of anger darted from her eyes. "That's ridiculous!" She finished buckling her sandals, stood up, and walked away, without looking back at him. Her heart pounded wildly as she made her way around the pool deck toward her cabin.

# # #

Michael sat at the black jack table looking at a queen of hearts and a seven of spades deciding whether or not to tap his finger for another card.

"Go for it."

Michael recognized the voice over his right shoulder. He glanced up to see Heather's chiseled features looking down at him. She and her boyfriend Matt were one of the couples he and Christine had met on the cruise. They shared the same dinner table most evenings over the last week.

"You think so?"

"You can't win without taking chances." Heather wrapped her lips around the straw in her drink and sipped it slowly.

Michael tapped his finger. The dealer drew the next card and laid it upright on the table in front of him. A four of hearts – perfect!

It wasn't long before Christine had showered, changed, and made her way to the Casino to find Michael. She was surprised to find Heather seated next to him at the black jack table. She leaned in and gave Michael a kiss before greeting Heather.

# # #

Hours later, she and Michael were preparing for the special black tie dinner scheduled on the final night of the cruise.

"I'm almost ready." She slipped into her evening gown.

"You look terrific." Michael scanned her through the mirror of the dressing table where he sat fixing his tie. Her floral silk dress with shimmering shades of pinks and plums clung to her slender waist revealing her tiny figure. Michael marveled at her shapely, five foot two inch frame and short blonde hair. She'd traded in her long blonde tresses after the birth of their second child for a more manageable hairstyle. The shorter cut accentuated her high cheekbones, large chestnut eyes, and sculpted nose.

As Michael observed Christine's reflection, he thought about how much she had changed since he married her eight years ago. She had been young and insecure back then. But now, she had developed into a mature woman with an insatiable intellect and the confidence to pursue anything she chose. He often felt himself slip into the shadows of her consciousness only to resurface when other stimuli were lacking.

She gazed back at him in the mirror. "You're not so bad yourself, handsome." He could still ignite a spark within her with just a casual, desirous glance. She snuggled up behind him, leaned in, kissed him on the back of the neck, and ran her fingers through his hair.

Michael turned to face her.

"Tease."

"Who's teasing?" She reached her hand behind her back, unzipped her dress, and let it slip to the floor.

# # #

Christine's sparkling brown eyes danced with childlike excitement as she surveyed the cruise ship's ballroom. The crystal chandeliers sent prisms of light skating across the burgundy tablecloths. The ice sculptured swan rose from the center of the buffet table while an array of exquisite tropical fruits coiled around it. The ship's guests walked leisurely to find their designated tables, as violins played Mozart in the background.

She and Michael found their usual table among the crowd of several hundred, joining the same three couples they had dined with most evenings throughout the weeklong cruise. One couple, Sue and Rick, had been at the poolside earlier in the day. In the afternoon, they had seemed cozy and cute with each other playing in the pool. Tonight, however, Christine felt a distance between them as she slid into her plush dining chair.

Heather and Matt were in their late twenties or early thirties. Christine had learned that Matt was a successful artist and Heather a pharmaceutical sales representative. The two of them lived together in California for the last several years. Matt resembled Michael with his broad build and light brown hair. Heather was sensual – long auburn hair, violet eyes, and a voluptuous body revealed by her low cut evening gown.

The third couple at the table was celebrating their twenty-fifth wedding anniversary. Their Caribbean cruise was a surprise gift from their six children. Bob and Marcia reminded Christine of her parents, married thirty-eight years. The attention they lavished on one another was constant, genuine, and respectful.

As Marcia spoke about their six children, Christine's mind drifted back home to her and Michael's little ones. Joseph was six. Elizabeth had just turned three. Joseph was a carbon copy of Christine - small framed, platinum hair, and deep brown eyes. At three, Elizabeth already had Michael's brawny build, hazel eyes, and darker hair.

The children were staying with her parents while they took "the cruise for two" gift from Michael's employer, Denver National Bank. Michael, the bank's Marketing Manager, was named employee of the year and the cruise was his reward. She smiled as she pondered what their future children might be like.

"Don't you agree, Christine?" Michael asked.

She jolted back to her plush surroundings and apologized. "I'm sorry; I drifted off thinking about our little ones back home." She smiled and wiped her mouth with her napkin. "I've enjoyed the cruise but I can hardly wait to see them when we return."

"We were just talking about how many people were ill last night as a result of the tropical storm." Conversation wasn't all she had missed while daydreaming. Heather's evening ritual of casual flirtation with Michael had become noticeably more direct.

As the conversation continued in small talk, she suddenly felt a tingle down her spine. She knew without turning around that the poolside stranger had entered the room. Every inch of her sensed his presence. Slowly she glanced over her shoulder. He was making his way down the staircase with a brunette draped on his arm. His eyes were focused in her direction. She quickly looked away. Though her back was turned, she felt them moving in her direction. Her pulse quickened. Every muscle in her body tightened. She felt his presence as they approached. They passed. He paused, glanced back, smiled at her, and continued on.

The stranger and the brunette sat at a table within view. Christine felt frozen in time, as if in slow motion. She groped her way through conversation, dinner, and dessert while the stranger occasionally glanced in her direction. She breathed a sigh of relief as dinner ended and she and Michael moved to the adjoining ballroom for dancing. Surely, she and Michael would escape the stranger's gaze in the crowd.

An unfamiliar song, with a waltz-like beat, began playing through the ballroom speakers as Michael excused himself and went to the restroom. She felt a hand on her shoulder and recognized the British accent.

"May I have the pleasure of this dance?"

"No thank you," she replied, "I'm married." She blushed as her response fell clumsily from her lips.

He chuckled in amusement. "I only asked you to dance, not to sleep with me."

She tried to refuse, but trancelike, she followed his guiding hand to the dance floor as the song played in the background.

'This world can break a body
Tear Dreams apart
But deep in the darkest hour
A miracle can start.'

She could barely breathe, much less dance. The song was slow and sweet. He held her at a distance as she felt herself quivering, trying to remain calm and in control.

'When I am old, darling
And dreaming back through time
I'll still thank God for giving me

A love like yours and mine.'

"You are like a frightened gazelle."

"I'm not frightened," Christine retorted. "Should I be?"

He laughed and for the first time, she took a long look at his regal face, childlike grin, and icy blue eyes.

'You don't take me for granted
You don't try to hold me down
You want to see me happy
You love me the way I am.'

"You see," he said, "the cruise ends tomorrow and I had to tell you what energy I felt from the moment I first saw you days ago. I have somehow known you since the beginning of time and yet I do not know your name."

"Christine, Christine Amory." She was caught in the magic of his movement, his words, his eyes. They glided across the dance floor.

'When I am old, darling
And dreaming back through time
I'll still thank God for giving me
A love like yours and mine.'

"And yours?"

"Maximilian Fairchild, Max for short." He stopped and looked into her trusting eyes. "It is all quite simple, don't you think?"

"What?"

"Life," Max answered. "We are born, we live and we die. Nothing more. Nothing less. And in between we struggle to survive and find pleasure the best that we are able."

Their eyes locked. "What did you say?" Christine asked.

"Your heard me, Christine. People overcomplicate life. It is much simpler than they make it."

"You don't really believe that's all there is to life, do you?"

"Indeed, Christine, I do." He slipped his business card into the palm of her hand and said, "Write to me, but the old fashioned way rather than on the computer. Truth flows better from mind to pen to paper."

The song had ended. She stood in utter confusion as he kissed her hand and walked away.

It was a moment or two before she reclaimed her senses. She made her way back to the table where Michael sat scowling. Her voice was animated, disbelieving. "He's the one that I mentioned I saw days ago. Isn't it strange, Michael?"

Michael listened as he always did to her honest confessions of attraction to other men over the last few years. He had been patient because he knew the men that intrigued her were never lovers. He wondered if she behaved this way because they had married young without either one of them dating much. He thought it was a phase she would outgrow. Her constant searching left him feeling drained and inadequate. "Yes, Christine. It's strange."

Michael failed to mention that on his way back from the restroom he had declined Heather's flattering invitation of seduction.

"Christine, I have a headache." He stood up. "Let's get out of here."

"Okay." She took Michael's hand, and led him toward the door.

Tropical air wrapped around them as they lingered by the

ship's edge. Countless stars salted the blackened sky as ocean smells wafted about.

She turned to face him. "I'm sorry, Michael." She leaned in to embrace him. "I didn't mean to upset you."

Michael took a step back, his agitation rising. "I'm tired of it, Christine. We've been over this so many times. You're always looking for something in someone else. You make it so clear that our marriage is not enough for you."

Her back stiffened. "That's crazy! You know I love you. I'm not interested in anyone else and you know it."

"You're not listening, Christine. Or, maybe you are, but you really don't understand what I'm trying to say." He sighed. "Let's go back to the room. I'm tired."

They returned to their cabin subdued. As they closed the cabin door, she turned to him, her eyes wide and sincere. "I really am sorry."

Michael couldn't resist her apologetic face. He reached for her. Passion pulsated through his veins. They wrestled fervidly as one, while the evening, the stranger, and the world evaporated into ecstatic oblivion.

Afterwards, Michael fell asleep but she lay wide-awake, struggling with the evening's events. Who was the stranger and what did he want? How was it possible that his presence created such an overwhelming response in her? Why did she feel like she somehow knew him but was sure that she didn't?

The night hours passed as she gazed out the porthole into a sky that appeared studded with diamonds.

As the sun peeked its shiny head above the sleepy horizon, the ship docked, and with luggage in hand, they departed. She glanced back from the cab as they pulled away; her mind was still riddled with questions.

TWO

"Michael, I can hardly wait to see the kids again!" They were headed toward her parents' home in Colorado Springs.

The surrounding mountains stretched into the sky, guarding the city below with their powerful presence.

"Me too." Michael adored Joseph and Elizabeth. From the moment he witnessed their births they had captured his heart. He treasured every moment with them – playing in the park, tossing a ball with Joseph, helping Elizabeth on her tricycle, and reading evening stories to them both. Time spent with them, left Michael feeling refreshed and renewed, as if rinsed in a gentle mountain waterfall.

They turned into the winding drive of the home where Christine grew up. The six-bedroom colonial estate loomed larger than life amidst the acreage surrounding it. A flood of memories warmed her heart as she took in the familiar structure with its freshly painted federal blue siding, bright white pillars and trim.

"Mommy!" Joseph and Elizabeth screamed as they raced toward her emerging from the car.

She bent down to catch each of them in a one-armed embrace.

"Daddy!" Elizabeth reached her cherub arms towards Michael.

"Hey, little princess." Michael crouched to join the joyous reunion. Elizabeth jumped on Michael's back while Joseph gave him a frontal hug. "How's my man?" Michael asked Joseph.

"Glad you and mommy are back." He pulled slightly away to

look Michael in the eye. "We had fun with grandma and grandpa but we missed you guys."

"You did?" Christine asked in a playful tone.

"Me too," Elizabeth insisted, ensuring her inclusion.

"What a welcome reunion," stated Christine's father.

Christine stood up and turned to face her parents. They'd be turning sixty this coming year. Her father's presence was still commanding. He towered over her at six foot four, two hundred twenty pounds. Her mother was petite like Christine with natural blonde hair, cropped close to her head.

"Mom, dad, do you have any idea how good it feels to see them again?" She nodded in the children's direction.

"Of course we do." Her mother wrapped her arms around her. "How was your trip?"

"Great, but there wasn't a day I didn't think of you two." Christine tousled Joseph's hair and gently pinched Elizabeth's chubby cheek.

Elizabeth hung on Michael's back like a monkey; her arms were clenched around his neck and her legs wrapped around his middle.

"Speaking of trips," Christine interjected, "I bet you two can hardly wait to leave for Italy in a few months. December fifth, right?"

"That's right," her father confirmed, "but we'll be back on the nineteenth, in time to spend the holidays with our 'little ones'."

Christine laughed. "Dad, I hate to be the one to break it to you, but Kathy, the youngest of your 'little ones' turned twenty-two several months ago."

"I know, I know," he said smiling, "but somehow even when your children are grown and gone, they always remain your 'little ones' in some way. You'll see. Just wait till these two grow up."

He pointed to Joseph and Elizabeth. As they approached the front door he paused, took his large hand and swept it in the direction of the house and outlying fifty acres. "You see, Christine, I've worked hard for all of this but if I lost it all tomorrow and still had your mother and you kids, I'd remain a wealthy man in the truest sense."

The words hit her like an unexpected snowball on the first day of winter. She remembered similar comments throughout the years but she couldn't recall a time her father had spoken with such intensity and conviction.

They all bounded into the house for a delicious buffet of cold cuts, fresh breads, raw vegetables, and salads.

"So, tell us all about your trip," prodded her mother.

Joseph methodically finished his Jell-O salad and Elizabeth scrambled for another strawberry yogurt.

"Well," she began, "the food on the cruise ship was out of this world and the islands were beautiful." She took a bite of her sandwich and switched gears. "You know what? There was this couple that reminded me of you two. Their six children sent them on the cruise as a surprise for their twenty-fifth wedding anniversary. They had a glow about them." She turned toward her mother. "What's your secret? How have you managed to stay in love after all these years together?"

"It helps if you focus on the good things in one another rather than on the things that annoy you." Her mother took a sip of her iced tea.

"It's a choice," Christine's father interjected. "It's easier if you try to appreciate each other rather than finding fault." He shifted in his chair and reached for a freshly baked chocolate chip cookie.

"No one is perfect and no relationship or marriage is perfect. You can always find reasons why a relationship 'won't' work.

We've chosen to find all the reasons we love each other and why the relationship 'does' work." Her mother took another sip of her iced tea. "It's not always easy but commitment gets us through the tough times."

There was something in her tone that seized everyone's attention. Christine's father broke the silence. "But it's a lot of fun too." He winked at his wife and his smile lit the room.

After they finished eating, everyone moved to the den. They sat enveloped in the fall glow. The setting sun cast shades of blues, purples, and pinks through the bay window, creating quilt-like patterns across the rich, russet carpet as she and Michael shared stories of their weeklong cruise. As the evening wore on, Elizabeth stretched and gave a big yawn. Joseph tried his best to keep his drooping eyes open. Michael was tired from the drive. "Hey you two, let's head upstairs and get some sleep. We'll let mommy finish talking."

A huge grin emerged on Elizabeth's sleepy face. "Okay daddy."

Joseph was resistant. "Do we have to?" He pleaded with Christine. Evenings were his favorite time of day. Joseph never wanted to miss a thing and he always had an excuse for staying up just 'fifteen more minutes'. Waking up in the morning was never easy for Joseph. Once awake, he was fine, but the effort it took to get there, annoyed him.

"I'm afraid so." She pulled him close for a goodnight hug.

Both children gave goodnight kisses to their mom, grandma and grandpa. They took their turns thanking their grandparents for taking care of them. Joseph loved the way grandpa shared the ice cream he wasn't supposed to eat. Elizabeth loved that grandma could be silly. Michael, Joseph, and Elizabeth raced up the steps bidding their goodnights.

After they were gone, Christine's mother turned to her.

"Christine, I get the feeling that your questions on marriage had a purpose. Are you and Michael having problems?"

She shifted on the couch. "It's hard to explain, mom. I've changed so much these last eight years. I've grown a lot. I feel a distance with Michael, not sexually," she said, then added, "more emotionally, I guess." She sighed. "Oh, I don't know. Maybe it's because I'm more independent."

Her father awoke to their conversation from his quiet dozing in his favorite recliner. He looked directly into her eyes. "Christine, a marriage can't work if one person feels their independence is more important than the relationship. It's always a matter of give and take." He stood up and stretched. "With those unsolicited words of wisdom, I'll say goodnight. I'm tired. It's been a good week, but a long week." He bent down and gave Christine a kiss on the forehead. "You'll be okay, sweetie, as long as you don't lose sight of what's really important."

Her mother stood up. She gave her husband a hug and kiss before he headed to bed. Christine debated whether or not to tell her mother about her encounter with Max. She took the risk and told her.

"Christine, you talk about growing but you haven't, if you're interacting like that with strangers when you're married."

"Oh, mom, it wasn't like that. You just don't understand."

"Maybe that's true." Her mother stood up and started tidying the room. "Maybe this is something that *shouldn't* be understood."

Christine rose from her chair and moved toward her mother. She spoke softly. "I'm obviously not communicating very well so let's drop it, okay?" She caught her mother's eye and gently touched her shoulder. "Okay?"

Her mother shook her head and rolled her eyes. A faint smile peeked out from the corners of her mouth. "All right, Christine.

But don't say I didn't warn you." She pulled her close and gave her a hug.

As Christine lay in bed later that night, thoughts of her family, childhood, and young adulthood floated through her mind. She remembered how her mother stayed home to raise the five children while her father had worked long hours as a neurosurgeon before retiring.

Christine realized how much she thrived on family interaction. From the time she was a child it was her safe-haven. Although reserved and anxious when she was young, she felt secure within her family. Sure, she and her brothers and sisters had their normal share of sibling rivalry and dysfunction growing up, but overall her memories were of fun-loving holidays, road trips, and the closeness that had developed between them. Her family was her cocoon, her parents the silk that bound them together.

Her parents had often been concerned about her serious, overly sensitive nature as a child. She chuckled as she remembered herself as a young girl, her father leaning over her desk in her bedroom. "Christine, are you still lost in those books? Close them up, go outside, climb some trees, and have some fun."

In high school, she felt safer in academic achievements and intellectual pursuits than in boys and dating. The world of books was far less frightening than the painful world of emotional development and relationships. When she reached college and met Michael, she found another dependable and stable force in her life. Upon graduation, she traded her dreams of graduate school in History for the security of marriage with Michael. He stepped in where her parents left off. She had slipped from one cocoon to the next without ever taking the necessary time or steps to emotionally develop into her own.

Her insecurities increased when Joseph was born. They were

heightened by the self-doubt that new motherhood inherently brings. Michael was always the strong one, the mainstay, during her rough emotional moments when she felt overwhelmed by the simplest of tasks. But soon she began to adapt to life – real life – by watching little Joseph grow. As the weeks and months passed, her neurotic housekeeping was replaced with strewn toys and playful romping. She took a part-time administrative job at a local law firm and never lost sight of her dream to someday return to academics. Elizabeth was born three years later. At times, despair imprisoned Christine's soul, as her dreams of an advanced degree drowned in a tidal wave of diapers, work, laundry, and meals. Yet, here she was, three years later, thinking of entering law school. She intended to discuss it with Michael when they returned home. Bit by bit, she finally felt she was coming into her own.

# # #

The next morning, they packed up Joseph and Elizabeth's belongings, ready to head home. The children gave their grandparents a long embrace.

"Thanks, grandma and grandpa. I had fun." Joseph shifted from one foot to the other.

"Me too." Elizabeth kissed them both and jumped into her car seat, waiting to be buckled.

"Someone's anxious to get home," Christine's father noted.

Emotion overcame Christine. She reached for her mother and hugged her tightly. "Thanks, mom and dad," she whispered.

"It was our pleasure, sweetie," her father replied.

"No, I don't' mean just for watching the kids," she tried to explain, "I mean for 'everything' over all the years." She turned to hug her father. He wrapped her snugly in his arms and she lingered in the safety of his strong embrace.

He smiled, released her, and patted her on the head. "It's our pleasure, sweetie. It has always been our pleasure." She felt overwhelmed with gratitude and appreciation as she buckled her seat belt, pulled out of the driveway, and waved goodbye.

THREE

It was ten in the morning, London time, when Maximilian Fairchild's limousine stopped in front of his office building. Max had renovated the twenty story brick building several years earlier to house his international architectural firm. Bold, brass letters on the black glass door entrance displayed 'Fairchild Enterprises'.

Max stepped onto the sidewalk and straightened his navy blue Armani suit. He turned to his chauffeur. "Thank you, Charles. I won't need you any more today. I'll call you if something changes."

Charles stood tall, fit in physique, professional in demeanor. He tipped his hat in salute, revealing his thick silver hair. "Very well, Mr. Fairchild. I'll be available if the need arises. Good day sir." Charles closed Max's door and returned to his post behind the wheel.

Max nodded and walked briskly toward the building, his Gucci briefcase in hand. His pulse quickened as he entered the structure in which he made his fortune. He'd been gone a week on the cruise and was glad to return. He thrived on remaining one step ahead of his competitors in the game of commercial architecture. To him it was like playing chess; strategy and cunning were paramount.

"Welcome back, Mr. Fairchild," smiled Robert, the enthusiastic doorman. Max nodded as he slid past him.

His chest swelled with pride as he perused the lobby from the intricate gold inlay ceilings overhead to the Italian pink marble underfoot. Expensive mauve wall coverings housed original artwork. His intent on overall design had been achieved, modern yet majestic.

Max pushed the button to beckon his private elevator. While he ascended the twenty flights to his office, his mind raced from business deals, to the women and party the night before, then back to the moment at hand.

The elevator door opened. He paused, admiring the two Rembrandt's that adorned the walls. Judith Forsythe, Maximilian's administrative assistant, stood at attention, anticipating his arrival. "Good morning Mr. Fairchild. You have quite a few messages and a Miss Gillian called here continuously in your absence. She has - -"

"Good morning Judith," he interjected with a charming smile. He walked past her, reached into his pocket, took the key to his office and opened it. The pungent scent of floral bouquets assailed him as the door swung open. "What the hell is this?"

"That's what I was trying to tell you, Mr. Fairchild." Her tall, young frame stood confident. Her cropped black hair created a dramatic contrast to her flawless, milky complexion. Judith was plain, but crisp and efficient in both appearance and ability. "Miss Gillian called continuously while you were on the cruise. She didn't believe you were out of town and kept sending you flowers. We had nowhere to put them except in your office."

He waved his hand in annoyance. "Remove them immediately. Feel free to give them away or keep them. Just get rid of them." He turned to enter his office, then turned back. "And Judith, if Miss Gillian calls again, put her through. I'll take care of it."

"Yes, Mr. Fairchild." Judith nodded her head, turned on her heels, and headed for his office to remove the flowers.

Max made his way into his immense office. His window spanned the length and height of the room, providing a panoramic view of London. He strode past his solid cherry wood desk to the window and gazed out at the marshmallow clouds billowing lazily across the fall sky. Sporadic sunbeams spotlighted the landscape, creating a collage of light and dark. He glanced down to the streets below with nameless faces racing, rushing, scrambling – unaware of their motion, blind to their freedom.

Suddenly, Christine's face flashed before his mind's eye. An unfamiliar rush poured through his veins. It wasn't the usual sensation when he thought of the beautiful women he wanted, would get, and then deliberately forget. This was different. "*Absurd.*" He shook his head in disgust. He eradicated the vision of Christine from his mind by grabbing the stack of messages that Judith had placed on his desk.

He plunged into the moment at hand with ferocious mental discipline. Within minutes, the room disappeared from his consciousness as he completed a memo, discussed an upcoming deal, and arranged a meeting. He paced with concentrated energy, feeling the power rise within him as he took each breath.

Several hours passed. Judith knocked gently on his door. "Mr. Fairchild?"

It startled him back to his physical surroundings. "Yes, what is it, Judith?"

"It's Miss Sarah Gillian. She's here to see you."

He paused a moment, registering the name. "Show her in."

The door opened. Sarah strolled into his office – a tall blonde, with pale blue eyes, and tanned olive skin. This striking face and svelte body that had enthralled him three weeks before the cruise, was now nothing more than a past moment barging into his office.

"Max." She reached to hug him. He stood motionless,

unresponsive.

"What do you want, Sarah?"

Sarah beamed. "Did you receive my messages? Did you see the flowers I sent? I've been thinking of you and anxiously awaiting your return."

He pulled back and tilted his head in bemusement. "Why?"

Sarah blanched. "Well, because I - -"

"Look, Sarah." He cut her off, his tone gentle and detached. "We had a fun couple of weeks. I don't need flowers or follow up telephone calls. I told you from the start not to expect anything more, didn't I?" He held Sarah's stare.

Shock and surprise sent Sarah reeling. The time they'd spent together in Rome was consuming. Max had treated her like no man ever had. He had anticipated her every thought and desire. He had fulfilled her every fantasy. He'd been attentive and caring. "But why?"

"It was what it was, Sarah, a moment in time - nothing more, nothing less. It was everything and nothing." He paused and tenderly lifted up her chin. "So, I would appreciate it if you'd stop trying to make it something more than it is." He smiled kindly, took her shoulder and opened the door, inviting her departure. "Now, I have a lot to catch up on so if you'll please excuse me."

Sarah's eyes widened as she clenched her jaw. She turned in a fury and stomped out of his office, fighting back the tears. She blew past Judith like tumbleweed, swirling in a sand storm.

Max watched her depart, then closed his office door. He gazed around his office, touched the leather on his chair, and glanced again at the view through his window.

He tried to return to his work but he'd lost his concentration for the moment. He relaxed, knowing that he accomplished more in several hours than most people do in several days. He knew the power wielded by his concentrated energy and brilliant mind.

Sarah might have thrilled him longer if she hadn't tried to capture him in some mundane, possessive relationship. Every woman he spent time with intrigued him for a while. Some lasted longer than others but none lasted for any length of time. Continuity was not important. The thrill of the moment was. When the thrill was gone, so was Max.

It wasn't always like this. There had been Rachel. But after that, everything changed.

Now he wanted a woman who understood the thrill of being alive - someone who understood that his one commitment in life was to life itself – to his freedom and the opportunity to live each moment fully, then let it go. Yet, he didn't really want anyone to understand him. He flattered himself on being an enigma. Those who tried to capture him were left submerged in the stream of consciousness that he lived, never to resurface in any meaningful way.

Again, he envisioned Christine's face. This time, it bothered him more. This simple creature electrified him. There was something different about her that eluded labeling or definition. He exchanged only a few words with her, yet he was drawn to her. He went to his briefcase, opened it, dug through to the pocket in the back, and pulled out a tiny piece of paper. As he opened it, the blood in his veins surged. "*Christine Amory*" he recited to himself. His friend in reservations for the cruise ship had retrieved her telephone numbers for him. As he reached for the phone, an unwelcome feeling flitted in the pit of his stomach. He placed the receiver back in its carriage. He grabbed his coat and glanced around his office one more time to drink in the pleasure of it all, then locked his office door and headed for the elevator.

He took a long breath as he greeted the streets of London. The crisp, fall air rushed through his nostrils. He lifted his face to catch a passing ray of sunshine, feeling its warmth and absorbed the view above, intermittent puffs of white, dotting the cobalt sky.

Max walked purposefully to his favorite pub up the street. He frequented the pub often, for an afternoon, or a lunch that turned into an afternoon that then turned into an evening. He enjoyed the ambiance and the alcohol. He enjoyed the anticipation of the next beautiful woman that might somehow pique his interest. As he entered the doorway, the regulars greeted him with their usual gaze of bewilderment and respect, reserved for the man who never left the pub alone unless he chose to.

He sat in his favorite booth. Angela sauntered over to him. She was willowy, with shoulder length, dark brown hair, emerald green eyes, and large breasts. She brought him his favorite drink, Grey Goose vodka, with a touch of cranberry juice. Angela worked at the pub in order to pay for her studies at the University. She was savvy, sophisticated, and self-supporting – determined to finish her degree, regardless of the time and effort it would take. She met Max two years ago when she started working at the pub. She had slept with him occasionally since.

Max sipped his drink as his mind shifted from the surroundings outside to the pub within. He liked the simple but efficient furnishings of this place. Dark blue leather cushions accented the enormous, solid oak booths, trimmed in brass. Colorful tiffany shades hung over every booth, each different in design, and unique in shape as well as color. Though not fancy, the pub was warm and welcoming. When he wanted high visibility, he would frequent the more exclusive London clubs on Regent Street, but today was a day for the pub.

As the alcohol began to perform its magic, slowing the rapid firing of neurons in his brain and numbing the intensity of his thoughts, Max entertained himself with one of his favorite pastimes, watching people in motion - unconscious, unaware motion. He observed a couple at one of the tables. They were probably in their early thirties and both wore wedding bands. The woman's face projected a proud pout while the man desperately groveled to regain her graces. He studied them, detached and amused. He noticed an attractive woman sitting alone at the bar. He observed two men enter the pub and take their strategic positions a little further down the rail. He watched as they planned the details of their mission to gain the woman's attention and favor. They launched their initial approach. Rebuffed – maneuver failed. Max grinned.

The entire time, Angela watched him from the corner of her eye. She enjoyed his charismatic presence, frequent visits, and the impact he had on those around him.

Max continued in silent amusement, analyzing the mind games being played by the pub's characters. He watched as they acted out their various, often humorous roles, as their egos rallied for center stage. The hours passed. He glanced at his watch. It was half past ten in the evening. He paid his bill, stood up, and nodded goodbye to Angela as he headed for the door. He was tired, tired of watching people, tired of being all too familiar with how they operate.

FOUR

Michael, Christine, Joseph, and Elizabeth were happy to be home. Though only away for a week, the comfort and familiarity of their two story brick home in Colorado was a welcome sight. The four of them sat at their kitchen table, finishing breakfast. Christine looked at Michael. Her chocolate colored eyes sparkled. "I've been thinking. I love the work I'm doing at the law office." She paused and moved her face closer to his, trying to gain his full attention. "I'm considering going to law school. What do you think?"

He stopped chewing his pancakes. "I don't know, Christine. Do you think it's really necessary?"

She stiffened. "Well, Michael, I guess it's not so much whether it's necessary as much as it's something I think I'd really like to do." She stood up and began clearing the dirty dishes. "I have my review with David today and I think I could work out part time hours in conjunction with taking classes. It might take me a little longer to get the degree, but I wouldn't be away from home any longer than I am already with the hours I'm working."

"You sure have the intellect for law school." Michael leaned back in his chair. "I guess we could work out any schedule changes between the two of us."

"Mommy, will you be at school like me?" Elizabeth interjected after swallowing a spoonful of her cereal.

Joseph and Elizabeth were enrolled in a nearby Montessori

school. Joseph was starting first grade and Elizabeth attended preschool.

"Yes, something like that. It will be school but not quite like yours." Christine grinned and looked over her shoulder as she reached the sink.

"I wish it were my school. That would be really fun!"

Joseph smiled, saying nothing as he continued chewing his toast.

"That would be fun," Christine agreed.

Michael stood up, pushed in his chair and carried his dishes to the sink. He turned to Christine. "I think I'll head out a little early this morning. After being out a week, there'll be a lot to catch up on."

He gave her a kiss on the forehead. "I think you should mention law school to David. I'm sure he'll agree that it's a great idea." He walked back to the kitchen table, picked Elizabeth up, hugged her tightly, and kissed her cheek. Then he shared his same goodbye gestures with Joseph.

"You two have fun getting back to school. Be sure to tell everybody all about your fun visit with grandma and grandpa."

"We will, daddy," Joseph said as he sat up tall, straightening his little back.

"See you later," Michael added as he headed for the door.

Christine finished the dishes and helped the children with their final morning preparations. When she dropped Joseph and Elizabeth off at school, she gave them each a big hug. "Remember, you two, have a good day. Okay?"

"I will, mommy." Joseph furrowed his tiny eyebrows with seriousness.

"Me too, mommy," Elizabeth said with another quick kiss before bounding down the hallway. She shouted over her tiny shoulder, "Have fun at your new school."

Christine laughed and gave Joseph another hug and kiss before he turned on his heels and also raced off to the school's meeting room.

Her heart swelled as she watched her two small children gallop down the hall. A grateful smile rested on her face as she turned to leave, how fortunate to be their mother and to be married to a man like Michael.

# # #

Christine beamed as she walked in the front door of the law offices, Montgomery, McCarthy, and Steinberg. The spacious entranceway of etched glass and chrome greeted her. She smiled at the security guard. "Good morning, Tom."

"Welcome back, Christine," Tom greeted her with a grin. He was a retired policeman, hired eight years ago by the founding partner of the firm, David Montgomery. Tom remained a friendly fixture in the lobby ever since. "We've all missed you."

"That's very kind of you to say, Tom, but I'm sure everyone managed just fine without me." She shook her head as she pressed the elevator button.

"All kidding aside, Miss," Tom continued in earnest, "this place just isn't the same without you. You're a ray of sunshine around here."

She blushed, flattered by his innocent accolade. "Well, thank you, Tom. I appreciate the compliment." The elevator door opened. "Have a great day."

"You do the same," Tom replied before the elevator door closed with Christine behind it.

She looked forward to her annual review with David. She worked well with all three partners but David was her favorite. He had hired her six years ago as his assistant when she was looking for part time work after Joseph was born. David had taken her under his wing. He was flexible with both her schedule and workload especially after Elizabeth's birth. Once Elizabeth started preschool, she began working full time at the firm. She developed a passion for the law and respected the integrity with which David practiced it.

She admired David's unique and rare combination of traits. He had the tenacity of a pit bull but an underlying warmth and sensitivity rarely found in any individual. He was tough but fair, honest and authentic. He listened more than talked, but when he spoke, people listened. Each word spoken, carried precise meaning and purpose. David was in his late thirties, slightly under six foot tall, stocky build, deep black skin, dark curly hair and incisive brown eyes. He wasn't married. David's career was his life. He was always the first to arrive at the office and the last to leave. David started his law practice right out of law school and worked hard to develop it. He hired his associates within a couple of years and the three of them gained recognition as the leading corporate litigation firm in the city of Denver. The fact that the firm was minority owned added to its prestige.

She often wondered why a man like David hadn't married. He was bright, successful, warm, and handsome. Last year she had asked him. His response was twofold. He hadn't found the right woman and he didn't have the time.

She poked her head into his office. "Good morning, David."

David glanced up from his massive oak desk. "Christine, welcome back." A smile spread across his face. "How was your trip?"

"It was wonderful! I'll have to tell you all about it sometime." She stepped inside his office. "What time would you like to meet for my review?"

David checked his watch. "Just give me five minutes."

"Great. I have quite a bit to catch up on." She turned and glided down the hallway to her office.

As they sat down to begin their discussion, Christine started in her usual energetic way. "David, I want to run something by you." She leaned over the edge of David's desk as she spoke. "I've been thinking about going to law school." She paused and took a deep breath. "What do you think?"

David leaned back in his chair and laced his fingers together, taking several moments before responding. "Well, as a matter of fact, Christine, in preparation for your review, I've been thinking quite a bit about your contributions and capability. I think that law school is an excellent choice for you. We can hire someone to help you with the administrative duties so I can get you involved with more legal work. Then you'll be free to work your hours around your school schedule and your family."

She bounced up from her chair. "Oh, David, do you mean it?"

He let out a slight laugh. "Consider it done. We'll start interviewing as soon as possible and begin transitioning you to your new responsibilities." Never losing her gaze, he continued, "You'll have to take the entrance exams but with your intelligence, Christine, it shouldn't be a problem. You'll be challenged in law school but you'll do fine. When you are finished with school you can join us here at the firm as an attorney."

She blanched as she sat back down in her chair and nervously bit at her lip.

David leaned forward on his desk to regain eye contact. "You can handle it. You are very bright and you'll make an excellent attorney." He looked closely at her as he spoke. "Relax, Christine. Take one thing at a time, one class at a time. Trust me, you'll be fine."

She took a deep breath. "Thanks."

After completing their discussion, she stood up and straightened her suit. "Well, I better get back to work." She turned to leave, then turned back. "Thank you, David."

"You are more than welcome."

FIVE

Michael arrived early to his office at the bank. The tellers were busily preparing for their day. Rebecca, a teller in her early twenties, batted her eyes and smiled cutely as Michael walked by. He responded with a wink and a grin. Walking through the regal hallways on plush red carpeting always brought a confident smile to his face.

Michael was anxious to return to work. The cruise had left him feeling more drained than ever in his relationship with Christine. What bothered him was that he didn't believe he was a participant in her changes, but rather an outside observer, almost an inhibitor to them. Once he knew her every thought and feeling but not any longer. Their physical closeness remained as strong and as enjoyable as ever and yet he felt alone.

"Good morning," Michael said as he approached Evelyn Costello, his assistant. Evelyn's back was to Michael as she replaced a file in her cabinet.

She spun around in her chair, stood up, and reached for his hand. "Welcome back, Michael." Evelyn's handshake was firm and welcoming. "I took the liberty of arranging the messages on your desk by priority."

Evelyn had been Michael's administrative assistant for the past three years. She anticipated his response to almost every business situation and demand. Evelyn was tall and broad, her hazelnut hair cut short with just a touch of curl. She wore colorful, tailored suits that revealed a surprisingly fit shape for a woman approaching fifty-five years of age. Evelyn was widowed with no children. She filled her days with work at the bank and volunteering at the Children's Hospital.

He placed the palms of his hands on her desk and leaned forward. "What would I do without you, Evelyn?"

She blushed and adjusted her glasses. "I have no idea."

The telephone rang. Evelyn picked up the receiver. "Mr. Amory's office, this is Evelyn, may I help you?" She listened, then replied, "Just one moment please, I'll see if he's available." She pressed the hold button and looked at him. "It's a Miss Heather Smithstone. She said it's personal. Would you like to take it or should I take a message?"

"Heather Smithstone?" He mused. "I don't recognize the name, Evelyn, please take a message." He turned and walked into his office.

His intercom line buzzed. "Yes, Evelyn?"

"She said to tell you she's Heather from the cruise."

Michael's pulse quickened. "Oh- uh - that Heather." He fumbled for composure. "You can put the call through, Evelyn."

"Very well, sir."

His mouth felt dry, as if lined with cotton. "Michael Amory speaking."

"Hi, Michael. This is Heather Smithstone." Her voice leapt through the line like lightning through a rod. "We met on the cruise last week. How are you?"

His tongue thickened. "I'm fine. How are you and how did..?"

"How did I get your number?" Heather interrupted. "During dinner on the cruise, you mentioned the bank where you work. Truth is, I've been thinking about you ever since we met so I thought I'd call, say hello, and see how your trip back was."

"Well, the trip back was fine and, uh, things are fine." He wanted a sip of water.

"Did I call at a bad time?"

"Well, sort of. I just got in the office and I'm trying to dig out from the stack of work on my desk." He paused. "Let me have your number, Heather, and I'll try to give you a call back." He wrote down her number before pleasantly saying goodbye.

Michael felt flushed, flattered, yet taken aback. He remembered the night on the cruise when she had tried to seduce him. Adrenaline raced through his body.

The telephone rang again. This time it was Michael's direct, private line.

"Michael Amory speaking."

"Michael?"

It took a moment for him to recognize Christine's voice on the other end of the line.

"Michael? Are you there?"

"Yes, Christine."

"What's wrong, Michael?"

Michael took a deep breath and cleared his head. "Nothing, Christine. I'm just trying to get back in the swing of work. What's up?"

She exploded with excitement. "Michael, I'm thrilled! I spoke to David and he'd been thinking along the same lines, I mean about law school." Her words flew fast and furiously, like bullets from an automatic. "He's even going to help pay for it and he offered me a job with the firm when I finish." She paused to catch her breath. "Isn't it wonderful?"

Michael listened before responding. "That's great. You've worked hard for this and you deserve it."

"Michael, are you sure you're all right? You just don't sound like yourself."

He resisted the urge to share his brief conversation with Heather. "I'm sure. Just a bit overwhelmed with the work facing me. That's all."

"Okay, I'll take your word for it," she replied, not sounding convinced. "Well, I won't keep you. I just wanted to share my good news."

"Christine, how about I take you and the kids out to dinner tonight to celebrate?"

She smiled into the phone. "Thanks, that's thoughtful of you, Michael, but I'll just fix something fun at home and we'll celebrate there."

Michael acquiesced, knowing it was futile trying to convince her once she made up her mind.

"I love you, Michael."

"I love you too."

Michael's stomach dropped with the resounding thud of the receiver as his mind raced. The call from Heather was spontaneous and meaningless. It was something to be flattered by, not something worth mentioning.

# # #

Heather sat back in her desk chair as she hung up the telephone with Michael. She worked out of her home office in her two thousand square foot condo in Beverly Hills. Her parents helped with the down payment over five years ago. She had since paid back every cent. Heather thrived amidst the hustle and bustle of LA.

Her condo was roomy and modern with stark white walls and black leather furniture that curved its way around the living area. A print of Monet's Waterfall hung on the wall adjacent to the large bay window overlooking the city.

Heather walked to her kitchen and reached for a mug. She made some green tea, returned to her living room, and nestled into her soft leather sofa. As she sipped her tea, her thoughts turned to Michael and the cruise. She had sensed Michael's animal magnetism from the moment she first saw him, but her attraction to him was more than that. Heather had admired Michael's undivided attention and focus on Christine and she had noticed that the devotion didn't seem mutual. Christine seemed pleasant enough, but appeared to pay as much attention, if not more, to everything going on around her rather than to Michael.

Heather's five-year relationship with Matt had ended months ago. It had died a slow, boring death but they had remained close just as they had promised. Since the cruise had been planned and paid for a year in advance, they agreed to take the cruise together just as friends.

As Heather took another sip of her tea, she wondered if all relationships started out exciting and fun and ended up tedious and boring. It sure had with her and Matt. She smiled as she stood up, stretched, and pictured Michael's face.

"*Enough*," she thought to herself. It was time to get moving. She stretched again before heading out the door for a six-mile morning jog.

SIX

Max leaned back in his chair with one leg crossed over the other and his arms folded across his chest. A relaxed, knowing smile, rested on his face. Roger Demerly, his competitor, sat across from him. Roger leaned forward on the table, elbows firmly pressed to the wood underneath, eyes fixed on Max, lips taut. Roger's firm was competitive in the London area. Their connections were extensive, their reputation outstanding, but not nearly as renowned as the international acclaim that *Fairchild Enterprise's* had achieved over the last fifteen years. Roger's attorney and top architect accompanied him at the table. Max pondered as he observed Roger's anxiousness. "*Check*", Max thought to himself.

The renovation project was a two hundred thousand square foot warehouse, a prime location for a restaurant or nightclub. Both Max and Roger had designed plans for its restoration. Both knew the potential financial gains involved. The stakes were high, the competition steep. The property owner, Jonathan Miller, entered the room with his entourage. They exchanged introductions and pleasantries as they took their places at the boardroom table.

Max inhaled slowly as his eyes moved around the table from one player to the next. He approached every situation with detachment. This deal was important to his firm, but there was never a deal he 'had' to have. From inception of his business, he had taken the same approach. At any point, if something didn't please him, he felt free to walk away, completely and totally.

Fear didn't factor into Max's mental framework. He understood that people were driven by egos and personal agendas. His keen consciousness allowed him to fathom the constructs of others, anticipate their thoughts and strategies, and prepare for their reactions. His presence radiated confidence and surety. He was focused, calm, and in control. This unnerved many that interacted with him. It unnerved Roger. Max could see the tension and uncertainty in Roger's every move. He reminded Max of a deer during hunting season, slowly making its way through the woods, listening, watching, waiting, and sensing the danger surrounding him. "*Check Mate,*" Max thought.

The negotiations began. Roger presented first. Roger's plans for the property included a combined, high-end restaurant and jazz club. The architect's drawings were impressive and unique. Then it was Max's turn. He unveiled his brainchild that included five different nightclubs of varying themes, décor, and layouts – acoustically buffered by an ingenious design. Each nightclub would provide a distinct, limited bar menu, supported by a centralized kitchen, and would attract crowds that enjoyed everything from classical, jazz, and rock, to new age and heavy metal. The concept was unbeatable, the design inspired and comprehensive. The response was unequivocal acceptance.

Roger tried to find solid footing while the floor beneath him slowly turned to quicksand. Within an hour the transaction was completed and Max was the victor. Roger slumped in his chair, swathed in defeat.

"Good try, Rog." Max placed his hand on Roger's shoulder. "Maybe next time," he added as he excused himself from the meeting. He grabbed his overcoat and headed for the elevator.

He moved with a playful stride toward one of his favorite nightclubs. It was late Friday afternoon and enjoyment was beckoning him. This nightclub was one of many establishments that had grown familiar with Max over the years. As recognizable as Max had become to many people in the city, he remained an enigma to them all. Max appeared detached yet engaged, separate yet connected. The personas he displayed were as versatile as each moment that he lived. His charismatic presence seemed to create reality around him. People felt alive and important in his presence as his calculating mind entangled them in his web of intellect and pleasure.

Everyone knew the financial heights Max had achieved but no one knew the man who had achieved them. Some tried to define the mystery behind the man. They ultimately drowned in their swirling sea of curiosity, more questions raised than answered.

Max's senses heightened as he walked down Regent Street toward Piccadilly Circus. His consciousness wrapped itself around each step that he took, every glance that he offered. He felt the briskness of the air as it disheveled his hair. He turned his head to catch the sound of traffic rushing by.

As he entered the nightclub, he was greeted by the loud buzz of the crowd. Many locals ended their workday early to commence their weekend entertainment.

Max glanced up after situating himself at his table and saw Sarah stomping in his direction. It took him a moment to remember why her face was curled with anger. He recalled the conversation in his office several weeks ago when he returned from the cruise.

Sarah stormed up to him. Her voice was loud, her tone fuming. "Maximilian Fairchild, I'll have you know that there isn't a woman on this premise with a brain that would have anything to do with you anymore. I've spread the word about you." Sarah shifted her stance and waved her arm. "I've told them how callous and shallow and empty you are. They now know how you use women and then hang them out to dry." Sarah's white complexion had turned as red as a cayenne pepper. "So you better find a new place to stalk your prey."

"Whoa, Sarah." Though Max hadn't expected this, he rebounded quickly. "Sarah, you don't need to be so hostile."

"Oh, I don't?" Sarah's jaw reminded Max of a clenched vise-grip. "I thought we had something special. I thought I actually meant something to you, but I guess not." She stopped to catch her breath. "I wonder if anybody does, or ever has."

"Sarah, look." Max reached his hand toward her. She jerked away. He spoke calmly, consoling her. "Sarah, you caught me the first day back from a ten day stint out of the country. I was bombarded with work. Quite frankly, in that moment I wasn't thinking of anything 'but' work."

"That didn't give you the right to say those awful things to me," Sarah glared.

"Awful?" Max titled his head. "How? By saying we had a wonderful couple of weeks - nothing more and nothing less? Maybe it's how you perceived what I said, versus what I actually said."

Looking into Max's eyes, Sarah's jaw slowly began to loosen. She lowered her head. "Well, Max, it just seemed to me that - -"

"Sarah." Max stood up, put his arm around her waist, and drew her close. "Please let me buy you a drink."

"I don't know what to think anymore Max." Sarah said softly.

He watched her closely, waiting for her to continue.

"I really thought we shared something special – that's all."

"We did," Max replied. "But it doesn't change the fact that it was a moment in time, one to be lived fully but not clung to. There are always new moments waiting to be lived."

Sarah's defenses dropped. She wanted to stay angry and walk away. She couldn't. Somehow this moment was different. This was the same man who shared her weeks of bliss in Rome. Max had a bad moment that day in his office. That was all – nothing more, nothing less.

Max pulled out a chair at his table and Sarah joined him. He ordered her favorite drink, a Black Russian made with Absolut. They drank and danced into the wee hours of the morning as Sarah melted within his magnetic embrace, his wit, his charm. When the nightclub closed, Sarah followed Max home without a questioning word or thought. She welcomed his passionate touch.

When they ceased making love, Sarah lay quietly on Max's chest. She glanced up at him and whispered, "Max, I think I love you."

Max looked at her, cocked his head, and responded, "Sarah, I'm somewhat surprised at you. I've been honest with you from the start. I promised you a good time and I showed you one. I also made it clear not to expect an ongoing relationship, didn't I?" He sat up and squared his face with hers. "I tried to explain this again to you when I returned from the cruise but you were offended." His tone remained warm, calm, and detached. "I never misled you. I enjoyed you again tonight, but I can't promise there will be a tomorrow. We've shared another experience – another wonderful moment in time."

Sarah was dumbfounded. "But, Max, how can you say that? Don't you care about me at all?" She choked on her words as tears welled in her eyes.

"I do care, Sarah." Max took her face in his hands. "I care enough to be honest, now and always." He reached for her.

The Unexpected Awakening

Sarah pulled away from him. Reality slapped her like someone trying to rouse her from a sound sleep. She was stunned at the realization that Max meant what he said. Confusion and disillusionment riveted her. She dressed and left without another word. Tears streamed down her face as she closed the door behind her.

Max rested his head on the back of his bed. He understood Sarah's need to leave. He didn't try to stop her. Images of all the different women he had known over the years floated through his sleepy mind – all except Rachel. Max kept a barrier as thick as concrete between his thoughts and her memory.

He was forty years old, never been married, and probably knew more women across the world than most men dreamt of. He was honest with every woman he met. He promised to treat them well and enjoy them fully. He never promised more than that. Relationships lasted from one night to months at a time. He loved the chase, the challenge, the catch, and the passion. He found that momentary and intermittent pleasure kept things enjoyable, intense, and uncomplicated.

He sat up in bed with a start. Again, Christine's face flashed before his mind's eye. From the moment he first saw her, something unfamiliar had swept through him. This woman, not even the most beautiful of women, had somehow seized his interest.

He got out of bed and began pacing. He went to his stereo and put on one of his favorite musicians, Dulcie Taylor. Her voice reminded him of Rachel's, many years ago. As the music seductively drew Max in, he was overtaken by an urge to write Christine a letter. He reached for a pen and let his thoughts flow to the paper in an unrestrained stream of consciousness.

He finished writing, then sealed and addressed the envelope.

He dared not reread the words that poured from pen to paper. He would not second-guess his expressive outburst, foreign as it was. He dressed and made his way to the post office before he could change his mind. The cold night air heightened his senses to attention as the letter slipped from his fingertips into the mail slot.

SEVEN

A week later, Christine came home from work and glanced through the mail. Her pulse quickened as she spotted the envelope with the UK return address. She reached for her letter opener and slowly slid it across the top of the envelope. Her stomach quivered with curious uncertainty.

Dear Christine,

Strange as time goes by I seem to move closer to you. When I think of you, I ponder reality and existence.

I am a person who thinks deeply about many things, things that most people don't even see or want to see. As I sit now writing to you, I am listening to one of my favorite musicians, Dulcie Taylor. Ironically, we danced to one of her songs on the cruise. Her music moves me to write many things to you.

When we danced and I said you gave me energy, I spoke bluntly because time seemed short. I knew you felt the same, yet you were frightened like a gazelle being hunted. All I wanted was to be close to you. I am about to close, but before I do, I ask only that you tell me your story.

Max

Her mind surged with wonder. Who was this man? What did

he want from her? Why did her entire being react so strongly to the thought of him?

Michael arrived home shortly after Christine. She asked about his day then told him about Max's letter. She reached her hand out and offered Michael the letter to read.

"I really don't care to read it, Christine." Making sure the children were out of earshot, he added, "What is wrong with you, anyway? It's just not right. He doesn't belong in our life."

"What are you talking about, Michael?" Her back stiffened. "It's only a letter for heaven's sake."

"Christine, I am too tired to get into this right now. Save it for another time," Michael said firmly, then headed for the den to say hello to Joseph and Elizabeth.

As they went to bed that evening, she pondered the letter and the man who'd written it. Then she turned her attention to Michael. "I'm sorry if the letter disturbed you."

Michael rolled away from her. "I really don't want to talk about it tonight."

The next morning, Christine awoke early and slipped out of bed, leaving Michael sleeping. She removed the letter from the desk in the den and slowly reread each word. Something stirred deep within her. Michael was right. Maximilian didn't belong in their lives, but she couldn't shake the feeling that she was somehow destined to know and understand this stranger. She knew Max wasn't someone to be in love with, or to share life with, just someone to understand. That was all she knew and she knew it to be true with every ounce of her being.

# # #

Christine worked diligently at the law firm throughout the morning. At lunchtime she drove to the nearby music store and purchased Dulcie Taylor's CD, Mirrors and Windows. She blared the music through her car speakers as she drove to her favorite park.

When she arrived, she pulled into a parking spot facing the mountainside. The sun sprinkled the trees with speckled light.

She listened intently as the powerful melody rolled out of each chord, trying to grasp insight to Max as it played.

She replayed the music over and over again. Each time, the music resonated deeper within her soul. As she listened, she gazed at the Aspen trees standing at complete attention on the mountainside, like soldiers guarding their palace. The golden leaves radiated while sunlight scattered effervescent hues across the landscape. The flowers in the field began to sway in lifelike motion as the clouds overhead became translucent, mirroring the sun's enchantment. The air itself became rippling waves of vibrating energy. She felt elevated and connected to all the beauty that surrounded her. She was overwhelmed with awe, tranquility, and understanding. She suddenly saw everyone and everything in the universe as an integral part of a unified, evolving life process. Everyone and everything that had existed - existed now, or would exist in the future - was a necessary, meaningful, and vital part of the whole. She remained in a state of heightened consciousness for several moments. Gradually, the landscape and her mind slowly returned to their prior state. She sat motionless. She didn't understand what had just happened to her, but she knew she would grow to understand it. She had to.

Because of her experience in the park, the rest of her day resounded with enhanced significance and purpose. She felt more connected to everyone and everything. When she arrived home that evening, Joseph, Elizabeth, and Michael seemed more important and special than ever before.

After the kids were safely tucked into bed, she and Michael

returned to the den and snuggled on the sofa. She attempted to tell Michael about the things she experienced throughout her day. He looked at her as if a total stranger had invaded his home.

When she had finished, Michael turned her shoulders to face him. "Christine, what has happened to you? What has happened to us?"

She stroked the side of Michael's head with her hand, her voice calm and soothing. "Michael, I've just changed and grown, that's all. I love you more than ever. Don't you understand that?" Her eyes twinkled with eagerness.

Michael continued to stare at her in disbelief. His eyes and voice drooped. "No, Christine, I don't understand. I see your changes these last couple of years and I'm glad for your growth. The problem is that all of your changes seem to happen because of someone outside of our marriage, not *because* of our marriage." Michael cast his eyes toward the floor. "God, Christine, now you're talking about some 'enlightened experience' because of some stranger from the cruise." He looked up and glared at her, his voice rising with anger. "How the hell do you expect me to understand 'that'?"

She grasped Michael's face with both hands and held it close. "But, Michael, don't you see? It doesn't matter how my changes have happened. All that matters is that we can be stronger and better because of them."

Michael pulled her hands away from his face and stood up. "No, Christine, I disagree. It 'does' matter how the changes happened." He turned and headed to bed without saying another word.

She curled her legs up under herself on the sofa and shook her head with confusion. Her words had fallen like water over the edge of a cliff, plummeting downward without a basin to catch them. Somehow, Michael could not, or would not, understand what she was trying desperately to communicate.

She loved Michael completely. She believed now, finally, she was capable of being his true partner and yet, he was slipping away from her. These last few years she felt more secure in herself than ever before and was excited to share it all with Michael. Sure, there had been several men that had caught her attention and interest over the years but they were nothing more than friends. Why couldn't Michael see that? It just didn't make any sense to her. She stood up, stretched, and yawned. Michael would come to understand, she thought. Everything would be fine. In time, everything would be better than it had ever been.

EIGHT

As Michael drove to work the next morning, sadness wrapped around him like a thick fog on a chilly day. The surrounding mountains were draped in the ominous darkness of winter's approach. Heavy clouds muted any hope of the sun. He felt cold and alone. Christine was a stranger to him. Her vibrancy and enthusiasm eluded him. What happened to the woman who he married eight years ago? What happened to the woman who thrived on their relationship? How could she be attracted to a total stranger who was thousands of miles away?

All morning at work Michael struggled to concentrate and focus on the tasks at hand. He felt as though he was being sucked into a vacuum of darkness. When lunchtime arrived, he reached into his desk and pulled out Heather's telephone number. He dialed it without hesitation, as if in a trance.

"Hello," Heather answered.

Michael was silent as he jolted back to the reality of what he'd just done.

"Hello?" Heather repeated.

"Heather, it's Michael Amory," Michael announced slowly.

"Michael, you sound as if something is wrong. What's up?"

Michael's jaw stiffened as he shifted uncomfortably in his chair. "Nothing, really. How are you doing?"

"I'm doing just fine," Heather said, then paused a moment before continuing. "I have some time before leaving for an appointment. What's on your mind?"

Without further coaxing, Michael succumbed, like a dam giving way after years of erosion from storm upon storm. Michael talked and talked and talked.

Heather listened. She could hear Michael's love for Christine in every sentence. She also heard his quiet cry for help and understanding within each word spoken.

Michael talked nonstop for close to twenty minutes. Finally, he caught himself. "Heather, I'm sorry. I didn't intend to go on like this. I called to see how you're doing and instead I - -"

Heather interrupted. "Michael, it's all right. That's what friends are for." She paused for a moment before adding, "You know Michel, at first, I just wanted your luscious body but I'll settle for friendship." She laughed, trying to ease the seriousness of the moment. "All kidding aside, Michael, I know I made you uncomfortable the last night on the ship and I apologize for that. I drank more than I should have and became a tease, as usual." She reached for her cup of green tea on her desk. "I sensed something was out of balance between you and Christine, but I never intended any harm to either one of you." Heather took another sip of her tea and continued in a playful tone. "Actually, I would have been scared to death if you'd taken me up on my offer that night."

Michael's limbs relaxed as he let out a slight sigh.

Heather paused again. Her voice grew serious. "Even when I first called you, it surprised me. I've never been involved with a married man. Too many complications and, besides, someone always gets hurt in that scenario. There are plenty of single men to have a good time with." Heather waited a moment to see if Michael had something to add. He remained silent. "I made up my mind not to call you again. But, Michael, I'm glad that you called me." Her voice deepened. "We can just be friends, and since we're miles apart, our friendship will be safe, no one will get hurt."

"You know," Michael said, "I can't believe I just spilled my guts to you like that." He sighed. "There's really no one, other than Christine that I'm open with. Even then, Christine teases me about being a nonverbal communicator. I guess both Christine and I are acting out of character these days." Michael hesitated, then added, "Thanks for listening, Heather."

"You are welcome."

Glancing at his watch, Michael said, "Heather, I just realized I have a meeting that starts in three minutes. I'm sorry, but I have to run. I'll call again soon and next time, you do the talking and I'll do the listening."

"Sounds like a plan."

"Promise?"

"Promise. Talk to you soon."

Michael hung up the receiver. The tautness in his shoulders and back had dissipated.

# # #

That evening, Michael did not tell Christine about his telephone conversation with Heather. He decided it wasn't necessary. After all, Heather was just a friend and lived in California. She wasn't a threat to their marriage. He would tell Christine if and when it seemed appropriate or necessary. For now, it was his secret to keep locked deep inside the pocket of his weary heart.

As they went to bed that evening, passion surged within Michael. He reached for Christine and they made love into the wee hours of the morning.

NINE

Max created a cyclone of activity as the days and weeks ensued. Ever since he had written the letter to Christine, he'd thrown himself into work. Something was struggling to be rekindled within him, and he wanted nothing to do with it. Max wanted to experience the pleasures of life - one moment at a time - with no commitments and no concerns. He wanted to let each and every moment flee his consciousness, as quickly as it arose and was experienced.

It was Wednesday evening. Max left work after another triumphant day at the game of commercial architecture. He stopped by his flat to change his clothes and check the mail before heading out for an evening at the pub. The light purple envelope from the US, addressed in feminine penmanship, jumped out at him as he perused the mail. His pulse quickened as he slid his letter opener across the top of the envelope. Faint traces of lilac taunted his nostrils as he read.

Dear Max,

It has taken me a while to respond to your letter. I am happily married with two wonderful children, but it did not escape me that something transpired between us. I have thought a lot about it, and it seems there is some sort of "spiritual" connection between us, for lack of a better word. It's not a feeling of lust or physical attraction, but rather a need to understand just who you are as a person. I cannot explain it any better than that right now.

I listened to Dulcie Taylor's music over and over again. You know what, Max? I had the strangest thing happen to me. I suddenly felt as though the universe opened up to me. For a few moments, it 'all' made sense. For a few moments, I felt connected to 'everything'.

That probably sounds crazy, but somehow I think you know what I'm talking about. Actually, I think you understand completely but for some reason, you have chosen to turn away from all that you understand.

As for me telling you my story, it's a rather simple but happy one. I honestly believe I am one of the truly blessed people in this world. I have a great set of parents, four siblings that are as much my friends as brothers and sisters, a loving husband, and two great kids. That probably sounds too good to be true, but it is surprisingly true. That's not to say that I haven't had my share of ups and downs, but I believe that's all a part of it. The bottom line is that I have a lot of love in my life and because of that I know I am a very fortunate person. After all, Max, when it's all said and done, love is all that really matters. So, you probably anticipated something a lot juicier but that's it, in a nutshell.

Now, please tell me your story as well.

I hope this letter finds you healthy and happy. Take care of yourself.

Sincerely,

Christine

Max placed her letter in his desk drawer and walked across

his white marble floor to the glass and brass bar that lined the east wall of his great room. He grabbed a bottle of vodka, tilted his head back, and lifted the bottle to his lips, letting the vodka slowly slide down his throat. He glanced in the mirror behind the bar, decided not to change his clothes, took the keys from his pocket, and walked out the door. He would go to his favorite local pub, get extremely drunk and obliterate every word of Christine's letter from his consciousness.

At the pub, Max tried to engage in conversation with different women, but none could hold his interest. The more he drank and the harder he tried to forget Christine, the more her dark, knowing eyes flashed before him. Finally, as the pub was emptying out, he pulled out the paper with Christine's number, and dialed it from his cell phone. With the time difference, it was only six in the evening in Colorado. Christine was fixing dinner and Michael was on his way home when the telephone rang.

"Hello," Christine said as she tucked the receiver under her chin so she could finish peeling the potatoes. She heard loud noise in the background and the voice on the other end was barely audible.

"Christine? It's Max,"

Her heart skipped several beats, then seemed to stop altogether. "Max?"

"Yes, Christine. I received your letter today."

Max paused momentarily, then spoke with a voice both distant and dreamlike. "So, Christine, that day in the park you had a glimpse of life from the mountaintop. For a moment, the universe made sense and you felt connected to everything around you." Max paused again, this time for several moments. To her, it seemed like hours. Max's tone grew melancholic. "Indeed, Christine, simple physics explains that all things are made of the same core elements. You 'are' physically connected to everything at some level in some way." Max took a long, slow breath. "But regardless, Christine, in the end, it always comes back to a matter of survival."

"I disagree," she replied automatically. "There is more to life than that, Max."

"Is there, Christine? Have you ever really thought about it?" Max spoke calmly, with unyielding confidence. "Unfortunately, most people are too busy trying to survive, or too afraid to think for themselves, to question life's purpose." He stopped speaking for several moments while she waited patiently on the other end of the line. "It is far easier for people to live by beliefs they have been taught, and obey rules they have been given, than to dig deep inside themselves to seek their own answers."

Her brain spun wildly as she processed Max's words. Joseph and Elizabeth bounded around the corner from the den and into the kitchen. "Daddy's home. Daddy's home." Their excited little voices leapt through the phone lines and smacked Max on the other end.

"I must go," Max stated and abruptly hung up.

She stood in disbelief, the telephone still cradled to her ear. She jumped when Michael caressed her shoulders from behind, gently kissing her neck. The receiver fell to the floor as Michael whispered, "Hi hon."

She took a deep breath, turned to face Michael and smiled. "Michael, you startled me." She kissed him softly on the lips, then bent down to pick up the phone. She decided she'd tell Michael about Max's call after the children were in bed.

# # #

Max sat motionless as he hung up his phone.

Angela was passing by with a tray of drinks for one of her

tables. "Max, are you okay?"

He glanced at her with a somber face. "Yes, Angela. I'm just fine." He opened his wallet, took out enough money for his tab and tip, then departed.

# # #

When the children were sleeping, Christine repeated word for word the conversation that had transpired with Max. Michael listened, excused himself, and went to bed without a word. She sat a while longer on the sofa in the den with her head still whirling in thought. Then she got up, went to the desk, and reached for a pen from the top drawer. She sat down in the oak desk chair, grabbed her lilac scented stationary, and began to write.

TEN

Several weeks passed. Michael thought of Heather often but could not bring himself to telephone her again. A part of him longed to, another part feared it. His ability to confide in Heather was comfortable but confusing to him. As another long day at the bank slid to a close, Michael glanced out his office window. The golden leaves had abandoned the trees, making way for winter's arrival. It wouldn't be long until the holidays were here. Thoughts of the past, glided across Michael's memory like the scattered clouds making their way across the fading autumn sky.

#

As a child, Michael had been reserved, serious and private, more reflective than interactive. His older brother, and only sibling, William, had been the shining star of the family. Michael had excelled in academics, just not as much as William. Michael had played several sports and the piano, just not as well as William. Michael knew his parents loved him, maybe just not as much as William. Michael learned to be quietly content with his accomplishments, without striving for the limelight.

He had dated in high school, but not much or often. He was too busy with academics and sports to create the time for a serious relationship. When Michael met Christine in college, everything changed. He remembered the first time he saw her, the fall of freshman year. It was the second day of orientation. He was looking out his dorm window, taking in the picturesque view of soft green lawn, sculptured shrubs, wrought iron benches, and the majestic Colorado Blue spruce that decorated the center of the campus. This tree, in its simplicity and solidarity, was the crowning glory of the elaborate campus landscape.

Michael couldn't help but notice Christine. She was sitting alone on the grass, beneath the magnificent spruce, reading. From that first moment, she had fascinated him. He observed her, unnoticed, wondering why she was always alone. Michael watched for her throughout each day during that first week on campus - at registration, in the bookstore, and the cafeteria, but to no avail. At the end of each day, however, he would again observe her from his room while she read beneath the protective shade of her tree. She seemed to belong there, an integral part of the beauty that surrounded her. He wanted to introduce himself but didn't want to disturb her privacy, her sacred reading ritual.

The first day of classes, Michael raced into his English Lit class after sprinting from the other side of campus, to find 'her' sitting in one of the front rows, notebook open, ready for class to begin. His heart pounded wildly as he took a seat near the back. He barely listened to the professor, distracted by her presence and the possibility of meeting her. Her blonde tresses glistened as they cascaded down her back. When class was finished, he mustered his courage and approached her in the hallway.

"Hi, my name is Michael Amory," he announced, surprising even himself.

She looked at him, bit at her bottom lip, and after a long pause, she smiled. "I'm Christine Morgan." She extended her hand to greet him. "It's nice to meet you, Michael."

"Now what?" Michael thought to himself. Trepidation tackled his confidence and threw it to the ground. "I, uh, have seen you on campus, underneath that tree and, uh, I just wanted to

introduce myself." Shades of pink and crimson slowly inched their way up his neck like streaks across the sky at sunset.

She looked into his eyes. Their hazel color, a blend of brown, green and grayish-blue, were mesmerizing. Their sincerity and shyness touched her. "I'm glad you did." She tried to alleviate his discomfort. "Boy, this class is going to be a tough one, don't you think?"

"Yes, it sure is," Michael responded, knowing full well he couldn't tell her the first thing about what went on in that classroom, hoping she wouldn't discuss specifics. His focus and attention had been elsewhere.

"What other courses are you taking this semester?" Michael asked after taking a deep breath, slowly recovering from his awkwardness.

And so it began. Conversation flowed freely. Instant familiarity and comfort connected them. Michael walked her across campus to her calculus class. They decided to meet at the cafeteria for dinner, then go to the library to study. This became their routine, day in and day out.

They spent the next several weeks sharing class, dinner, studying, and late night talks. One evening after a two-hour library session, she suggested they take a walk on the outskirts of campus. It was a magnificent autumn evening, clear sky, crisp air. There were so many stars that it reminded her of her mother's blouse, the one with countless numbers of little white dots on a background of solid black silk. She sat on a patch of grass, beyond campus buildings, traffic, or other distractions - just the grass, beneath the speckled sky.

"Christine," Michael said as she crossed her legs and settled into the dewy, lawn beneath her, "there's a bench just up a little further. That might be more comfortable and less wet."

She smiled. "No thanks, Michael. I prefer the grass. I grew up around nature and the outdoors. We had acres of land to run through, hide in, play in, and just 'be' in." She stretched her arms out behind her and leaned back. "I think that's why I love reading underneath that tree so much."

Michael joined her on the grass. They gazed upward, drawn to the glistening umbrella overhead. Christine finally broke the spell of silent awe. She glanced sideways at Michael, with her head tilted, a coy smile, inviting eyes. "Michael, I feel so at home with you. It's hard to explain." She bit at her lower lip. "But I've never been this unguarded and open with someone before and it feels good." Her smile broadened as her eyes traced a pattern from his eyes to his lips and back again.

Michael reached over, placing his hand gently on the side of her head. His fingers flowed through the golden mane that adorned her tiny face. The gaze between them guided their lips closer and closer to their long awaited union. This first kiss created an explosion within each of them, an instantaneous fusion of flesh and heart. It was a moment they would talk about for years, a moment they would remember forever.

They rolled within an impenetrable embrace, flattening the dewy blades of grass beneath them, delighting the winking stars overhead.

# # #

"Michael," Evelyn Costello interrupted his reflective trance. "Is there anything else you need before I leave for the day?"

Michael shifted his gaze from the window to Evelyn standing at the doorway to his office. "No, Evelyn. I'm all set. Please, feel free to head home."

Evelyn studied Michael's face closely. "Are you all right, Michael? You seem more distracted than usual."

He stood up, stretched his arms, and forced a reassuring smile. "I'm fine, Evelyn, just a little tired. That's all."

"If you say so." Evelyn reassessed his demeanor. "You haven't been yourself for weeks. I hope whatever is pressing on you, eases up soon."

"Really, Evelyn, I'm fine." Michael moved toward the doorway and teased. "Now why don't you leave while you still have the chance, before I find something else for you to do?"

"Say no more. I'm on my way. See you tomorrow, Michael." Evelyn grinned, turned, and departed.

Michael waited to hear Evelyn's footsteps fade down the hallway before closing his office door. He plopped down in the comfort of his soft, leather desk chair. The telephone stared at him, begging to be engaged. He hesitantly accommodated by raising the receiver and dialing Heather's number.

The telephone was on its fourth ring when Heather breathed heavily into the receiver. "Hello, this is Heather."

"Hi, Heather. It's Michael Amory. Did I catch you at a bad time? You sound out of breath."

"Oh, Michael, hello." Delight resonated in Heather's voice. "I'm out of breath because I raced down the hall to catch the phone before the machine picked up. I just got back from a sales appointment and I'm expecting a call to confirm another large contract I have in the works."

"I can call back another time. I wouldn't want to stand between you and a business deal," Michael teased.

"Don't be silly. I thought it might be my client, but I'm thrilled that it's you. Besides, I have call waiting. If we get beeped, I'll put you on hold and see if it's him." She paused. "That's if you don't mind."

"Not a problem. I told you I'd call again and this time it's your turn to talk. Remember?"

"I remember." Heather placed her briefcase on her desk and walked toward the kitchen to get a glass of cold water. "Hmm, what would you like me to talk about?"

"Anything you'd like. I think it's only fair to give you equal floor time after our last conversation." Michael leaned back in his chair. "All kidding aside, Heather, it was helpful for me to let loose a couple of weeks ago. I thought I'd touch base and see how you're doing."

"Like I said, Michael, I was happy to listen and I'm here anytime you want to talk."

Michael leaned forward, pressed his elbows on his desk and propped the receiver on his shoulder. "Heather, does it upset Matt that I call you? I wouldn't want to cause a problem for you and your relationship with him."

Heather's breathing had returned to normal. "Matt and I aren't living together anymore. I thought you knew that." She took a sip of water. "He moved out months before the cruise. We took the trip together because we'd planned it long before we decided to split up. We're still great friends so it wasn't a problem for either one of us taking the cruise together." Heather returned to her office, sat down at her desk and continued in her perky tone. "I thought I mentioned that on the ship but maybe you didn't hear it. So," Heather chuckled, "the shorter answer to your question is, no, Matt doesn't mind that you call."

"Oh." Michael felt his insides take a playful leap. "I didn't realize that. It's nice that you're still friends but wasn't it hard to break up after living together?"

"Surprisingly, it wasn't," Heather was nonchalant as she sipped on her water. "We had some great times together during those five years but it was time to move on."

Michael was silent for a moment. "Didn't you love him, Heather? I mean you spent five years of your life with the man but you sound as if he was nothing more than a roommate that moved out because he wanted a new place with different décor." Michael leaned back in his chair, still cradling the receiver with his neck and shoulder. "Didn't you two ever talk about marriage and having a family during all that time together?"

Heather twirled a strand of her hair with her index finger. "When I met Matt, we just clicked. We were both passionate about our careers and loved our freedom." Heather's tone was warm but matter-of-fact. "We both entered the relationship with the understanding that it would be monogamous but probably temporary. You see, Michael, Matt and I agreed that it's unrealistic to expect one person to fulfill all of your needs for an entire lifetime." Heather leaned forward and released the strand of hair from her finger, letting it unwind. "We agreed that as long as it felt right, we'd stay together, when it no longer did, we would end it. The first couple of years we were on the same wavelength - best of lovers, best of friends, best of times. Marriage and children never crossed our radar screens." Heather paused. "Matt changed about a year or so ago. He wanted to talk about the future, marriage, a family, etc." Heather took a long breath as she resumed wrapping her hair around her finger. "Well, I thought about it but I just couldn't see my life going in that direction." Heather grew pensive. "Michael, it seems to me that relationships always result in an imbalance, one person needing or wanting more than the other person." She stood up, released her lock of hair, and walked to her bay window. "Anyway, we realized we wanted different things from the relationship. So, we moved on with our lives and stayed friends, just as we promised."

Michael listened without interruption. When he knew she had

finished, he said, "Heather, you didn't answer my question. Did you love him, I mean really love him?"

Heather stood still. Her gut wrenched as if an old wound had suddenly been ripped open. Her smile vanished as she stared out her window, her response barely audible. "Yes, Michael, to the extent I've ever loved anyone, I loved him."

"Heather, haven't you ever been 'in love'? Who was your first love, the one that made your heart pound, the one that kept you daydreaming and sweating bullets every time you thought of him?"

Heather swallowed hard. Her voice grew factual and void of feeling, almost flip as she turned and began pacing throughout her living room. "Michael, if you are referring to 'puppy love', I can honestly say that I never indulged in it. I've watched others writhe in the devastating aftermath of unrequited love. Why anyone would allow feelings for another person to control their happiness is beyond me. It just doesn't make any sense."

"Wow, Heather, that's sad." The words slipped from Michael's lips like Jell-O from a spoon to the floor, before he could catch it. He sat upright in his chair.

"Sad? Michael, think about it. No disrespect intended, but who is the sad one here, you or me?" Heather stopped in the middle of the room, straightening her back. "I'm very content with my life and I don't have the slightest bit of sadness or remorse for any part of it." She returned to her sofa, sat down, and crossed her legs. "You, on the other hand, are tied up in knots because of a marriage that's gone awry. So how can you label my thoughts or experiences sad?"

"I'm sorry, Heather. I wasn't trying to criticize," Michael recanted, shifting in his chair. "You're right that I've been tied up in knots but you know what Heather?" he continued with unexpected conviction, "I wouldn't trade one minute of the pain and confusion I'm feeling now, if it meant not knowing the happiness I've shared with Christine." He leaned forward on his elbows again. "I guess what I meant to say is that life without real love would be sad," Michael stopped, then quickly added, "For me."

Heather's back tightened as she absorbed each word that Michael spoke. They stung like hypodermic needles as they reached beneath the surface of her skin. The telephone suddenly beeped, alerting her to another call.

"Michael, the other line is beeping. Do you mind holding for a moment?"

"Sure, I'll hold."

Heather's back loosened as she pressed the button to receive the other call. After several moments she returned to the line with Michael. "Sorry about that." Her voice bubbled with victory. "It was the call I expected. They signed the contract. The deal is done."

"Congratulations, that's great!" Michael mirrored her enthusiasm before shifting to an apologetic tone. "Heather, please don't misunderstand anything I said. I certainly wasn't judging you and I hope I haven't offended you."

"I understand, Michael." Heather stood up and strolled into her office, reaching for her briefcase. "I really do. You and I define happiness differently. That's all." She pulled a contract out of her briefcase and laid it on her desk. "We're free to decide those things for ourselves, so no offense taken. Still friends?"

"Still friends," Michael reiterated with a warm smile. "I better wrap things up here at the office and head home. Heather, it was great talking to you. Congratulations again on your deal."

"Thanks. Next time it'll be my dime. I'll catch up with you

sometime soon and see how things are going."

"Sounds good," Michael confirmed. As an afterthought he added, "Oh, Heather, let me give you the number to my private line here at the bank. That's the best way to reach me."

Michael hung up the phone, checked the time, finished a few things, and left for home.

Heather turned to her paperwork and follow-up calls.

Christine and the kids finished the final touches for dinner, awaiting Michael's arrival home.

ELEVEN

The sun was slipping below the horizon, leaving streaks of pink and plum. Max reached down and opened the bottom left office desk drawer and slowly retrieved the unopened letter he had received from Christine over a week ago. He had debated whether to read it. Once decided, he savored the waiting. Now was the time. He rubbed the lilac colored parchment between his fingers and held it up to his nose, inhaling the soft scent. Gingerly, he opened it.

Dear Max,

Needless to say, our brief conversation left my head spinning with thoughts I feel I must share.

You seem to believe that life is nothing more than the physical world in which we find ourselves and that our purpose as human beings is nothing more than to seek survival and/or pleasure. I agree with you that we have the physical component to life. I also agree with you that survival and pleasure play a role in life. But Max, as I said on the phone, there is so much more to life than that. There is meaning and purpose and value in so many things. Each of us is a spiritual being as well as a physical being. Life would be so empty if there were nothing more than this physical existence. Just think how unfulfilling life would be without love. I don't mean romantic love but rather a more generalized human love – the genuine care and concern for someone or something outside oneself. Just think about it, Max.

I will close for now.

Wishing you pleasant thoughts and meaningful moments.

Sincerely,

Christine

Max smiled, folded the letter, replaced it in its envelope, and returned it safely to his desk drawer. He reached for a pen and began to write.

TWELVE

The following Friday, Christine worked later than usual. The Courtney case had heated up. She and David were preparing for the upcoming trial. Michael picked up the kids from school and decided to stop for pizza before heading home.

The smell of freshly baked dough, pizza sauce, and melted cheese welcomed Christine as she opened the back door. "Yum! Something sure smells good."

"It's pizza, mommy." Elizabeth's voice arrived in the hallway before the rest of her little body came racing around the corner.

"Oh, is that what it is?" Christine reached down and pulled Elizabeth into a bear hug. Elizabeth nodded her head yes against Christine's chest as Joseph made a quiet entrance and waited his turn to be greeted.

"Hi, big guy!" Christine said as she pulled Joseph close. "How was your day?"

He smiled, thrilled to be first to share. "It was fun. We started a new book on different animals." His dark eyes darted with animation as he shared the details of what he learned about his favorite passion, animals. She and Michael often mused about Joseph ending up a veterinarian or landing his own television show for animals.

Elizabeth waited patiently while Joseph finished the recap of his day. She took her turn when he was through and chatted nonstop while Christine hung up her coat, placed her purse on the counter, took both Elizabeth and Joseph by the hand, and went in search of Michael. She found him sitting on the sofa in the den, watching the news.

"Hi hon," she greeted as she leaned down to give him a peck on the cheek.

Michael's gaze never left the television as he returned a perfunctory, "Hi."

"What's wrong, Michael?"

"Nothing," he replied, denying his coolness toward her. He stood up and looked at the kids. "How about we tackle that pizza, guys? I don't know about you but I'm starving."

"Me too," Joseph and Elizabeth chimed in unison. They all walked toward the kitchen. As Christine passed the desk in the den she noticed the mail lying on the desktop. Michael must have brought it in. There was one envelope set off to the side. It had multiple stamps and a UK return address.

After dinner, reading with the kids, and settling them in bed, Christine turned to Michael on the sofa. "I noticed the letter from Max on the desk. Is that what has you upset?"

"No," Michael retorted as he glared at the television, "should it?"

"I don't understand why his letters bother you." She sighed. "I really don't. You are welcome to read them."

Michael shifted on the couch but didn't shift his gaze. She grew agitated. "Michael, please, I'm trying to talk to you. This is important to me and I'm trying to share it with you."

Michael muted the television and turned to face her. "Christine, you'll have to excuse me if I'm not interested in 'love letters' you receive from another man."

"Michael, this is only the second letter from him and that conversation I had with him was, uh, oh, it was philosophical, not romantic in nature." Ignoring Michael's total lack of interest, she continued, her voice gaining momentum and enthusiasm as she spoke, "Michael, it's hard to explain but what he says makes me think about things. What people believe and why, how people view life, why people view life the way they do." She took a deep breath before continuing. "I've been thinking so much about so many things that sometimes I think my brain will explode."

Michael shook his head and mumbled, "I'm glad he can do that for you." He pressed the mute button a second time and returned the sound to the television as he turned away from her and focused back on the program he'd been watching.

"Damn it, Michael. Why won't you let me talk to you anymore?"

Michael hesitated a moment, still staring at the television, then replied, "Because, Christine, I don't want to listen to how a total stranger excites you." Michael turned to face her, his words snapping like piranha. "What don't you understand about that?"

"It's not about 'him'. What don't you understand about 'that'? It's about 'me' and the things 'I'm' thinking'."

Michael's voice escalated. "Things you're thinking 'because' of him." He stood up, took a deep breath, and tried to calm down, then glanced down at her. "Look, Christine. I don't want to fight about this. Just understand that I'm not going to talk about it. I told you from the start that he didn't belong in our lives. I'm not about to make him more a part of it by having ongoing discussions about him." Michael exhaled; his tone softened. "Christine, that's the best I can do."

She acknowledged the pained look on Michael's face. She stood up and took his hands in hers. "I'm sorry, Michael. None of this is meant to hurt you. I feel I'm becoming a better person, a better partner, not the opposite." She wanted to explain further but recognized the futility of her effort.

"I just wish I was enough for you."

"But you are, Michael, as my spouse and partner. Other people enter our lives and affect us, regardless of age, sex or background, but not in the same way our lifetime partner does. Don't you see the difference?"

Thoughts of Heather skipped across Michael's mind. He internally debated whether now was the time to tell Christine about his new friendship but decided against it. "I guess," Michael acquiesced, "but, Christine, can we drop this conversation for now? I'm tired and really don't have the energy for it."

"Sure." As the word left her lips, aloneness filled her heart.

Michael yawned. "I think I'll head to bed early if you don't mind."

"That's fine. I'll join you in a little bit." She tried to smile as Michael gave her a kiss on the forehead before turning and heading toward the bedroom.

She plopped back down on the sofa. In her mind, Max could just as easily be a seventy-year old woman with the same ideas and have the same impact on her. Maybe she was being unfair expecting Michael to understand. Maybe it was wrong for her to share all of this with Michael but she had never hidden anything from him, nor did she want to. He was her best friend. As she mused, she remembered Max's letter on the desk, still unopened. She jumped up to retrieve it, anxious to discover its contents. She snuggled back into the couch as she tore it open and began to read.

Dear Christine,

Your letter was interesting and refreshingly naive.

Isn't 'love', irrespective of the type, merely another form of pleasure? Christine, different people define pleasure in different ways by making different choices. Some people find pleasure in the basics - food, sex, expensive toys and the freedom to pursue them all, exactly how they want. Others find pleasure in being married, raising children, helping others, trying to make a difference in this world. Even altruism brings pleasure to those who choose it.

Christine, everyone, when push comes to shove, will make choices that promote their individual survival and/or pleasure over everything else, however they define that for themselves. It's in our nature as a species. The more civilized man has become the more civilized his way of surviving and seeking pleasure. It all comes back to the same thing – time after time –person after person.

I will close for now.

Max

Christine's mind raced from one thought to another, about life, people, choice, free will, meaning, purpose or lack thereof. Time passed as thoughts flooded her brain. It was hours later that she finally slipped into bed, curled up behind Michael, and fell asleep.

THIRTEEN

Several weeks of hectic meetings and sales calls left Heather both tired and elated from her growing success. It was an early end to a long Thursday. She slipped out of her confining business suit into her comforting black sweat pants and matching t-shirt, poured herself a glass of Australian merlot, turned on Brahms, and settled onto her sofa. Heather reached for the phone as she remembered it was her turn to call Michael.

"This is Michael."

"Hi, Michael. It's Heather."

Michael had just returned to his office after a lengthy and taxing meeting with his team. The bank's biggest marketing campaign was less than three months away. With many details still needing attention, they'd been putting in some late nights. Heather's voice was an unexpected reprieve.

"Hi, Heather. How've you been?" Michael's pulse quickened.

"I've been great. I'd have called sooner but it's been a crazy couple of weeks for me. I've had one meeting after another but," Heather said as she took a sip of her wine, "I'm happy to report that I'm selling even more than I expected!"

"That's terrific," Michael replied. "You really love your career, don't you?"

"Absolutely." Heather leaned her head back against her sofa and twirled her wine glass in her hand, watching the red liquid swirl about. "I look forward to getting up every morning and tackling the day. It's a buzz. I love it."

"You're one of the fortunate ones." Michael grew reflective. "So many people just go through the motions with their job. They feel trapped and unhappy rather than excited and charged."

"I know. I see it all the time with different doctors that I meet." Heather pulled her left leg up and tucked it underneath her. "Some of them are passionate about their profession; others are disillusioned and marking time until retirement." She sighed. "What a sad way to live. You enjoy your work, don't you, Michael?"

"Most days," Michael chuckled, "I'm also one of the fortunate ones that thrive on what I do. Some days are obviously more enjoyable than others, but, overall, I enjoy it."

"I thought so, but just wanted to make sure you weren't living a life of quiet desperation without telling me." Heather laughed.

Michael grew silent as Heather's remark ripped through him like a scythe.

"I'm sorry, Michael. That was insensitive. I didn't mean it the way it came out."

Michael leaned forward on his desk as he rubbed his forehead. "That's all right. My nerves are a little raw lately. Don't worry about it." He stood up and stretched his neck in a circle, then settled back into his chair. "Heather, tell me about your family. Do you have brothers or sisters?"

"Nice transition, buddy," Heather replied. "Let's see where to begin."

With that Heather told her story without edits. Michael sensed the words she didn't speak and understood the pain she communicated with her omissions.

# # #

Heather was an only child. Her father was a senior executive at a Fortune 500 technology firm and her mother, a partner in a prestigious investment firm. Both her parents traveled incessantly. Madeline, the live-in nanny, was responsible for Heather's care. Heather lacked nothing - except her parents' love and attention. Madeline was twenty when she joined the Smithstone household as Heather's nanny. She adored Heather from the moment she first saw her. Madeline loved her as if she had carried her in her own womb and had given her life.

Heather's stunning looks were present at birth and increased as she grew. Her early childhood was filled with luxury, traveling, and tutors rather than neighborhood games, nearby parks, and school friends. Madeline was her only anchor.

Heather attended a private school for junior high and Beverly Hills High School after that. her parents bought her a Jaguar for her sixteenth birthday and sent her to Paris to celebrate. Unfortunately, they weren't able to accompany her because of their pressing business demands. They sent Madeline and one of Heather's high school friends instead.

Heather's looks and presence commanded attention everywhere she went. She dated off and on but never seriously. Her expertise was teasing the boys, leaving them breathless and longing. It was a game to her.

She was as bright as she was beautiful and attended Stanford University. She majored in marketing and graduated with honors. It was at Stanford that she lost her virginity. She had decided it was time. Her target - a prominent, divorced professor, fifteen years her elder. The relationship lasted several months before she grew tired of him and moved on, mission accomplished.

Upon receiving her Master's Degree in Business, and researching various options, Heather decided on a career in pharmaceutical sales. The income potential was high; beauty and brains would be a tremendous advantage. Heather's success and achievement came swiftly, with relative ease. That was five years ago. The accomplishment and dollars associated with it had become addictive. She looked forward to embracing each day, new faces, new challenges, more success, more money, more recognition.

Through every change, Madeline remained a constant. Madeline married the year Heather left for Stanford but never lost touch for long. Several years later, at age thirty-eight, Madeline still hoped to give birth to her own flesh and blood. At forty-two, she was successful and Christopher Robert came bounding into the world at ten pounds, two ounces, after a difficult pregnancy and horrific labor. Madeline died four days later from complications. Her death burned a hole deep within Heather's fragile heart, the heart that only Madeline knew and shared. Heather lost the only part of her where love existed. Her shield of emotional protection became impassable.

She met Matt later that same year. Five years her senior, Matt was already an accomplished artist with a faithful following. Their common interests abounded – devotion to their prospective careers, moving in fashionable circles with prestigious people, and partying. It provided everything that Heather was capable of needing or wanting at the time.

# # #

"Wow," Heather paused and swallowed her last sip of wine. "I can't believe I'm telling you all this." She suddenly felt exposed and nervous. She stood up and headed for the kitchen to refill her glass.

"Don't worry, Heather. Anything you share with me will stay only with me." Michael sat at his desk, straight-backed and attentive. "That goes both ways, I trust."

"Of course. It's just that I--."

"What? Heather, what is it?"

Heather reflected for several moments before answering. "Well, it's just that this isn't like me. I don't mind telling you things but I don't usually share this much information." Heather paused, then tried joking to relieve her discomfort. "I'm used to giving the facts, sir, just the facts."

"Join the club. That's exactly how I felt the day I unloaded everything on you. I've never talked about my marriage with anyone except Christine. I felt awkward at first but then I realized I could trust you. I don't know why I know that, but I do." Michael paused. "I hope you feel the same."

"I do." Heather let another sip of wine slip down her throat. "It's just different for me to open up like this and it'll take some getting used to, I guess." She felt naked, exposed, as if under a roving spotlight that revealed each and every flaw as it illuminated her flesh.

"Heather, you still sound ill at ease." He waited for her response but she was silent. "It's okay; your thoughts are safe with me. I promise."

"Thanks, Michael," Heather whispered as his voice rushed over her like a summer breeze, making her feel secure again.

Michael's line began beeping, signaling another call was waiting on his private line.

"Heather, I hate to do this to you but my other line is beeping. Do you mind holding for a quick minute?"

"That's fine, go ahead." She welcomed the chance to regain her balance.

Michael clicked to the second line. It was Christine. He could feel the tenderness in her voice. "Hi, I just wondered if you knew how much longer you might be. I fed the kids but they'll want to say goodnight over the phone if you think you'll be much longer."

Michael glanced at his watch. It was after eight. "Oh, I'm sorry, Christine. Please tell the kids I'm sorry for missing dinner but that I'll be home in time to read to them before bedtime."

"Okay. We'll see you when you get here."

"I'll leave shortly."

Michael switched back to Heather. "Heather, I didn't mean to leave you on hold for so long. It was Christine wondering what time I'll be home. Boy, I didn't realize how late it was."

"That's all right. It gave me the chance to collect myself." Heather set her wine glass on the end table. "I better let you get home to your family." Her stomach growled as she headed to the kitchen to fix herself a salad.

"Yes, I better get moving." Michael glanced out his office window at the stars making their entrance into the sky. "It was great talking to you again, Heather."

"You too, Michael. I'll talk to you soon." As she hung up the receiver, a warm flush rushed through her body. She wrapped her arms around her chest and considered herself hugged.

# # #

Throughout the weeks that ensued, Michael and Heather talked often. They shared everything from their favorite color to their deepest thoughts and dreams. Michael felt alive again. He felt needed and wanted again.

Michael still hadn't brought himself to tell Christine about his relationship with Heather. He believed the right time would come. For now, it was his private oasis of renewal. It kept him sane while he listened to Christine's endless conversations of the new ideas that permeated her thoughts.

The daunting question remained. How did this all come to pass? Why in the hell did he feel that Christine was slipping away from him with no way for him to hold on? At times, pain gnawed at him like a tick burrowing deep into his skin. Other times, he'd shut it all out and pretend that everything was fine. Deep inside, Michael grappled with the uncertainty that surrounded him.

FOURTEEN

Judith handed Max his stack of mail. The lavender colored envelope from Christine lay on top, awaiting his opening touch. Max set the mail aside until Judith's departure. Then he leaned back in his grand leather chair, rested his feet on his desk, and opened his scented treasure.

Dear Max,

Your letter was interesting, but I respectfully disagree that my thoughts are naïve. You see, Max, I think free will allows us to choose what we believe or don't believe. You are free to believe that there is nothing more to life than hedonistic pursuits and I am free to believe that there is an undeniable spiritual dimension to life. That doesn't make either one of us naïve. We just have different perceptions and make different choices. We are free to choose to believe in God or not. We are free to love or hate, to respect or judge, to appreciate or condemn. It all comes back to choice and in the end we are all accountable for the choices that we make.

Max, you know what really struck me as I was thinking about all of this? It's something quite simple, actually. How we choose to live life really does make a difference. Since we are all connected and a part of a larger life process, it does matter if we try to do the right things for the right reasons, not just for ourselves, but for others as well. The choices we make do affect others, often more than we realize.

Max, since everything is all made of the same 'stuff', isn't life a process of becoming more 'conscious' of our 'inherent relationship and interconnectedness' with other people, nature, life itself?

My guess is that you understand exactly what I'm trying to communicate but that something happened, or didn't happen, along the way, to turn you away from living the truth that you know, to make you protect your soul with such vengeance. You still have not told me your story.

I'll close for now. As always, I wish you pleasant thoughts and peaceful choices.

Sincerely,

Christine

Burning energy reverberated throughout Max's body while each word ignited Rachel's memory and the dying embers of soul left within him.

FIFTEEN

Christine awoke, remembering that today was the day her parents would leave for their trip to Italy. Even though they were together the prior week for Thanksgiving, she wouldn't miss an opportunity to chat with them before they departed. She picked up the telephone, anxious to wish them a wonderful time.

"Hello," her father's deep voice resonated through the phone.

"Hi dad. It's Christine. I just wanted to wish you and mom a great trip."

"Well thanks, sweetie. We sure are looking forward to it."

"I imagine you are, and I also imagine that Italy will be gorgeous. You might even get some Christmas shopping done while you're over there," she hinted with a smile in her voice.

"I don't know about that. I left the daily scheduling up to your mother. Hold on, I'll let you talk with her." He paused, then added, "We love you." He handed the phone to her mother before Christine could respond. She chatted with her mother then hung up the phone to get ready for work.

The day was exceptionally busy, from answering phones to assisting David with the preparation of several briefs.

At three o'clock that afternoon, Michael unexpectedly appeared in the doorway of her office.

She glanced up from her desk and then took a double take. "Michael what are you doing here?"

"Christine," Michael said as he closed her office door behind him, "I'm so sorry to have to tell you this." He started choking on the words as he made his way to her desk.

"Michael, what is it?" Her stomach dropped with a thud. Her hands began to tremble as she stood up and grabbed Michael's arms. "Is it Joseph or Elizabeth?" she asked in a panic, tightening her grip.

Michael took her by the shoulders and held her tightly. "No, Christine, it's not the children." He swallowed hard. "It's your parents."

"My parents?" She bit her bottom lip hard as she straightened her back, bracing herself. "What about my parents?"

The words lodged in Michael's throat. He found it hard to breath. "Your sister Melanie called." He spoke slowly, intermittently sucking in air, trying to breathe normally. "She said that they were killed, in a head on collision on their way to the airport a few hours ago."

Christine stood motionless, enveloped in utter disbelief. The words rolled over her like an eighteen-wheeler racing out of control down a steep hill.

She pulled away from Michael. "That can't be! There must be some mistake," Christine insisted, her eyes glaring.

"Oh, Christine," Michael whispered as he pulled her close again. "How I wish it were a mistake."

Michael hugged her tightly but she stood perfectly still, unresponsive, her arms hanging listlessly at her side. Time stopped as reality came crashing in, numbing every inch of her, inside and out. She heard the words but couldn't make sense of them. It wasn't conceivable that the two people she loved so deeply, needed so much, and still depended upon, were gone. It just couldn't be.

As Michael led her down the hallway after gathering her

things, David quietly approached. Michael had forewarned him by telephone before his arrival. David was stunned by the news. He knew that Christine cherished her parents and he could only imagine what this would do to her. "Christine and Michael, I'm terribly sorry." Looking at her he said, "You take all the time that you need. Don't worry about anything here."

Christine nodded in a daze. "Thanks, David," she managed to whisper. David turned and walked back toward his office, visibly shaken.

She was on autopilot – awake but in a trance, moving but not feeling.

# # #

They picked Joseph and Elizabeth up from school. They waited until they were home before explaining the sudden change in daily routine. Christine sat them on the couch in the den. She knelt in front of them, and looked them straight in the eye. She took a tight hold of their small hands before she began.

"Joseph and Elizabeth, this is going to be very hard for you to understand right now but grandma and grandpa have died. They were in a car accident on the way to the airport. We're going back to their house to be with the rest of the family."

Christine paused to gauge the children's absorption of the information and their reaction to it. Their wide-eyed faces reflected attentiveness and confusion.

Elizabeth broke the silence. "Mommy, I don't understand. You mean they are dead – dead? I won't see them again?"

"That's right, sweetie," Christine said as tears escaped and inched their way down her cheeks. "We'll all miss them but we just have to know, deep inside, that they're together and somehow this is meant to be." Christine's tears gained momentum. She inhaled deeply, struggling desperately to find a way to ease this horror for her children. "They will always be with us, in here." She pointed to her chest. "They will always be in our hearts." She heard the words coming out of her mouth as the tears poured down her cheeks. She knew that she was speaking the truth but she didn't know how she'd ever be able to live without her parents. They were her foundation, her lifeline. For now, she had to focus on the children. Anything more was too much for her to handle.

Elizabeth began to quietly sob. Joseph wiggled his foot and stared at the ceiling without saying a word. Christine joined them on the couch, nestling in between them. She pulled Elizabeth into a tight embrace and placed her other hand on Joseph's leg. "Joseph, honey, do you want to talk?"

Joseph pulled his leg away from her, turned his head in the opposite direction, and did not respond.

"Joseph," Christine tried to soothe him, "it's all right if you don't want to."

His leg wiggled wildly during several moments of silence before he blurted out, "I don't believe you." Angry tears exploded. "They can't be dead. They can't be dead."

"Joseph, I would never lie about something like this. They are dead. I understand that it hurts and it's okay to be angry."

Joseph pounded his little fists on the couch. "It's dumb. It's really dumb." He then covered his eyes with his hands. Christine wrapped her other arm around him and he fell against her chest and sobbed. Michael joined them on the couch and they held one another tightly.

SIXTEEN

It was a little after ten in the evening in London on the same day. Max sat at the bar in one of his favorite pubs, conversing with Deborah, the owner of a local fashion boutique. His thoughts abruptly switched to Christine. Something was terribly amiss. The feeling created an unwelcome pit in his stomach. It had been like this with Rachel. He could sense if something was wrong irrespective of physical proximity. His heart pounded faster as tension surged through the muscles of his limbs. He excused himself, without explanation, and headed home. When he arrived, he quickly called Christine's office. With the time difference it would be three-fifteen in the afternoon in Colorado. Christine had just walked out the office door with Michael.

David noticed Christine's private line flashing and picked up the receiver on the third ring. "Montgomery, McCarthy and Steinberg, may I help you?"

"Is Christine there?" Max inquired as he began pacing throughout his flat.

"No," David answered as his grip tightened around the receiver. "Christine will be out of the office for several weeks. Would you like to leave a message for her?"

"Is she all right?"

"May I ask who is calling?" David asked, not recognizing the voice or the accent.

Max stopped pacing and retorted with impatience, "This is

Maximilian Fairchild, a friend of hers from London, and I just bloody want to know if she is all right or not."

"Christine had a personal emergency that arose and is headed out of town with her husband and children."

"I knew something was wrong. What the hell happened? Is she all right?" The intensity of Max's voice surprised both David and Max.

David couldn't recall Christine ever mentioning a friend from London, but sensing the desperation in Max's tone, he answered, "Christine's parents were killed in a car accident today and she is going to her parent's residence to be with her family."

"Do you have a number where I can reach her?"

"I am sorry, Mr. Fairchild, I do not." David unclenched his grip around the receiver. "I'm sure I'll be hearing from them. Would you like me to relay a message for you?"

"Yes, please tell her this," Max hesitated for a moment and then spoke with forcefulness, "Tell her I can feel her sadness. Tell her my thoughts are with her and to call me as soon as she is able." Max recited his office, cell and home telephone numbers to David before hanging up.

David replaced the receiver in its carriage. He leaned back in his chair, astounded at the conversation that had just transpired. It surprised David that he was unaware of this stranger's presence in Christine's life. Who was Maximilian Fairchild? How long had she known him? How did she meet him if he lived in London? One question after another raced through David's mind.

# # #

Max hung up the phone and resumed pacing throughout his flat. He wanted to reach Christine, to let her know that he felt her struggle. He didn't try to escape his feelings but rather he let them pour in, and through him. He walked to the desk in his den, sat down, and fervidly began to write.

With each word he wrote sentiment swelled within him. The fortress of stone that encased his heart and soul, burst. Feelings rushed in with the force of all the years he had repressed them.

SEVENTEEN

As Michael and Christine pulled into her parents' driveway, emptiness swept over her. She could not grasp that her lively, loving parents would not be greeting them at the door. She lowered her head and wept.

Two of her siblings, John and Melanie, had already arrived with their families. They greeted Christine and her family at the door with tearful faces and embracing arms. Joseph and Elizabeth ran off to the family room to join their four cousins in play, temporarily escaping the reality that surrounded them. The adults went to the den to wait the arrival of their other two siblings. Snowstorms in Chicago and Boston delayed both Kathy and Sam.

The entire family was finally together under one roof by nine o'clock that evening. They shared tears and even laughter while telling stories, reminiscing, and mourning. Time passed through a surrealistic haze of disbelief. They talked about practical arrangements and planned for the Memorial Service. Any mention of the upcoming holiday season, reduced them all to tears. This would be the first time in all their lives that they would not share Christmas with their parents. All five children managed to come home each and every year for at least part of the season. There would never be another Christmas with their mom and dad.

Michael watched Christine with wonder. She shed tears with the others but then she would focus on the realities that lie ahead.

It was after midnight when the circle of siblings and extended family finally retired for the night. When Joseph and Elizabeth were fast asleep, Michael and Christine headed to bed.

Michael reached for her and pulled her close. She reciprocated the hug and whispered, "Thank you, Michael, for being so supportive."

He blanched. He thought she would crumble, turn to him and need him during this devastating life trauma. Instead, she appeared sad, but centered, mournful but in control.

She lay there as Michael faded into slumber. Restlessness overcame her. She slipped out of bed, grabbed her clothes, and crept out of the house, making sure not to disturb anyone. As she walked across her parent's property, she listened to the whisper of the wind as it echoed through the barren trees. Suddenly, the pain of death's reality grabbed her like a violent flu, shattering her shock and disbelief. She fell to the ground, gripping her stomach and screamed, "Why? How? Oh God, mom and dad, how can you be gone?" She began sobbing so deeply that her consciousness took flight. She felt as though she was spinning through a dark vortex as waves of grief crashed upon her and through her, with unyielding force, leaving her reeling and gasping for air. She couldn't think – only feel – the churning emptiness, the engulfing void of pain. She felt as if it would never end, that her family would find her sobbing and writhing uncontrollably, forever. Fleeting insights and thoughts interrupted the raw, untamed emotion ripping through her. She didn't know how much time elapsed before conscious thought slowly returned.

She always knew death was out there, hiding in the shadows like an assassin, waiting for his time to strike and steal life away without mercy or sentiment. She'd lived every day as if there'd never be an end to life or the life of her loved ones. She lived each day being caught up in all the minutia of its demands. Now, mortality struck her in the face with its fierceness and its finality. For the first time she fully realized that life is a precious gift, transient, temporary, a momentary blip on the cosmic radar screen. Simultaneously, she grasped death's universality. Life is a gift and death is a certainty, such simple truths, that she'd never seen or fully understood before this devastating moment.

She suddenly had the same feeling she had experienced that day in the park, as though someone had switched the view on her mental telescope. The small, myopic lens through which she had seen life was again transformed into a panoramic, macroscopic, view in which everyone and everything could be seen as a necessary part of the whole. Sadness, tears, and pain were as integral to the life process as happiness, laughter, and joy.

In that moment, she *knew* The Universal Life Force existed and not as something taught or something believed in blind faith, but as an unquestionable reality. She *felt* it in every fiber of her being. She *saw* it as an eternal life process – present everywhere, in everyone, and in everything. She *understood* it as the core of life itself, the source of all that ever had been or ever would be, and the inherent purpose that unifies all physical and spiritual reality by its very existence.

She lay on the cold ground, her eyes swollen shut from crying, shivering with cold. She thought about how wonderful her parents had been. She realized that she had no control over their death; the only control she had was how she responded to it.

She sat up, took a long, deep breath, and looked around. The field glowed brightly in the moonlight. The bare trees stood tall, saluting the whispering night. She stood up, brushed off her achy body, and walked slowly back to her parents' home. Sadness, peacefulness, emptiness, fullness – all moved within her tired, struggling heart. She crept quietly into the bedroom, where

Michael lay sleeping soundly. She glanced at the clock. It was nearly five in the morning. She closed her eyes to catch an hour of sleep before the new day began.

EIGHTEEN

She awoke within the hour. She rose from bed, slipped into her robe, and left Michael still sleeping. Thoughts of Max crept through her brain like a chameleon, ever-present and ever changing. She reflected on how Max had been a catalyst to the transformation she was experiencing. She was grateful that his letters had pushed her to think in new ways and analyze things she had never considered.

The painful day ahead crashed upon her as she looked in the bathroom mirror and saw that her eyes were red and puffy. Her parents were still dead – gone – never to return. She let her tears fall unrestrained before washing her face, brushing her teeth, and heading to the kitchen. She found her brother John staring at a cup of coffee.

"Good morning, John", she whispered and patted his back.

"You know, Christine, I just can't believe this." John kept his eyes focused downward on his coffee cup. "Mom and dad are both dead. As crazy as this sounds, it struck me that even though we're all adults, we're now orphans." His jaw tightened as he pushed back his tears.

"I know what you mean." She pulled up a kitchen stool to join him at the counter. "Last night I walked to the backfields and just started screaming, then sobbing. First I was angry. Then I was sad. It consumed me, completely consumed me." She paused a moment as she relived the memory of last night's experience.

"Then, John, this might seem insane," she hesitated again before finishing, "but for a moment, I realized it's all okay. For whatever reason, it's meant to be."

John stared at her in bewilderment. She became animated, oblivious to John's reaction. She shifted on her kitchen stool. "You know what, John? I'd rather have had the short thirty years of my life with mom and dad as parents than to have sixty years with other parents not as caring or loving." She stopped. She looked past John through the kitchen window to the landscape outside. Silence hung between them for several minutes before she looked back at John. "We have so very much to be grateful for so I've decided to focus on how lucky I've been, rather than all I will miss."

John's jaw hung open wide in disbelief as he stared at her. "Are you crazy? Mom and dad are dead less than forty-eight hours and you are spewing this philosophical bullshit?" John pushed his stool back from the counter and stood up.

"But, John," she stammered, "I was just trying to share my feelings with you and---"

"Spare me, okay?" John turned and stormed out of the room without another word.

Tears rolled down her shocked face. Another wave of grief pounded down on her and she sobbed.

The rest of the day passed in slow motion. Even walking was an effort for her.

The family divided the chores that needed to be done and went about the day. With John's reaction fresh in her mind, she decided not to share her prior night's experience with anyone else. The internal seesaw of gripping grief and subtle peace, rocked within her as she faced each unending task of the day. Her eyes were too tired to let tears flow out of them. She moved within time as if balancing on a high wire in a circus, no safety net below. She couldn't look down – only place one foot in front of the other – hoping to reach the other end without falling.

Suspended animation held the entire family within its trancelike grip the rest of the week. They cried together, laughed together, mourned together, and worked together. The Memorial Service was standing room only in spite of the unexpected snow that blanketed the landscape. Her brother, John, gave her father's eulogy and her sister, Kathy, gave her mother's. Their words projected their parents' lives like a kaleidoscope, creating colorful images of the love, laughter, and foibles that had brightened their home.

The gathering after the service was more of a party than a funeral. In their will, her parents had requested to be cremated, to have a Memorial Service, and then a gathering where people could celebrate their memories and enjoy one another. And so it was. Cocktails flowed along with the tears and laughter. She glanced around the room and knew her parents were pleased. Her brother John sent her an apologetic wink from across the room and she returned it with an understanding smile.

Christine spotted David in the crowd and made her way over to greet him.

"David, I never expected you to travel through this weather to be here."

David reached out and hugged her gently. "Of course I'd be here Christine. It's the very least I can do."

"It means a lot to me." She forced a smile with her puffy, grateful eyes. "Thank you."

David pulled back and perused her closely. She looked tired, thin, and frail.

"Come, David, let me introduce you to the rest of my family," she said as she took his arm.

"Oh, Christine, before I forget," David interjected, "a man called the office looking for you. He was concerned about you and said he sensed something was amiss. His name was Maximilian Fairchild."

She stopped in her tracks. "Really?" she deliberated, her eyes questioning.

"Yes," David confirmed. "He was quite demanding and very frustrated when I wouldn't give him your cell phone number or the telephone number here. You've never mentioned him, Christine, so I chose to be respectful of you and your family's privacy." David paused, watching her closely.

"Oh," she fumbled. "Sure, David, that's fine." She glanced out the window and murmured, "I just wonder how he knew."

"That I can't answer, but I did tell him what happened and that you'd be gone for a couple of weeks," David finished, then remembering Max's message, added, "Oh- he asked me to give you a message. He said that he could feel your sadness, that his thoughts are with you, and to call him as soon as you can. He left his telephone numbers with me if you'd like them."

On one level David's words surprised her. On another level, they did not. Somehow Max had sensed her tragedy. She didn't know how or why, but her connection with Max transcended time and space.

"Thanks for taking the message, David. Do you have the numbers with you?"

"Yes, I do." David reached inside his suit jacket to retrieve the paper he'd written them on. He hesitated, then handed her the numbers and asked, "Christine, who is Maximilian? You've never mentioned him."

Her eyes shifted downward. She wavered before responding.

"David, I met him on the cruise that Michael and I took several months ago. He's quite unusual. It's hard to explain." She bit softly on her lower lip. "It's ..."

As she struggled to find words of explanation, Michael approached to tell her that several guests were leaving and wanted to say their goodbyes.

"Hello, David." Michael extended his hand in a warm handshake. "It's thoughtful of you to be here today."

"My deepest sympathy, Michael, for all of you." David reached for Michael's hand in return. Looking at Christine he added, "You go ahead with Michael. I'll make my way around."

"Are you sure, David? I hate to leave you in the midst of all these strangers."

"I'm sure. I'll be fine. You go ahead." He nudged her arm gently toward Michael.

"Okay, but please don't leave before we have the chance to spend more time with you, David. Promise?" she asked.

"I promise," David agreed. Michael and Christine turned and walked away, arm in arm. David stared after them, wondering how Maximilian fit into their lives.

NINETEEN

On the following Saturday, Christine, Michael, and the children returned home after a long, emotionally draining ten days. The goodbyes to her siblings left her feeling like a new puppy, prematurely lifted from its litter. She longed to stay with them indefinitely but knew it was time for each of them to return to their individual lives.

On their ride home, they were unusually quiet as their thoughts wandered separately through the landscape of changes this traumatic life event bestowed upon them. Joseph and Elizabeth fell quickly to sleep.

Michael reeled in awe at Christine's newfound strength. The woman he married eight years ago never could have handled this shock so well. She would have been incapable of functioning in any meaningful way. Instead, she was an active participant in the fabric of focus and strength that helped bind the family together as they managed their way through the pain, decisions, and necessary activities. He admired her but felt the gap of misunderstanding widening between them.

Christine reached for Michael's hand as if she could read his thoughts.

"Michael, thank you for being so helpful during all of this."

"You're welcome, Christine, but quite honestly, you didn't seem to need much help."

"Michael, it's so strange. Sometimes I sob and feel like I'll never stop. Other times I'm filled with a sense of peace. There's a part, deep inside of me that understands this is just meant to be – like so many things in life." She looked over at Michael, reached for his hand and squeezed it. "We can't control when loved ones die, get ill, or any other life trauma waiting in the wings. The only control we have is how we choose to handle both the good and the bad things that happen to us. It's up to us to make the best of it." She turned away from Michael and stared out her car window, still holding his hand. "You know Michael, even though I understand it intellectually, it sure is hard to internalize it emotionally."

Silence wrapped around them. Several minutes later she continued as if she had just momentarily paused. "Death brings out so many emotions – anger, shock, resentment. It hurts so deeply." She took a long, deep breath, still staring at the mountains. "But I'm determined to focus on the good things still in my life, like you and the kids, and the rest of my family and friends." She turned her head to look back at Michael. "Michael, I think I'll grieve for my mom and dad for a long time but someday, I'll be at peace with all of this, all of the time and not just some of the time. I'll learn to live with the loss instead of fighting it."

She looked closely at Michael and suddenly noticed his stiff posture and motionless face staring ahead as he drove. "Michael, I'm sorry for rambling. This is the first chance I've had to share anything with you these past ten days. I just wanted to..," she started to explain but Michael interrupted her.

"Christine, it's fine that you want to talk." There was a bite in his tone. "I don't know how to respond to you anymore." Michael removed his hand from hers and placed it on the steering wheel. "You seem to have all the answers."

Her shoulders dropped along with her smile. "Michael, I don't have all the answers. I'm struggling with the biggest loss I could ever imagine. I just need to share the things going on inside of me." She lowered her head as tears began to trickle down her cheeks.

Guilt rushed through Michael as he reached over and patted her hand. "Look, Christine, I'm sorry. It's been a long ten days for all of us and I'm doing my best to handle this as well. Don't forget, I lost your parents too."

Her eyes opened wide as awareness took hold. "Oh, Michael, I'm sorry. I really haven't been there for you through all of this. I've been so preoccupied with my family and the kids that I've neglected your feelings altogether." She sighed. "God, Michael, how insensitive of me."

Michael glanced over at her and forced a smile as he slipped into the ever-widening space between them. She completely missed what he was trying to communicate. How could she feel that she should've had the strength for him instead of the other way around?

"It's all right, Christine. Don't worry about taking care of me. I'll be fine."

They finished the drive home in silence.

As they pulled into the garage, the children didn't budge from their sound sleep. Michael lifted Joseph while Christine gently removed Elizabeth from her car seat. They carried them to their bedrooms and the children barely stirred while Michael and Christine put on their pajamas and tucked them into bed for the night.

After unpacking the car and their suitcases, Christine and Michael were ready for sleep.

"I'll check the answering machine and be right in," Christine said as she left the bedroom for the den.

Among the messages, there were two from Max. Each of them

stated in a very matter-of-fact tone that he was thinking of her and sending her positive energy. Max's accent and words wrapped around her like a warm embrace. A gentle smile surfaced on her weary face as she returned to the bedroom.

"Anything important?" Michael asked as he slid between the sheets and pulled up the covers.

"There were several messages of sympathy from people at your work and mine, a couple of sales calls, and two messages from Max just sending his sympathy," she answered.

Michael cringed. In an accusatory tone, he asked, "When did you have time to call Max and tell him what had happened?"

Her brow furrowed. "I didn't call him, Michael. He called David because he sensed something was wrong and wanted to make sure I was all right. David mentioned it at the memorial gathering." She dropped her robe and slid into bed next to Michael, curling up behind him. "Michael, forget about Max. I love you – not him."

Michael looked into her loving, chestnut eyes. He recognized the beauty of her flesh but not the spirit within it. They reached for one another. Sadness held them close as they embraced. She grieved for the loss of her parents; Michael longed for the understanding he once had for the woman he loved more than life itself.

TWENTY

It was early the next morning, Sunday, and another unusual snow was falling steadily, powdering the landscape. It was changing from heavy wet flakes to a light mist. Christine rolled over to hug Michael and found his side of the bed empty. She draped her blue fleece robe around her and went to the kitchen in search of him. She found Michael with a cup of coffee, staring out the bay window. He looked like a little boy waiting for the return of his lost puppy.

Michael had been awake for several hours grappling with his tugging emotions. He loved Christine but wished he knew her the way he once did. His feelings for Heather left him riveted with guilt. He was confused and drained.

Christine wrapped her arms around the back of his neck. "Good morning." She kissed him. "A penny for your thoughts."

Her entrance startled him. "Oh – good morning Christine. I – uh – have been thinking about everything we've been through these past few months." He turned to face her.

"It's been a lot, hasn't it?" She sighed as she pulled up a kitchen chair next to him.

"It sure has." Michael yearned to tell her about his friendship with Heather but he didn't know how to explain it. How could he justify it when he disapproved of her relationship with Max? Christine would never understand the difference. Max had come into their lives and changed everything. Heather came along and befriended Michael; she renewed his weary spirit. Michael thought all this craziness would pass and then he would tell her everything. Telling her now, with the death of her parents, would only make things worse.

Elizabeth interrupted his thoughts as she came bouncing around the corner with a smile planted on her face.

"Mommy, daddy, can we go sledding today?"

She and Michael looked at one another. Their children's resiliency amazed them both. They watched their children's angry and sad moments arise, be shared, then pass as quickly as they had arisen. Joseph was still angry and wiggled his foot a lot. Elizabeth was still sad and cried often. Christine and Michael knew it would take years for the children to fully understand and integrate the loss of their grandparents. Today, it seemed Elizabeth was ready for some fun. After the last ten days, they were all ready for some fun.

"You bet princess. We rarely get snow like this so let's have some fun in it." Michael said as he drew Elizabeth up into his arms.

Christine chimed in, "Hey, you two, don't you think we should check with Joseph and make sure he also wants to go?"

Michael laughed. "Joseph? That's a 'gimme'," he said as he twirled Elizabeth in the air. "He's the adrenaline king of sledding."

"What's 'adredadin'?" Elizabeth asked, trying to reproduce the new word.

Michael tried to explain. "Adrenaline is the feeling you get inside when you're really excited about something."

"Oh," Elizabeth paused for a moment, internalizing her father's words, "like when mommy fixes banana nut pancakes with chocolate chips?"

Michael and Christine's eyes locked and they chuckled.

"Something like that," Michael replied. "I'll have to think of a better way to explain it."

"Okay," Elizabeth offered as Michael helped her into her chair at the breakfast table.

"After breakfast, I'll make hot chocolate and sandwiches to take with us. How does that sound?" Christine asked the hugging duet.

"Sounds great," Michael replied.

"What sounds great?" Joseph asked as he came around the corner of the kitchen, rubbing the sleep out of his eyes.

"We're going sledding," Christine announced.

Joseph's drowsy eyes opened wide as the good news sunk into his sleepy mind. "Really?"

Christine and Michael nodded.

"Cool!" Joseph replied.

Within an hour they were on their way to their favorite park. The sun shimmered off the ground, mesmerizing them as they drove. The trees bowed gracefully beneath the weight of their decorative powdered robes while the mountains loomed overhead like crystalline prisms. The virgin landscape humbly displayed its unblemished purity.

They arrived at a secluded part of the park that she and Michael had discovered years ago. The snow lay untouched other than a few tracks left by the wildlife that called the forest home. She smiled as she remembered back to the afternoon Joseph was conceived. It was fall and she and Michael had made love on a bed of fallen, crisp leaves while the towering trees stood guard. She glanced at Michael, wondering if he, too, might be remembering that breathtaking afternoon, but he was reaching down to pick Elizabeth out of an angel she had just imbedded in the snow.

They spent hours racing down the hill on their sleds. She and

Michael took turns accompanying Joseph and Elizabeth. Christine loved the cold mist whipping into her face, through her nostrils, and around her eyes as the slicing motion of their flying sabers created patterns across the hillside. Every ecstatic ride down the hill meant another grueling walk back up it but it was a small price to pay for such fun. Michael's heart filled with delight as he watched Christine and the kids prance through the snow. Sounds of playful shrieking and loving laughter penetrated the silent woods surrounding them.

They finally took a break to indulge in the hot cocoa and sandwiches she had made. They ate voraciously and after finishing, they sat on the blanket to let their stomachs settle. As she began to clean up, Michael reached up and pulled her down to him on the blanket. She giggled as they playfully wrestled in the snow. Elizabeth and Joseph clapped their hands and joined in the fun. Puffs of snow flew, creating swirling, white billows as all of them tumbled and rumbled on the ground.

Michael's mind flashed back to the fall afternoon over seven years ago, when Joseph was conceived. He thought about all the years with Christine, how he had known her insecurities and issues but had supported her through each trial and tribulation. He loved this woman as he loved no other. He knew he would never love this way again.

Happiness surged through him. It had been an unfamiliar sensation these past few months. Today, he was enjoying the three people he loved most in this world. This day, there was no mourning or doubt, only laughter and love.

Contentment filled each of them as they returned home. Elizabeth was asleep within minutes while Joseph chatted, still flying high from the sledding. This was life, Christine thought, the very life of life

TWENTY-ONE

Monday morning came quickly. Christine looked forward to getting back to work. She viewed it as a helpful diversion from the prior ten days spent at her parents' home. Thinking about normal things would feel good for a change. Then again, 'normal' as she knew it was gone, forever. As she dressed for work another wave of reality washed over her. Her parents would never see Joseph and Elizabeth grow into adults. They'd never attend another school play, dance recital, or sporting event. They'd never share another birthday or holiday. There was so much that they'd miss, not just in their lives, but in all of her siblings' lives as well.

She lay back on her bed, curled up tightly on her side, and cried. She lost track of time as sorrow seized her. She rocked back and forth sobbing until her tears finally subsided. As she raised her head from her bed, she now understood that this was the grieving process. It would envelop her when she least expected it, completely consume her, and then gradually release its powerful grip. Each time it happened, the feelings of loss and sadness were as intense as the first time, but she knew now that each emotional storm would eventually subside and she would regain the ability to focus on the moment at hand. At first, the waves of grief came several times each hour, then several times each day, but yesterday she had escaped their daunting force. The day of sledding was full of fun, not grief. She began to understand that grieving is a process of letting go. Each wave of grief that washed over her helped her to accept the finality of her parents' death, one wave at a time, one tear at a time. Someday, she thought, her heart would catch up with her mind's understanding and acceptance of this. For now she could only do her best to get through each minute of each day.

Michael noticed her reddened eyes when she finally came to the kitchen. "Are you okay?"

"I'm as good as I can be this minute," she replied in a soft voice. "I realize these 'sad attacks' are all part of it," she sighed, "but boy, sometimes it's tough."

Though Michael didn't know how he expected her to answer, this was definitely not a response he anticipated. He was used to her emotional responses, not the detached and analytical replies she recently verbalized. He gave her a hug, then realizing the time said, "Christine, I better get going if I'm going to beat rush hour." He pulled back from her and looked in her eyes. "Are you sure you're up for going back to work so soon? I'm sure David will understand if you need more time."

"Yes, Michael, I'm sure. I actually think work will be good for me," she said as she gave him another hug. "I guess I'll find out."

"I love you," Michael whispered as he held her.

"I love you too," Christine replied as she leaned in to kiss him.

"What about me?" Elizabeth asked as she came down the hallway from her bedroom.

"We love you too, sweetie." A faint smile crawled across Christine's weary face. "You never have to worry about that. We'll love you always and forever." She leaned down and kissed Elizabeth on the forehead. "Now, give daddy a big hug and kiss. He needs to get going."

Glancing down the hallway she beckoned, "Come on, Joseph, daddy's leaving for work and it's time for us to get going." Joseph was a notorious procrastinator, always choosing the pace that suited him best, depending on the activity. He finally joined them in the kitchen and added his goodbyes.

As Michael started up his car and began his drive to work, contentment washed over him. Joseph and Elizabeth filled him with a sense of purpose, and as difficult as it was for him to understand Christine's changes, he knew that she really did love him. As daylight sprinkled patterns of orange and gold across the landscape, Michael's spirits lifted.

His thoughts suddenly shifted to Heather. She might be worried about him. They'd been talking several times a week for the last month or so. He'd left a quick message on her machine the day he'd received the news about Christine's parents. He'd not found the time to call her since. He picked up his cell phone and dialed her number.

"Hello," Heather answered.

"Heather, it's Michael. I'm sorry I've kept you hanging all of this time," Michael explained, "but this is the first chance I've had to give you a call."

"Michael, it's good to hear your voice. Don't worry. I knew it would be difficult for you to call." Heather paused, then asked, "How are you doing? How are Christine and the kids? Oh, Michael, what a terrible shock for all of you."

"It's been the longest ten days of my life. I really can't believe all that's happened. I loved Christine's parents as I if they were my own and the thought of them..." Michael's voice trailed off.

"I wish I could be there to give you a hug and ease your pain. I can't imagine what you're going through but please, know that I'm here for you. I lo..." Heather stopped abruptly before the rest of the thought could cross her lips. She didn't want to add to Michael's struggles, only ease them. Expressing her feelings might make him uncomfortable, though she had no doubt he felt the same. She knew Michael looked forward to their conversations as much as she did. Her initial lust for him had long ago been replaced with genuine care and friendship. Heather now realized somewhere along the line, and for the first time in her life, she had fallen deeply in love, and it was with Michael. This wasn't something she intended or wanted to happen. She knew how much he loved Christine and his children.

"It's all right, Heather. I love you too," Michael stated. "You've been my best friend during this difficult time in my marriage and I'll never forget that."

"Michael, you talk as if you're saying goodbye. Are you?"

Michael hesitated before beginning. "Heather, I realize I'm turning more and more to you for the friendship I should be finding in Christine." He spoke swiftly. "Heather, you should see how strong and brave Christine's been these past ten days. You should see how she's helping the kids handle all of this." He stopped for a moment and took a deep breath before continuing. "Yes, she's changed and there are times I feel alone but there are other times when I feel close to her. I know she loves me. Yesterday the four of us went sledding in the mountains and it was a perfect day. I love them, Heather. I really do." Michael paused again, letting the truth of his words flow through him.

Heather remained silent, waiting for him to continue. "The problem is," Michael went on, "that I've grown to love you too. I try to tell myself its only friendship but the more I talk to you, the more I want to talk to you. The more I share with you, the more I want to share with you. I..." He couldn't continue. How could he say goodbye? He knew he must, but he never realized how painful it would be.

Heather listened as each word pummeled her vulnerable heart.

"Michael, it's all right," Heather consoled him. "Please, I understand. You've been through so much. The last thing I want is to cause you pain in any way. I'll be here, Michael, if and when you want to talk again. For now, just know that I love you in a way that I've never loved before." It was Heather's turn to struggle for words. "I'll care about you whether we ever talk again or not." She paused again before adding, "Please take care of yourself, Michael." Tears cascaded down her cheeks as she hung up the phone.

Michael felt as if someone had reached down his throat and pulled out his lungs with his bare hands.

TWENTY-TWO

Christine dropped Joseph and Elizabeth off at school before making her way through morning traffic to the office. The sparkling, snow-covered landscape glistened around her as she drove. Thoughts of her parents, her children, and Michael shifted throughout her consciousness like the pages of a photo album – each thought revealing a precious look, a funny moment or an unforgettable event. Her sadness dissipated as warm memories of her childhood and family filled her mind and heart. She realized that the loving foundation her parents had provided now needed to be self-sustained. More than that, she knew it was up to her to keep the spirit of her parents alive for her children, as they grew older without them.

"Welcome Back, Christine," Tom, the security guard greeted her. "We missed you and, uh," he was unsure how to broach the unspoken subject, "I'm sorry about your loss."

Tom's words felt like a bandage being ripped off an open wound. "Thank you, Tom," she murmured, barely looking at him, afraid she would begin to cry. She wanted to dash to the elevator but instead she forced a pleasant smile, wished Tom a nice day, inched slowly toward the elevator, and robotically pushed the button. Once safely inside, she leaned her back against the elevator wall and tried to hold the tears inside. She never expected to feel so raw, wounded, and at a loss in front of others. She wanted to run home and stay cocooned with her loved ones and family. She didn't anticipate that returning to daily routine and the outside world would leave her feeling so alone and vulnerable.

"Good morning, David," she said as she peeked around his office door.

David looked up from his desk, his eyes widened with surprise. "Christine, I didn't expect to see you this soon. You know you could've taken more time, don't you?" He motioned her into his office.

"Yes, David. You've been wonderful about all of this, and I appreciate it, but I really think it's time for me to get back at it." She forced another pleasant smile. "I actually think the diversion and focus will be good for me." David noticed the dark circles under her brown eyes.

"I don't know if I mentioned this to you, Christine, but we found a temporary that's been handling the administrative work in your absence." David leaned forward in his chair, placing his elbows on his desk and resting his chin on his folded hands. "Her name is Tina Ludlow. Let me know what you think of her work. If you like her, we can hire her full time and free you up to start working on more legal related issues."

"That's great," she replied, without her usual enthusiasm. "I'll look forward to meeting her." She turned to depart.

David stopped her. "Christine, how are you holding up?" He held her gaze, trying to fathom the loss of both parents simultaneously. "I can't imagine what you are going through."

She straightened her shoulders and calmly answered, "Actually, David, this minute I'm fine. Other times, when I least expect it, like this morning when I entered the building, sadness overtakes me." She took a slight breath. "But then it passes and I can focus again on all of the positive things."

David considered her response. It seemed analytical and

detached, though her expression was sad and sincere. There was an inner strength in her words that he'd never heard before. There she stood beautiful, self-assured, emanating confidence. He shifted in his chair and glanced away.

"Well, Christine, let me know if you need anything to get back in the swing. I'll be happy to oblige." David shuffled some papers on his desk, signaling to her that their conversation had ended.

"Thanks, David. I'll be sure to let you know as I start digging into things. And, David," she paused as she turned to exit, "I can't tell you how much your presence at the Memorial Service meant to all of us. It was thoughtful of you to drive over seventy miles to be there. Thank you."

David nodded and returned to his files.

Tina suddenly appeared at the doorway. She struck Christine as pixie-like, short in stature with cropped, bright red hair.

"Oh, I apologize," Tina stammered, not expecting anyone in David's office. "I didn't mean to interrupt. I can come back later." Tina's slight build and southern drawl blanketed her forty-two years of age well, leaving an early thirties impression.

"You're not interrupting," David said. "We just finished. Tina, I'd like you to meet Christine. Christine, Tina." David nodded back and forth between them.

Christine extended her hand. "Nice to meet you, Tina. Thanks for doing such a great job covering for me in my absence. I'm looking forward to working with you."

"Christine it's a pleasure to meet you. Everyone sings your praises daily," Tina replied with a firm handshake. Remembering the reason for Christine's absence, she solemnly added, "My condolences. I'm terribly sorry for your loss."

"Thank you."

Tina shook her head. "Oh, I almost forgot what I came in here for. Actually, I was going to leave a message with David, not knowing when you'd be back," Tina said looking at Christine. "You just missed a call from a," Tina glanced down at the paper in her hand, "Maximilian Fairchild. He said he's been trying to reach you and wondered if I knew when you'd be returning to work. I told him I would check and get back to him but now you can call him back directly." Tina handed her the pink slip of paper.

David caught himself frowning as Tina announced Max's name and forced the tension away from his forehead.

"Thanks, Tina," she said as she reached for the paper.

Several hours later Christine decided to ask David for an overview of the cases that were in process when she left. They were in the middle of discussing the Courtney file, the criminal case involving embezzlement, when Tina peered into David's office.

"I'm terribly sorry to interrupt the two of you again but Maximilian Fairchild is on the telephone. He's upset that no one called him back." Tina's lips were pursed as if she'd just bitten a lemon. "Would you like me to take another message, Christine?"

"Tina, I'm sorry. I forgot that he'd asked you to call him back. I planned on giving him a call this evening, off work hours." She stood up. "I didn't mean to put you in a difficult situation." She started out of David's office. "Just put the call through to my office, Tina. I'll explain what happened." As an afterthought she glanced back at David. "Is that okay?"

He nodded approval and waved Christine off with his hand.

"Hello, this is Christine," she said as the transferred call came through. Her insides suddenly felt like confetti.

"Christine, you are back. How are you?"

"I'm okay, I guess," she hesitated before adding, "or at least the best I can be right now." She launched into rapid explanation.

"Max, I want to explain why Tina didn't return your call from this morning. I asked for your number and told her that I would call you. I intended to call you this evening, after work, so please understand she wasn't ignoring you."

"Christine, that's fine. I really don't give a damn about your receptionist, or her lack of response. I just want to know how you are – really." Max inhaled before continuing. "I knew something terrible had happened. It was there – within me. I tried reaching you but I couldn't get a number to call you."

His tone reminded Christine of a parent, sick with worry.

"Max, I know. David told me and I can't tell you how nice it was to know that you were thinking of me during this time." Her words were slow, deliberate. "Thank you for caring."

Her detached composure sent a cold chill down Max's spine.

She struggled to explain. "It's hard for me right now to know what I'm feeling any minute of any given day. You have no idea the times you've run through my mind during these past weeks." Her breath grew shorter as her words flew faster. "I'd get flashes of insights and thoughts that I knew somehow you'd understand. Whether you'd agree with me or not, I just knew you'd somehow understand. I've been thinking about how grateful I am that our paths crossed. How much I've grown and learned just through growing to know and understand who you are, who you really are." Her words reeled faster and faster like a top spinning out of control. "I see things so differently now." She pulled herself in, but only momentarily. Conviction wrapped itself around her next words like a noose around a condemned man's neck. "Ironically, Max, so much of this resulted from contemplating your writing and the emptiness resulting from a life of hedonistic choices. Oh," she stammered, "it's so hard to explain." She paused to collect her thoughts and realized that her animated voice had drawn her coworkers' attention. "Max, this really isn't the time or place for me to have this conversation, so I better say goodbye for now. I'll try to call you tonight to talk more."

"Goodbye it is, Christine."

It took her several moments to realize that Max was no longer on the other end of the line. She reflected on all that had fallen from her mouth. She wanted to express her appreciation and care, not judgment, but had he taken her words differently? Had she hurt his feelings? No, she thought, he had no real feelings, only sensations that rose and fell with each second of each minute of each day. Max never stopped long enough to feel, only to think, about the blood running through his veins and the physical world that he manipulated around him. This was Max; this was the man she had grown to understand over all these months. She never would have believed that someone could live their life with such a detached, pleasure seeking, approach but indeed, this was Max. He wasn't shallow. That implied a lack of conscious thought or intelligence. No, it was just the opposite. Max's lifestyle and choices were very conscious, hyper conscious, a deliberate response to the fuller reality that he, too, had glimpsed.

She had thought about all of this. The more she thought, the more she had grown to believe that life was a process of change, growth, and development with meaning, purpose and direction – if one chooses to recognize it and live it as such.

Max had chosen a life of self over others and physical pleasure over spiritual development. Max knew his personal power and freedom, more than anyone she had ever met. She had become awakened to her own freedom of choice by analyzing the life Max had chosen the live. She believed Max's choices had arisen from a sense of isolation, from a lack of genuine human understanding and love.

"*Choice*" kept ringing through her brain. Didn't it all come back to choice? Aren't the choices we make, each minute of every day, what truly defines who we are and who we are continually becoming? Don't we become more accountable for our choices the more 'conscious' we become of their potential consequences?

Her head felt like a balloon being filled with helium, on the verge of explosion. Why did she have to think about these things? Why did she ever have to meet Max? Why did she have to become so 'conscious'? Why couldn't she go back to the simple things she used to think about and just be happy?

"Christine," David said, trying to interrupt her thoughts. He had stepped into her office after she hung up the telephone. "Christine," he tried again. This time he approached her and gently tapped her shoulder. "Christine, are you all right?"

"O-oh, Da-vid," she stammered as she pulled her consciousness back to her concrete surroundings. "We-ll, yes, I-I'm fine," she faltered, attempting to shake her clouded brain as if awakening from a deep sleep, filled with foggy dreams.

"Christine," David said, closing her office door. "I couldn't help but overhear you as I was heading down the hall." He paused a moment, then looked into her eyes. "I'm concerned that this Maximilian person upset you." David knew his words lacked presentation but it was the best he could do at the moment.

"Thanks, David." A smile poked at the corners of her mouth. "But really, I'm fine. Now, should we pick up where we left off? The day is rapidly gaining on us." Her smile reached across her face as she picked up some additional notes and walked back to his office with him.

She had changed so much the last few months. Now there was a part of her that David no longer fully understood. He was beginning to realize that Maximilian was a powerful influence in her life, in spite of her denial.

TWENTY-THREE

As Christine drove home that evening, her mind again began swimming in new thoughts. She realized how exploring new ideas felt similar to when she would go scuba diving in the ocean, where unfamiliar creatures and vibrant coral reached out, surrounding her, luring her into their private, unknown world. The deeper she dove, the brighter the colors and more unique the life forms she encountered. Awe and wonder gradually replaced fear and consternation as she grew more comfortable, more relaxed within the motion of her new awareness.

Before heading to the children's school, she needed to make a quick stop at the drug store to pick up some vitamins. As she hurried down the aisle, a woman, probably in her mid-sixties, brushed past her. The unexpected smell of Nina Ricci perfume wafted through the air and landed on her nose like a sledgehammer. She halted her steps as tears welled in her eyes. It was her mother's favorite scent. She wondered if there would ever come a day when a certain smell, or sound or sight, wouldn't trigger a memory of her parents that reduced her to tears.

She listened as both Elizabeth and Joseph shared her/his story about their first day back to school, amazed at how they were both growing and changing by the day. How quickly the years seemed to be flying. Joseph would be seven in July and Elizabeth would turn four in August. It seemed like yesterday that she'd given birth to them both. She remembered back to the feelings she experienced while carrying each of them inside of her. Every flutter and movement had been carefully etched and safely stored within the permanent memory of her womb. Her pregnancies had been healthy, free of morning sickness, and absent from complications. Her deliveries were lengthy and challenging, but well worth the struggle.

Her thoughts set sail. Would Joseph and Elizabeth continue to change and grow at what seemed like lightning speed? What further heartaches, losses, and disappointments lie ahead for them? Were she and Michael doing all the right things to guide and help them grow into well-adjusted, happy adults? As her mind started spinning with the questions only time could answer, they pulled into the garage. Michael's car was absent. He sometimes made it home before they did, depending on rush hour. If he were going to be held up for long, he'd let them know.

After hanging coats and putting school things away, Joseph and Elizabeth joined her in the kitchen. "Do you want to help?" Christine asked them as they made their rowdy entrance.

"Sure," Elizabeth volunteered.

"Good, you can wash the potatoes." She wasn't going to give either one of them the chance to change their minds. As she seated them at the table with tasks at hand, the telephone rang.

"Hello," she answered.

"Hi, hon, I'm going to be another hour or two here at the office. There's a lot to catch up on and we've got that national marketing campaign coming up. I'll give you a call before I leave so you'll know when I'm on my way." She felt the stress in Michael's voice. "I probably won't be home before the kids go to bed so can you please put them on the phone so I can ask about their day?"

"Sure, I'll get them for you," she replied and added, "Are you okay? You really sound beat."

"I'm all right, just a bit overwhelmed," Michael explained, "I'll feel better if I stay tonight and get my arms around this workload."

"What if I feed the kids now and then wait to eat a late dinner with you? How does that sound?"

"Not tonight, Christine." Michael was matter of fact. "I really don't know how long all of this will take. There's no need for you to wait. I'll order in and eat while I work."

"Oh, okay." She was surprised but understood. "Let me get the kids for you."

"Kids, it's daddy," she announced. "He won't make it home until very late tonight, after bedtime, so he wants to talk to both of you now."

Elizabeth's face lit up as she reached for the phone. She repeated every detail of her day to Michael. As they finished their conversation, Elizabeth held out the phone to Joseph. He was equally animated in describing his part in constructing the 'awesome' snow castle at school. When Joseph completed his story, he handed the receiver back to Christine. "Daddy wants to talk to you again."

"Christine, I do love you. You know that don't you?" Michael declared with unfamiliar solemnity as she took the receiver.

"Of course I do, Michael," she replied as if she'd missed the seriousness of his tone. "Don't worry about it. It's fine. Think of the times I've had to work late and you've juggled everything for me. It's really not a problem."

Michael didn't pursue it further. "I'll give you a call when I'm finished."

"Michael, I do know how much you love me, even though it isn't easy these days." Christine paused. "Good luck with your work," she added softly before hanging up.

After finishing their meal of chicken, tossed salad, green beans, and baked potatoes, Joseph, Elizabeth, and Christine snuggled up on the couch to share their nightly ritual of reading. Christine, Michael, or both, would spend the hour before bedtime, reading to Joseph and Elizabeth. Each of them found it to be the highlight of their day – the cuddling, the quiet, and the closeness.

Elizabeth fell asleep on Christine's shoulder within thirty minutes. Christine carried her to bed, tucked her in, and kissed her forehead. Joseph's surrender to slumber wasn't long after.

As she returned to the family room to grab a book of her own, thoughts of Max encroached upon her consciousness. He had hung up abruptly when they'd spoken. She wanted to explain herself. She reached for her purse where she had tucked away the numbers David had given her and dialed Max's home number. She glanced at the clock. It would be several hours after midnight in London but she let the phone ring anyway.

The telephone rang several times before someone on the other end picked up.

"Hello," a female voice answered.

Christine was stunned.

"Hello?" Max's guest repeated.

"Hello," Christine hesitated, caught off guard. "Is Maximilian Fairchild there or do I have the wrong number?" She blushed as the question tripped off her tongue.

The woman on the other end of the line laughed. "No, you don't have the wrong number. He's here." Christine could hear her telling Max that the call was a woman and it was for him.

"Hello," Max said curtly.

"Max, this is Christine. I'm sorry to call you so late. I- I.," she stammered. "I didn't mean to interrupt anything. I-I just wanted to apologize for not being able to finish our conversation earlier.

People were listening to me and.," she tried to finish but Max interrupted.

"Christine, the conversation 'was' finished." His words were slurred from drink. "There was nothing more to say. There 'is' nothing more to say."

"Max, please," she pleaded, "I just want to talk to you. I didn't mean to hurt your feelings. I was..."

"Christine," Max interrupted her again, "as I said, there is nothing more to say. 'This' conversation is finished." He hung up.

Christine was flabbergasted. She 'had' offended him this morning. She 'had' hurt is feelings. Was it that he really 'cared' about her? Was she wrong about him? Had she lost sight of the fact that she'd been interacting with a human being, not just some intellect defined by his detached lifestyle and ideas? As thoughts ran rampant through her mind, the telephone rang.

"Hello," Christine answered anxiously.

It was Michael's voice that greeted her hopeful ears, not Max's. "Christine, I'm just about finished and should be leaving the office in another ten minutes or so. I just wanted to let you know."

"Oh," she sputtered. "Thanks for letting me know."

"Did I catch you in the middle of something?"

"No, not really, Michael. I was just off in thought. I'll see you when you get home."

"See you soon," Michael said and hung up.

Sadness swooped down on her. She couldn't imagine ending her relationship with Max on such a negative note. She wanted to reach out to him, to make him understand. She would write him a letter during lunch tomorrow and explain everything.

She picked up her book, trying to change her train of thought. After finishing several pages, she realized that she'd forgotten to get the mail on her way in from work. She went to the mailbox and pulled out a hefty stack of bills, advertisements, and bank statements.

As she sorted through it, an envelope with a UK return address jumped out at her. It was postmarked the day after her parent's death. Max must have written it after trying unsuccessfully to reach her through David. She tore it open. As she raced to devour every word, tears began to stream down her cheeks.

My Dearest Christine,

I feel your pain. I ache with your loss. I would like to hold your hand this very moment.

I reflect on the many years of distance between many people and me. Now let me tell you my story. I once loved someone with my entire being. Her name was Rachel. There is something about your energy and trusting spirit that remind me of her. She was my true love – my other half – my meaning and my purpose – my life. We met on a playground in the countryside when we were five years old and became steadfast friends and soul mates from that day on. Our families disapproved because she was Jewish and I was Protestant. They were traditional people that believed life was about following rules irrespective of truth and love so Rachel and I found ways to spend time together at school throughout the years. As we grew older we could never understand why they didn't see that all religions are different expressions of the same spirituality, like the different colors of a prism generated from the same light. What our families lacked in love and support, our relationship fulfilled. Our friendship evolved into passion by the time we were teens. We were inseparable and learned to communicate with one another in thought even from a distance. It's as if we were one spirit with two bodies. Our love knew no bounds.

We planned on eloping when we turned twenty. Rachel's parents somehow discovered our secret and decided to send her away to relatives in a different county. Before they could execute their plan, Rachel packed a few things and fled her home in the middle of the night. I am sure she was on her way to me and didn't want to risk being discovered. She never made it.

I awoke from a sound sleep that night. I could feel her terror. Though there were miles between us, I could see her face and hear her screaming. I dressed and ran wildly through the countryside toward her home.

I was too late. I will spare you the details but let it suffice to say that Rachel was brutally raped, mutilated, and murdered. To this day, those responsible for her death have not been found or held accountable. Officials eventually closed the investigation because of lack of evidence and labeled it a 'random incident' by some transient criminals passing through the countryside.

That night changed me forever. 'Random' – I have come to realize that everything is just that – random.

My life is an enigma to almost all who meet me, and though many people have tried to comprehend my book of life, you are the first that I have chosen to share it with.

Only as we are finishing life do we see that all of it has been a lesson, and we have been inattentive pupils.

Let me tell you how good I feel writing this letter to you.

I send you warm feelings of peace and love.

Max

Why couldn't she have received this letter before she spoke with Max this morning?

She reached for the phone and redialed Max's number. This time, there was no answer and no machine to relay her desperate plea for forgiveness.

As she hung up the phone, tears still flowing, Michael walked in the den.

"Christine, my God, what's wrong?"

She just sat there, letter in hand, crying.

Michael reached for the letter that she willingly handed to him. As he began to read Max's profession of love, his stomach dropped. Michael felt as if he were being tossed from the roof of a fifty floor high rise. With each word he read, he tumbled, head over heels, floor after floor, gaining momentum. Then – splat – he was obliterated – every ounce of him – from the impact of the fall. He stood there a while then handed the letter back to her. Without saying a word, Michael turned and walked away toward the bedroom. There was nothing for him to say. There was nothing left of him.

TWENTY-FOUR

Max hung up the telephone with seething, suppressed, anger. The anger was targeted inward, not at Christine. He loathed the fact that he had allowed himself to become vulnerable after so many years of living free from the burden of feelings and attachment.

"Are you all right, Max?" Deborah asked.

"I'm fine but I'd like you to leave now," Max responded coldly as he reached for his clothes. Deborah, the model who owned the boutique, was the first woman that Max had been with in weeks. After his conversation with Christine earlier in the day, he had left his office, went to the nearest pub, and did his best to drown his thoughts in alcohol. He hadn't touched the stuff in weeks. From the day he learned Christine's parents died, something had reawakened within him.

"But, Max, we just got started," Deborah protested as she tried to reach for him. Max looked down at her on his bed. She reminded him of a cross between an angel and a nymph. He was disgusted with himself and her.

"I said, please leave," he insisted as he pulled his arm away from her groping reach.

Deborah was shocked but sensed that Max meant what he said. She dressed, gathered her things, and left without saying a word.

Max sat down on his bed, his head pounding as the anesthetic effects of his all day drunk began to wear off. He reached for the bottle of vodka on his bureau, began lifting it towards his lips, and then hurled it against the wall. It shattered, spraying glass and vodka across the room.

No, Max thought, he would never allow anyone or anything to get the better of him. Not now, not ever. He was furious at his weakness to surrender to his emotions, in any way, on any level, even anger. He dressed, cleaned up the mess he made, and walked toward the door of his flat. As he opened it, the telephone rang. He walked back, switched off the answering machine and then exited, locking the door behind him.

He walked several blocks to his office building, nodded at the security guard, and proceeded up to his private suite. As he entered the room, he took in every detail of his exquisite surroundings, from the cherry wood desk to the Italian leather chairs, from the antique clock to the Waterford crystal pitcher and glasses that decorated his fully furnished bar. He walked to the window and looked down at the city of London. This was life, Max thought to himself. Emotions and feelings were fleeting and for the weak and vulnerable. Power, wealth, and pleasure were for the free and unattached.

Max tried hard to believe the things he was saying to himself but Christine's words from earlier that day kept echoing in his mind, as if spoken from a mountain top, reverberating from peak to peak, across the landscape between them. Her voice, her words, whispered gently back to him. Thanking him for the changes within her, the changes that resulted from contemplating his writing and the emptiness resulting from a life of hedonistic choices. She had been neither harsh nor judgmental but rather genuine and loving. Yes, Max knew that she loved him. There had never been another woman, or person, that had reached so deep within him to uncover the truth of who he was, his belief system, the core behind his choices. Many people were aware of how Max chose to live, Christine was the first with whom he chose to share why.

Choice, yes, Max had made a very conscious choice years ago that the only way to really survive was to remain detached. It was the only way to deal with the randomness and senselessness of life and death. He let his mind race through the paces.

We're born, we live, we die. That's it. Time – the manmade concept, designed to impose some control and power over the unyielding, chaotic universe. How ridiculous, Max thought. God – the manmade concept designed to give meaning and purpose to the random, physical universe; and organized religion –the manmade concept designed to control the masses. Even more ridiculous!

Real control, Max thought, lies in understanding how things really work, how people operate from fear, survival, and pleasure.

Max started pacing through his office. His hands clasped behind his back, his mind charging full speed ahead. Sophisticated people create an intricate internal web of morality, religion, or higher purpose to trap their basic human nature. They will lie, only if they really have to. They will take advantage of someone in business, only if it's really necessary. They will go to church every week, but remain a bigot or cheat on their spouse. Ah, Max thought, the power of self-deception, hypocrisy, and rationalization! At least, Max reflected, he was honest about who he was and did not pretend to be anything more or less. He had found it futile to share these ideas. That is – until Christine.

He had written to her some of his thoughts and she had written and verbalized some of hers. Max knew that his letters had triggered her internal journey that brought her to the other side of the mountain. He knew she had become mystical, not cynical. He sensed that her belief in life's universal and inherent meaning and purpose was unshakable.

Max remembered the time in his life, many years ago, when he and Rachel chose that path. They believed in life's inherent goodness irrespective of prejudice and challenges. They understood that they were somewhat isolated in a world that remained unconscious and people that remained self-absorbed. What they discovered was people often mistook their kindness for weakness. What they discovered was that it was difficult to walk that path without having one another to understand and share the path they were on.

After her violent and meaningless death, Max realized there was not enough 'real 'human pleasure – an understanding embrace, a knowing glance, a loving soul mate – to sustain him on that path for long. Yes, love – pure love, not ego driven but spiritually driven – was the key that unlocked that path, but he was human and needed more. He had decided way back then, to make other choices, to never look back at his forsaken love and efforts on the path he had once shared and now abandoned. And then, he met Christine. Thoughts of her began drawing him in, like the seductive scent of an exquisite but poisonous flower, tempting to the nostrils, but lethal to the lungs, slowly creeping its way into his being.

He turned on his heels, abandoning London's splendid view and headed for his desk with calculated steps. He knew what he must do.

TWENTY-FIVE

The next morning, Christine tried to reach out to Michael, to talk to him, to help him understand, but he wanted nothing to do with her. He was not angry. He did not act hurt. He was simply distant, detached, as if the love had gone out of him altogether – like a kite left unattended on a windless day, once buoyant but now listlessly lying on the barren ground.

"Michael, please talk to me," she pleaded as Michael finished dressing.

"Christine, there's really nothing to talk about."

"My entire relationship with Max has been about his soul, my soul, beliefs that determine the soul."

He turned to face her. "Fine, go ahead and say what it is you have to say." He walked back to the bed and sat down.

"Michael, I understand how this must seem to you but you have to believe me when I tell you that my love for you, Joseph, and Elizabeth has grown and been enriched, not diminished in any way through all my changes. Yes, I love Max, but it's different. It isn't the passionate, day in and day out love I have for you. It is spiritual for lack of a better word. I don't long to be in his arms. I don't long to share his bed or passion. I don't long to spend my days with him." She sat next to Michael and took his hand. "I don't know why but I know that I was meant to understand and care about him – about his soul, but I also know that I could *never* love him the way that I love you."

"Is that it?"

"It's the best I can explain right now."

"I'm sorry I'm not enough for you." Michael removed his hand from hers, stood up, and started out of the bedroom.

"But you are, Michael."

He kept moving.

She would try again later and trust that eventually he would realize the truth she was trying desperately to communicate.

Breakfast was respectfully quiet other than Elizabeth's chatter in anticipation of another fun day at school with Miss Julie and the gang. She and Michael had agreed before Joseph was born that any marital issues were not something to ever impose upon their children. They made it a habit never to argue or exchange harsh words in front of them.

Michael barely touched his food. When Elizabeth paused to catch her breath, he politely interrupted her. "Well, princess, I hope you and your brother have another good day at school but I have to leave for work." He reached down and pulled Elizabeth up with one powerful sweep. He hugged her long and hard. Christine noticed the sadness etched in Michael's somber, blue-grey eyes.

"Wow, daddy that was the best hug ever. Can you give me another one?" Elizabeth asked when Michael's grip lessened.

"Sure," he whispered and he embraced her once again, shielding his face, for fear of her noticing the unhappiness painted across it. Michael gingerly placed Elizabeth back in her seat. He leaned over and gave Joseph a hug and kiss, then gave Christine a peck on the cheek, before leaving without another word. Christine felt Michael's struggle with every step that he took. She would find a way to make things right between them.

Max, she suddenly thought. She glanced at her watch, realized it was too early to take the children to school and thought maybe she could reach Max in his office. She needed to make things right with him as well. Even if they never spoke again, she needed Max to understand what she really meant. If not, it would negate all that she had grown to know by learning to understand him.

"Joseph and Elizabeth, while you finish eating, I'm going to make a quick phone call from the den. Okay?"

"Sure, mommy," Joseph answered for them both. Taking his role as big brother seriously, he nodded his head in Elizabeth's direction and added, "I'll make sure she finishes."

She stifled her laugh. "Thanks, big guy. I knew I could count on you." She gave them each a quick pat on the head. "I won't be long."

She went into the den, dug the numbers out of her purse, and dialed the number for Max's office.

"Fairchild Enterprises, this is Judith, how may I help you?" A pleasant female voice with a lovely British accent, greeted her.

"Is Maximilian Fairchild available?" She inquired with her best business voice.

"I will be happy to check for you. May I tell him who is calling?"

"My name is Christine Amory and it's very important that I speak with him." She couldn't mask the sense of urgency that overcame her.

"Just a moment, please." Judith placed her on hold. Max had given her explicit instructions not to put her calls through to him.

Judith waited another minute before reengaging the line. "I'm sorry, Ms. Amory, but he is unavailable right now. He is in a meeting. May I take a message for you?" She sounded convincing.

"I would like you to interrupt him, please. This is very important."

Without hesitation, Judith replied, "I'm terribly sorry, but that is not possible. I have specific instructions not to disturb him. I will be happy to take a message and leave it with him."

Christine now sensed that Max specifically did not want to take 'her' calls.

"Judith, I don't mean to put you in an uncomfortable position, but I really need your help," she implored. "I understand that he does not want my calls, but this really is very important." Emotion yanked at her as each word of Max's letter flashed within her memory.

"I'm sorry, Ms. Amory, but I'm forbidden to interrupt him," Judith sympathized. "I just cannot disturb him with your call."

A long silence precipitated Christine's response. "I understand," she whispered. "Will you please give him a message for me?"

"I can try." Judith could hear the desperation in Christine's voice and appreciated that Christine wasn't arrogant, demanding, or condescending like some of the other women who called Max. "I will do the best I can. What message would you like to give him?"

Another awkward silence before Christine spoke. "Thank you, Judith. Can you please tell him that I didn't receive his letter, the one he wrote the day my parents died, until after I reached him briefly last evening?" She took a moment, trying to maintain composure. "Please tell him that I'm very sorry and that I really want to speak with him and explain." Her voice drifted off. "There's so much that I didn't have the chance to tell him. Please tell him," she took a long pause before completing her thought, "Yes, please tell him that I love him." As the words flowed from her lips, she realized the truth that lied within them. She wanted to reach deep within Max's ashen soul and relight its dying embers, the light that was dampened but not completely extinguished even after Rachel's tragic death. There was still hope if only he knew he wasn't alone, if only he knew how much he was loved as a person, not as a lover or spouse, just understood and loved for the person that he was and for all that he had survived.

"Is there anything else?" Judith interrupted her silent thoughts.

"No," she said. "Hopefully, he will understand."

"I will give him your message, Ms. Amory. Is there a number to call you back if he chooses to do so?"

She recited both her home and work numbers. She rarely gave people her cell phone number. She thanked Judith again for her kindness before hanging up.

She stared at the telephone, wondering if her words would be too late. Would Max believe her? Would he ever give her the chance to explain? What if he wouldn't? What if she never heard from him again? She couldn't bring herself to believe that was possible. He would reach out again, when he was ready to hear all that she had to say. She would write him a long letter during lunch. He would read it. She was sure of that. For now, she needed to focus on the moment at hand.

"Are you two all through with breakfast?" She asked as she rounded the corner into the kitchen.

"All done!" Elizabeth exclaimed.

"She did a good job," Joseph agreed with approval.

"Nice job by both of you," she complimented with a wink of thanks to Joseph. "All right then, let's get our coats and get moving."

# # #

Judith waited for Max's direct phone line to go dark, signaling that he had finished his call, before venturing into his office.

"Mr. Fairchild, Christine Amory called a little while ago. I did not disturb you, as you requested."

Max looked up from the papers in front of him.

"She did, however, ask me to give you a message."

"All right then, Judith, please leave the message on my desk."

Judith proceeded to verbally communicate Christine's message to ensure he would, in fact, receive it. Max looked at Judith as she spoke. When Judith finished, she thanked him and quickly returned to her desk.

Max stood up, went to his window, and leaned against it as he gazed out at the city below. No matter how hard he tried since last evening, he couldn't drown, destroy, or eradicate the feelings Christine had sparked within him.

He was determined to overcome this. He knew that Christine's love for him was spiritual, not carnal. He knew that her passion and devotion to her husband and children defined her. Max and Christine led different lives; the schism between them was as deep as the ocean that separated them. How ironic, Max thought, after all these years of isolation since Rachel, to finally meet a woman that reached his soul but could not share his flesh. Maybe he and Christine had been together in another life or maybe they would be together in the future, but he knew he did not belong in her life now. Max grabbed his topcoat.

"Judith, I'm going for a walk. I'll be back shortly."

TWENTY-SIX

All morning at work, Christine found her mind wandering, first to Michael, then to Max. How could she love two men in two such different ways? Why couldn't Michael understand the difference? Would she grow to verbalize her awakening in a way that was intelligible to Michael and others? Would Michael eventually be excited to share in her new world and reap the benefits of all his years of loving devotion to her?

And what about Max? Even if he reached out to her again, who could she ever really be in his life? She had her life with Michael, Joseph, and Elizabeth but Max had no one and nothing of real purpose in his life. Why was she drawn into understanding him? She realized all that she had gained over these months, but what could she possibly offer Max in return? Friendship? She doubted that would provide any meaning in Max's world. Maybe someday he would be able to love someone again the way he once loved Rachel but it certainly wouldn't and couldn't be her.

"Christine, are you sure you haven't come back to work too soon?" David asked noticing her puffy eyes and distant gaze.

She had neither seen nor heard David approach, but he was standing right in front of her desk, peering down at her with concern. She looked up at him. Her eyes were dull, faded from fatigue.

"David," she stumbled, trying to regain her bearings, "I'm fine, honest." She shifted in her chair. "I was just thinking about things." She looked up at him and pulled out a strained smile. "I'll try not to let my mind take walks on company time."

David's look of worry remained fixed on his face. "I mean it, Christine. You've experienced quite a loss. I just wonder if maybe you've returned too soon."

Christine's jaw tightened. She stood up and spoke with an intensity and conviction that caught David by surprise. "I appreciate your concern but the sooner I learn to live each day "as it is", the better off I'll be."

David stood by Christine's office window, watching and listening as she strode from one end of her office to the other and back again. She stopped by his side at the window and gazed down at the city park below. They stood side-by-side, soundless, contemplative.

Christine turned away from the window and began pacing again. "David, isn't it strange that death is the one thing that each of us will face – absolutely – for certain – no exceptions, and yet, we never take time to really 'think' about it?"

David didn't anticipate her question. He shifted his stance by the window as his hand rubbed his chin. He took his time in responding. "Well, Christine, I would venture to guess that most people don't think about it because the thought of their own death might frighten them."

She stopped and spun around to face him. The sunlight from the window pirouetted on her animated brown eyes, creating a flicker of amber. "But, David, that's just the point! If people don't think about it, then how do they ever know what their life really meant when their time comes to die?" Before David could answer, she turned toward the window again and moved in its direction as if drawn into the sun's alluring glow. As she gazed out at the world beyond the window, calmness rested peacefully on her face.

Christine placed her hand on the warmed glass and whispered softly. "Just think, David, of all we'll miss, all the possible regrets, if we never take the time to appreciate life while we have it."

As David pondered his response, Christine's intercom line rang. Tina was buzzing her. She excused herself from David and picked up the receiver. "Yes, Tina, he's here." She nodded her head. "Sure, I'll let him know." She hung up and looked up at David. "Mr. Bellamy has arrived. He's fifteen minutes early but Tina wanted to let you know that he's in the lobby whenever you're ready."

David checked his watch and then looked back at Christine. "I'd like to continue this conversation at another time."

She dropped her eyes to the papers on her desk and shrugged her shoulders like a little girl, suddenly self-conscious. "Oh, David, that's not necessary." Shifting her childlike gaze back at David she added, "But, thanks for listening to me ramble."

"That was far from rambling, Christine." He turned to leave her office. "I enjoyed the philosophical jolt this morning. It's better than the caffeine in my coffee."

Christine exhaled, relieved at his understanding. "Have a good day," she said as he reached her door.

"You can bet on it, Christine."

TWENTY-SEVEN

Depression descended upon Michael like putrid smog, slowly but steadily, surrounding him, from head to toe, leaving him sickened and disgusted. The landscape that was previously painted with glistening shades of gold and silver, now hung like a dull, vacuous canvas, absent color, only black and white remaining. The sun's morning arrival was incapable of penetrating Michael with its' healing warmth and comfort. He was immune to everything but the darkness that had enveloped him. His commute seemed endless.

How could this have happened? How could he have given his heart, soul, and entire being to Christine for all these years, only to find her being consumed by someone else? How could all their years together lead them to this point? How could she be so vulnerable to another man's attention and obvious desire for her? Where would they go from here? The feeling he once had for Christine now seemed like a distant memory, a flickering star, barely visible in the vast, barren sky.

Michael pulled off the road and surrendered to the emotional pain that he had suppressed for months, maybe years. He didn't know. At this moment he didn't know anything. He felt like a tree caught in a ferocious wind, pelted by unyielding rain, pushed to the point of breaking, struggling to hold on, wondering if his roots were deep enough, strong enough, to survive. He felt as if his insides were being sucked out of him, inch by inch, leaving him hollow and exhausted. As the storm of emotion subsided, Michael realized that for all these years his love for Christine had been the source of meaning and purpose in his life. He lived for her. He lived to know her every thought, need, and desire. He lived to make her smile, laugh, and moan in delight. Everything he did, he did for her. When Joseph and Elizabeth were born, it deepened and extended the love he had for Christine. He and Christine both loved the joy of parenting and it added more meaning to his life. He worked to provide for her and the children and he had grown to define himself by his love for Christine. He had given her his all. And now, he had lost it all. He had lost his sense of self. He realized that Christine didn't love him the same way he loved her because if she did, the relationship with Max wouldn't have happened, couldn't have happened. Michael had waited patiently all these years for her to grow to love him with the same total abandonment that he had for her, but she never did. He now realized she never would. He knew that she loved him, but not the same way. He was a part of her life, not the center of it. Christine had always been at the center of her own life. Michael had not. From this moment on, the rules would change.

He glanced at his watch and realized that almost an hour had transpired. He straightened his tie in the rear view mirror and put the car in gear.

When Michael arrived at the bank building, its tall, steel structure loomed with sterility, throwing gloomy shadows across the sunlit street. He parked his car in his reserved, underground space, grabbed his briefcase, and made his way toward the building entrance, his feet following the same path they had followed for the past nine years. Everything seemed different, surreal, as if he was no longer the person living his own life but rather an actor trapped in a bad movie that made no sense, playing a role with a script that seemed insane.

Michael didn't greet the flirting tellers with his usual grin and wink. He passed them quickly, head lowered, moving directly to his office, closing the door behind him. He looked out his sixth floor window at the sky that was darkening with the first signs of new snow. Large, heavy flakes fell slowly, clinging to each building and fixture in their path, claiming the pavement below as home. Usually, a new snowfall brought images of warmth and laughter, by the fireside with Christine and the kids. Today the only image Michael could muster was maneuvering his way through it at the end of the day. He sat at his desk and stared down at the file he was working on late last night. It seemed days ago now, a lifetime ago.

The marketing campaign was scheduled to roll out by the end of April. Being out of the office for ten days had set him behind his deadline. The upcoming Christmas holiday would set him back even further. He knew he needed to work late each night in order to meet the demanding schedule. He kept staring at the file in front of him as if it would somehow transform itself, like a moth into a butterfly. The longer he stared, the less he could focus. Yesterday, he had tackled his work with a vengeance. Today, it seemed meaningless. He surrendered to his procrastination and headed for the small kitchen down the hall to grab some coffee.

"Michael, I was just coming to your office to speak with you," Gary Hudson said as he met Michael in the hallway. Gary was the Senior Vice President of Marketing, Michael's boss.

Michael looked up with surprise, hesitating slightly as if not recognizing him. "Oh, Gary, what can I do for you?"

"Do you have minute to step down to my office, Michael? I'd like to discuss the upcoming rollout of the national marketing campaign."

"Sure, let me just fill my coffee mug and I'll be right there."

"I'll join you," Gary replied. "I can use some caffeine this morning as well."

After fixing their coffee, they walked down the hallway to Gary's office. Gary closed his door after gesturing for Michael to take a seat in one of his large, burgundy leather chairs.

"Michael, I've been thinking. You and your family have been through a traumatic time these past few weeks. I'd like to suggest that we tap an additional resource within marketing that can assist you with meeting the demanding deadlines over the next couple of months. I thought about changing the timing of the rollout but we have too much invested to do so." Gary sat erect, hands folded on his desktop. He observed Michael as he addressed him. "I know that you planned on personally handling the rollout in the San Diego, Los Angeles, and San Francisco markets, but let's talk about who might be capable of taking your place. I don't expect you to leave your family at a time like this to travel that week."

Michael listened carefully before responding. "Gary, the additional resource would be a big help and I appreciate your understanding of my family's recent tragedy. I do, however, intend to personally oversee the launch in California." Michael's posture was stiff, his tone determined. Yesterday Michael would have welcomed the opportunity to pass on the travel but today he wouldn't hear of it. "It's still several months away and I'm sure that Christine and the kids will be fine. I insist on handling it." He leaned forward in his chair and looked into Gary's eyes. "Trust me, Gary, it'll be fine."

"I find it hard to believe that Christine wouldn't prefer to have you home. I know that she's always been supportive of your career and the travel it sometimes demands, but the timing of this is different."

"Gary, I 'want' to go. It'll be good for me. Christine will be fine, believe me."

Gary was surprised at Michael's agitation. "All right, Michael, relax. Do me a favor, would you? Take the next several weeks to think about it. We'll revisit the topic sometime during the end of January or early February and go from there. How does that sound?"

Michael set his jaw and spoke slowly. "Gary, I don't need to think about anything. I'm going and I won't change my mind."

"Okay, Michael. We'll move forward as planned for now. I'll contact Sue Richmond and ask her to meet with you later this morning to determine the elements of the project she can assist you with. I think you'll be pleased with the results she's able to produce. I'd like an update on the rollout by Friday. Just let me know if you need anything else." Gary looked at his watch. "I have a conference call that started two minutes ago. Please excuse me, Michael." Gary nodded and lifted the telephone receiver as Michael stood and made his way to the door.

When Michael returned to his office he glanced out the window as he walked toward his desk. The snow was gaining momentum as it continued its assault. Longer commute. He reached for his private telephone line and dialed. After several rings, the answering machine picked up. "Hi, this is Heather. I'm not available right now. Please leave your name, number, and time that you called, and I will return your call as soon as possible." Beep.

"Heather, this is Michael. Give me a call."

Fifteen minutes later there was a gentle knock on his office door.

"Come in," Michael stated flatly.

The door opened and Susan entered. She was in her mid to

late twenties and Michael noticed the confidence in her step as she walked towards him with an outstretched hand of introduction.

"Hi Michael, I'm Susan Richmond."

Michael politely extended his hand in return. Her grip was firm and self-assured. He immediately liked her. "Nice to meet you, Sue. Please have a seat."

"If you don't mind, Michael, I actually prefer to be called Susan. I haven't yet been able to break Gary's habit of calling me Sue, but I really do prefer Susan, if you don't mind." Her broad smile revealed bright teeth, perfectly shaped.

"Then Susan it is," Michael replied, feeling the life slowly climb back up inside him, like the tingling that occurs when circulation returns to a limb that's fallen asleep. "Have a seat, Susan, and we'll get started." Their eyes locked momentarily, pleased with the mutual comfort established between them.

Michael opened the file that had daunted him all morning and began reviewing each facet of the project, items completed, and tasks remaining. Energy returned to his voice and resolve to the work before him.

They worked diligently for over an hour before Evelyn interrupted them.

"Michael, Heather is on your private line and insists on speaking with you. I told her that I was asked to hold your calls but she is adamant." Evelyn's frustration was evident in the tightness of her lips as she spoke. "Would you like to speak with her or shall I insist on taking a message?"

Michael's neck stiffened. He and Heather had agreed months before that she would never leave a message with Evelyn or ask for him directly at the office. They both thought it would avoid awkward questions until Michael had the opportunity to tell Christine about their friendship. Evelyn rarely answered Michael's private line but today he requested it, forgetting the message he left for Heather earlier in the morning.

"Yes, Evelyn, please put it through," Michael responded, acting nonchalantly. Susan began to get up but Michael motioned her to remain seated, indicating he would not be long.

"This is Michael."

"Michael, it's Heather. Your message sounded alarming. Has something happened? Are you all right?"

Michael's voice was pure business. "Yes, I'm fine. Actually, I have someone in my office right now. Can I give you a call back later?"

"Sure," Heather replied, confused

"Thanks for calling. I'll speak with you later," Michael finished and hung up the receiver.

Addressing Susan, he said, "I apologize for the interruption. Let's see, where were we?" He reached for the document they'd been reviewing prior to Heather's call.

Time flew as they tackled one item after another. They worked through lunch and all afternoon before Evelyn poked her head into Michael's doorway.

"Is there anything else that you need, Michael, before I leave?" Evelyn stepped fully into Michael's office. "This has been quite the year for snow," she said as she pointed to the window. "It will probably take forever to get home in this mess."

He glanced out the window at the swirling white mass still descending. "Evelyn, I wish you would have mentioned this earlier. I would have insisted that you both leave before it got this bad." Michael stood up and pushed his chair away from his desk. "Susan, we should call it a day as well. I think it's best if you both head home now before the snow gets any worse."

"I'm on my way," Evelyn replied. "Both of you drive safely and

I'll see you in the morning."

As Evelyn departed, Michael looked at Susan. "Susan, I can't thank you enough for helping me out with this project. By the end of the week we'll be right back on schedule. Thank you."

Susan looked Michael in the eye. "I appreciate your vote of confidence." Turning her head to look out the window she added, "I think I'll take you up on the offer to head home. I live about forty-five minutes from here on a good day. It'll be an eventful drive, I'm sure." Susan leaned down and gathered her things from Michael's desk.

"I'll see you tomorrow," Michael said as he replaced the documents in the project folder.

Susan stopped when she reached his office doorway and turned back. "Michael, Gary told me about the loss of your wife's parents," she said, nodding toward the picture of the blond with two small children on Michael's desk. "My sympathy goes out to her, to all of you. I can't imagine what she must be going through. I don't know if I could survive without one of my parents, much less both of them." She lowered her head and added softly, "My thoughts and prayers are with her, with all of you." She turned and left, shutting his office door behind her.

As his office door closed, Michael stood at his desk, stretched his neck, and sighed. Susan's parting comments hit him hard. Wouldn't Susan be shocked to see how well Christine was doing? Wouldn't she expect Christine to be in pieces rather than spouting philosophical ideas?

This morning's depression slowly returned. It crept under his skin, like a fungus, ever present, not always noticed. Michael plopped into his desk chair, put his head back, and placed his feet on his desk as thoughts of his own parents drifted through his mind. They were good, hardworking, people. He loved and respected them both but he never felt a deep emotional attachment to them. At least, not the kind of attachment that Christine and her siblings had for their parents. Michael originally envied the bond that existed in Christine's family. It was special. Then, he felt lucky enough to become a part of it. His stomach ached with emptiness when he thought of Christine's parents' death. Life wouldn't be the same without them.

When he glanced at the digital clock on his computer, it read six ten. He reached for the telephone.

"Hello," Christine answered.

Michael's voice was void of emotion. "Christine, I'll be working late again tonight and probably all the coming weeks leading up to our rollout." He sighed. "I'll let you know when I'm leaving. I'm not sure how long it will take me to get home in all this snow."

"I understand," she said softly. "Would you like to talk to the kids?"

"Sure." Just the sound of their voices brought life back into his tired limbs.

TWENTY-EIGHT

Heather stepped into her kitchen, filled up her teakettle, and placed it on the stove. She thought about Michael's reaction when she had called earlier as she fixed a cup of green tea. She had stopped home between sales calls and found his message on her machine; his voice was strained, his message curt. She thought something terrible must have happened considering only yesterday he had tried to end their relationship. Her emotions had gotten the better of her.

She leaned against the counter as she awaited her kettle's whistle.

She realized Michael had touched a part of her that no one had previously reached. She felt vulnerable, yet safe – selfless, yet fulfilled.

The kettle shrieked. Heather placed her tea bag in her cup and sauntered to her sofa where she curled up on the soft leather. She leaned her head back and closed her eyes. She knew that Michael felt close to her as well. There wasn't anything he didn't talk about. He'd chuckle at how she could finish his sentences after just a few words. They were connected in a way that neither one had experienced before. Michael told her how he once could finish Christine's sentences and read her thoughts but she was never able to do the same with him. He thought the day would come when she would, but it never had.

At times, Heather longed to be wrapped in Michael's arms,

laughing, hugging, kissing, making love. She tried not to indulge in fantasies because she knew how important Michael's marriage and family were to him. She intuitively knew that a choice to be with her would be a choice that might destroy everything Michael believed in and worked hard for. It might be a choice he would regret forever. She only wanted to see him free from the incredible burden he was carrying and the loneliness he embraced.

Heather jumped when the telephone rang and reached for the receiver.

"This is Heather."

"Heather, it's Michael." He sounded hollow and empty. "I apologize for being abrupt with you earlier. I had someone in my office and I couldn't talk. I hope you understand."

Heather sat up straight and held the receiver tightly. "I'm the one that owes you an apology. I should have known better." She placed her leg underneath her. "I shouldn't have pressed but I was alarmed when I received your message. It didn't sound like you. All I could think was that something terrible had happened again."

"That's all right," Michael said as he stood up from his desk and walked over to his window. "I never should have left that message when I did."

"No, I'm glad you called," Heather interjected. "After yesterday I didn't know if I'd ever hear from you again so it surprised me."

"Look, Heather," Michael began, "I probably shouldn't have called again because this relationship is unfair to you. It's just that – well." Michael paused, staring at the whirling snow outside his window. "Selfish or not, I like you in my life." He turned away from the window and returned to his desk. "I've decided that I'm done living for someone else. It's time I live for myself as well."

Heather stood up and began walking while she talked.

"Michael, this is 'not' unfair to me. Do you have any idea how much I've changed for the better because of our friendship? For the first time in my life I can truly place someone else's needs first. I want nothing more than to see you happy."

"I don't know anything anymore," Michael said, his back stiff, his shoulders tight. "I'm just trying to survive from one day to the next without going under."

"Michael, I've come to understand so much through knowing you – my motivations, defense mechanisms and above all the impenetrable shield I created to protect myself after Madeline died. You have been my emotional safety net. You have a way of removing the fear from truth and providing me a safe place where I can face my insecurities."

He was silent.

Heather returned to her sofa, sat down, and crossed her legs. "Michael, what happened to put you in this state?"

The silence lasted minutes, not seconds.

Finally Michael spoke. "I realized today that Christine has never, and probably will never, love me the way that I loved her." Heather caught Michael's use of the past tense when he spoke. "Last night, I came home late from work to find her sobbing over a letter from Max, professing his love for her. She tells me time and time again that she doesn't love him the way she loves me, that she doesn't want to 'be' with him, only me." He leaned forward and pressed his elbows into his desk. "I think she does love Max in a different way. I think she loves him the way that I loved her." He paused, trying to internalize the words spilling from his mouth. "Max has touched her in ways that I never could." Michael's voice grew cold, bitter. "She knows it and I know it." His elbows felt glued to the desk beneath them. "She tells me that now she can be a better partner to me because she realizes how self-absorbed she's always been. That might be true." His jaw clenched. The silence was longer this time. "I just don't know if I'll ever feel the same about her again."

They were both silent for a while. Heather took a sip of her tea, then spoke, almost in a whisper. "Michael, it breaks my heart to see you so sad. I hope you know how much I care, how much I want to see you happy." She sighed softly. "Please remember I'm here for you, okay?"

Michael softened as Heather's words took root in him. "Thanks, Heather. It does help to talk." As he spoke, a strained smile pulled at the corners of his mouth.

"I can tell you are trying to smile. I feel it," Heather teased. "I won't tell. Go ahead, let it rip."

Michael couldn't resist and a grin stretched across his tired, drained face.

"Okay, okay," he said as he lifted his elbows and leaned back in his chair. "I'm smiling, now are you happy?"

"I sure am," Heather laughed. "I just knew you had it in you." She stood up and went to the kitchen to make more tea. "You know something, Michael, as serious as life can be I think it's important we don't take ourselves 'too' seriously. Having a sense of humor is paramount to survival."

"True enough," Michael said as the muscles in his shoulders slowly relaxed. "Thanks, Heather."

"That's what friends are for, remember?"

"I remember," Michael said before adding, "and when I forget, please remind me. Deal?"

"Deal."

Michael looked at the clock. "Heather, I better go. We were hit with another unusual snowstorm today and it'll take me forever to get home. Oh, before I forget, I wanted to tell you that I'd be in Los

Angeles at the end of April. Remember the big marketing campaign I told you about?"

"Yes," Her heart thumped against the inside of her chest.

"Well, it'll be rolling out in California soon. I'll probably spend two days in the LA market. Once I know the dates, I'll let you know."

"That's terrific. I'll arrange my schedule so we can meet for coffee or lunch or something." Heather swallowed hard, trying to slow her racing pulse. "Oh, Michael. It'll be great to actually see your face again even though I think I can see it through the telephone half the time."

"I 'know' you can see it, most of the time. I'll give you a call when the trip is finalized. Take care, Heather."

"You too, Michael." Her stomach quivered with excitement as she hung up the receiver. She was going to see Michael again, after all these months.

Michael stood up and walked to his office window, his spirits lifted. Maybe Christine was right. Maybe he and Christine could grow closer in time. He knew he needed to keep trying but right now he felt he had nothing left to give. Maybe in time, that would change.

The snow outside his window was falling with renewed vigor. Michael called Christine to let her know he was on his way. He gathered his things, turned off the lights, and locked his office door behind him.

TWENTY-NINE

Max found it hard to concentrate. Each day he forced thoughts of Christine from his mind. He stayed at his office longer and worked harder. In spite of his efforts, Max found less and less pleasure in drinking, sex, and business battles. Nothing seemed to fill him as before. He moved from moment to moment, hoping the thrill would return with time.

It was Friday morning and Max's schedule was full. He arrived at a client's office at eight o'clock for another face off with Roger Demerly. There was another property to bid. Roger arrived early and was waiting with the client, Henry Jacobs, for Max's arrival.

Max exited the elevator and was greeted by the client's assistant. "Mr. Fairchild, Mr. Jacobs and Mr. Demerly are waiting for you in the boardroom."

"Thank you." Max nodded and headed down the long hallway lined with windows overlooking the city. The clouds were thick; the city lacked its normal charm and allure. He glanced down at the street below to view the everyday hustle and bustle of people, going everywhere and nowhere.

Henry and Roger rose to greet Max as he entered the boardroom. Henry's strong handshake was a welcomed contrast to Roger's sweaty palm. The muscles in Max's face tightened as they sat down at the table. He found Roger's lack of strength and confidence appalling. The sooner they could complete this meeting, the better. They were bidding on a building to be used for office space in the business district. Once again, Max's creative insight and conceptual capability reigned supreme. The meeting concluded within forty minutes. They shook hands and Max departed in silence. The normal thrill from winning was noticeably absent.

Max returned to his office and began sorting through his mail. His heart beat faster as he noticed the light purple stationary. He picked it up, took his letter opener, and slid it across the top of the envelope.

Dear Max,

I wish you had given me the chance to explain. I don't know if you'll read this or not but I hope and trust that you will.

I am so terribly sorry that I had not received your letter prior to our talking. I cannot begin to imagine the pain you have endured. I now understand even more the reason you are the way you are, why you have chosen the path you have chosen. Again, it is through growing to understand you that I have grown to understand so many things.

The last thing on earth I would ever want to do is to hurt you. It's amazing to me that you could sense something was wrong when my parents died. I meant it when I said I appreciate your concern because I do.

Max, please believe me when I tell you that I never meant to offend you. I love you for who you are because I understand who you are. I will be forever grateful for knowing you. I just want you to know that.

Love and peace,

Christine

Each word slowly made its way to Max's heart. He felt the genuine compassion in Christine's every word – detached with reason – not fiery with passion. He knew he shouldn't expect more, but some part of him did. He slid the letter back into its envelope and returned to his work.

THIRTY

The holiday season crept up on Christine and her siblings, catching them all unprepared and unenthused. She muddled through decorating the house and the tree for the children but each time she touched one of the ornaments her mother had given them, emptiness would erupt within her aching heart; tears would flow unconstrained.

John, Kathy, and Sam, three of Christine's siblings, were not up for traveling. Christine, Michael, and the kids spent a quiet Christmas Eve alone but decided to have her older sister Melanie, her husband James, and their two children, Chet and Hannah over for Christmas dinner. Joseph and Elizabeth always looked forward to spending time with their cousins.

The adults did their best not to dampen holiday spirits for the children, but the absence of Christine's parents left a hole that was deep and cold. They called each of their out-of-town siblings, trying to fill the gap but conversation was limited, tears were plentiful. The children spent as much time as possible playing alone with one another, insulating themselves from the emptiness. Everyone hoped that in time, the pain would lessen and holidays would once again become a reservoir of joy.

# # #

Max worked longer hours as the holidays came and went. He chose not to throw his annual party and avoided the pub and nightclubs altogether. Festive was not his frame of mind.

THIRTY-ONE

The next several months came and went. Some days were longer than others for Christine, but, bit-by-bit, step-by-step, tear-by-tear, she was learning to survive without her parents. Michael remained distant from her in ways she could not pinpoint but trusted time would mend the fissure that had developed between them.

It was Monday, April twenty-eighth, the day Michael was scheduled to depart for California. The preparation was complete; the marketing campaign was ready for launch. Michael and Susan had worked diligently to meet the deadlines. The work they delivered surpassed Gary's expectations and everyone felt confident of the upcoming campaign's success. Michael finished packing his suitcase as Christine and the children ate breakfast in the kitchen, waiting to say their goodbyes. Michael took one last look at the contents of his luggage, making sure nothing was forgotten. He grabbed his things, carried them downstairs, and placed them by the front door.

"Are you sure you wouldn't like me and the kids to drive you to the airport instead of taking a cab?" Christine asked.

"I'm sure. I have some additional work to do on the way, so this will be fine," Michael said. "Besides, there's no need for all of you to spend your entire Monday morning driving to and from the airport." The horn of the taxi signaled its arrival. Michael reached for Elizabeth, lifted her up in his arms, and hugged her tightly.

"I sure will miss you, little princess," he said as he kissed her forehead.

"I'll miss you too, daddy," Elizabeth replied as a frown knitted her tiny brow.

Noticing Elizabeth's gloomy scowl, Michael reassured her, "Don't be sad. I'll only be gone for a week. I'll call you every night and I'll be home before you know it."

He hugged her again, kissed her cheek, and gently set her down.

Michael leaned down and gave Joseph a big hug and whispered in his ear. "You're the man of the house while I'm gone. Take good care of them, okay?"

Joseph smiled broadly and straightened his small back. "You bet, daddy," he stated with the sureness of a young man rather than a boy of six.

Christine stood patiently waiting her turn for parting hugs and kisses. Michael looked into her trusting eyes, glanced away, then reached over, and pulled her into a long embrace.

"I love you, Christine," he whispered.

"I love you too, Michael."

They embraced a moment longer. The taxi beeped impatiently. She pulled away to let Michael gather his things but not before she kissed him one more time.

"Be safe," she added as she shifted her stance, trying to shake the apprehension from her bones. Since the death of her parents, traveling brought high anxiety. She hoped the heightened angst, like her continuing grief, would ease in time.

"I will. I promise."

He gave them each another quick hug, then made his way out the front door to the taxi.

# # #

After Michael settled in the cab, he pulled out his itinerary from his briefcase. First stop was San Francisco. He was to meet several colleagues this evening to review the details of the campaign launch. He would spend a day and a half in the San Francisco area, then head to Los Angeles for two days, and wrap up in San Diego on Friday. There would be kickoff meetings at each branch in each location, followed by speaking engagements in the various communities. It was going to be fast paced and demanding but Michael felt up to the challenge. He found great escape and relief in his work these last several months.

His heart beat faster when he thought about seeing Heather again. She had become his friend, a lighthouse guiding him across his turbulent seas. A steady beat of eagerness and anticipation pulsed through his body. Only a few more days and they could actually talk face to face.

He called Christine upon his safe arrival and reaffirmed that he'd call them at some point each evening during his trip.

San Francisco went well, better than expected. By midday Wednesday, Michael was packed and ready to leave for LA.

Michael called Christine and the children early Wednesday evening after arriving in LA. The meeting with the directors of the local branches later that evening lasted several hours but everyone seemed locked and ready to go the next day. Michael finally returned to his hotel room sometime after nine. He was tired but satisfied with the initial success of the campaign.

He undressed, unpacked, and reached for the telephone to call Heather.

"This is Heather," her voice was eager. Michael had told her his basic itinerary prior to leaving so she knew he would be in town today. She had busied herself the best she could throughout the day, trying to remain focused, but her distraction was insurmountable.

"Hi, Heather. It's Michael."

"I am so glad it's you. This has been one of the longest days of my life," Heather confessed as she nestled into her sofa. "Did you arrive on schedule? How did things go in San Francisco? Did you have your meeting this evening as planned?"

"Whoa," Michael chuckled, "slow down, one question at a time, please."

"I'm sorry." Heather leaned her head back against the sofa. "I've been thinking about you every minute today and wondering how your trip was going. I want to hear every little detail."

"In a nutshell, it's going extremely well. San Francisco went even better than expected and the branches here seem to be equally prepared for their rollout. Tomorrow will be telling but I have a feeling things will go according to plan. The timing for these products and services seems to be just right and timing is everything in marketing," Michael stated as he placed his briefcase on the dresser.

"I'm so glad for you, Michael. You've worked hard on this campaign for months and it's great that things are falling into place."

"Well, we still have quite a ways to go, but I think this one's a winner." He sat down on his hotel bed and kicked off his shoes.

"Do you know if you will have any free time to have lunch or dinner or even a cup of coffee?" Heather asked, hoping to set a time to meet with him.

"Actually, Heather, my schedule is crazy. Tomorrow I have to make presentations to different community groups at breakfast, during lunch and also over dinner." Michael's tongue felt thicker than usual. "The last event should end sometime around eight in the evening. I wondered if we could meet somewhere after that and share a cup of coffee or a nightcap." He stood up and stretched his neck.

"That'll work for me. Where is your dinner engagement?"

"It's at the Century Plaza Hotel in Century City."

"That's great, Michael." Heather leapt up and walked over to her bay window. "It's only two blocks from where I live. We can have coffee here and you can see my condo."

Michael swallowed hard, prying his tongue off the roof of his mouth. "I don't think that's such a good idea, Heather. I mean I would love to see your place but," he tripped over his words, feeling silly and inept, "I - well - I think it might be better to meet somewhere else."

"I understand." Heather glanced up at the star-studded sky. "Well, why don't you give me a call when you're finished and then I'll think of a place nearby where we can meet? How does that sound?"

"Sounds good."

"Good luck tomorrow, Michael," Heather said as she strolled back to her sofa and sat down. "I'm sure your presentations will be flawless."

"I don't know about flawless, but I at least hope the presentation makes sense to everyone." Michael stretched his neck again.

"I'm sure you will do fine," Heather added as she reached for a strand of her hair and began twisting it. "I'll talk to you tomorrow night."

"Talk to you then."

Michael tossed and turned in his bed, unable to fall asleep. Why was he suddenly acting cool and detached with Heather instead of sharing his excitement? He threw the covers off. Couldn't he spend time with Heather without violating their friendship or his marriage? He got up, went to the bathroom, poured a glass of water, and drank it down. Why was he so apprehensive? He returned to bed, turned on his back, and stared at the ceiling. After hours of fretting, he finally fell asleep.

When his alarm sounded at five o'clock, he jumped out of bed, afraid of being lulled back to sleep. He mentally rehearsed his presentations while jogging for forty minutes on the hotel treadmill. He showered, dressed, grabbed his briefcase, and headed for the hotel lobby. As he stepped into the cab, he felt refreshed, alert and focused, ready to meet his audience.

The day was non-stop but Michael kept pace with each presentation and meeting. The feedback was overwhelmingly positive at each engagement. It was eight-thirty in the evening before he bid his farewell to the dinner guests and returned to his room. He was exhausted but pleased with the days' events.

He set down his briefcase, and still standing, he called Heather, afraid that if he sat, his energy would fade.

"Hi Heather. I'm finally finished with my day."

"How did it go?"

"Well, really well."

"You sound beat, Michael. Do you still feel up to meeting or would you like to pass?" Heather asked, hoping for the best.

"I don't want to pass. I'm tired but not too tired to finally see you after all these months."

"How about meeting at Harry's Bar? It's located right on the Avenue of the Stars in Century City and I can be there in fifteen minutes."

"I'll see you there." A rush of adrenaline charged through Michael's tired limbs as he hung up the phone.

Suddenly realizing he hadn't called home yet, he hurriedly dialed his number.

"Hello," Christine answered.

"Hi," Michael said as he rubbed the back of his neck with his hand. "I'm sorry to call so late but this is the first minute I've had since five this morning. I missed saying goodnight to the kids, didn't I?"

"Yes," Christine explained, "they fell asleep quite a while ago but I told them you might not be able to call before their bedtime every night. They understood and told me to send you love, hugs, and kisses." Then she asked, "How was your day? Did it go as well as in San Francisco?"

"Yes, I think it did." Michael glanced at his reflection in the mirror on the dresser. "It's been long and exhausting, but a rewarding couple of days."

"I'm so glad." She smiled into the telephone. "If anyone deserves success, you do. You've driven yourself so hard on this. I'm happy that it's paying off for you, Michael."

"Thanks. Well, I have another crazy day tomorrow." Michael yawned. "I'll do my best to call earlier and please tell the kids I'm sorry I missed them."

"Boy, you sound beat. I'll let you catch some sleep but I'll be thinking about you tomorrow." She added, "Michael, I really miss you. It'll feel good to have you home in a couple of days."

"Yes, it – uh – sure will. I'll call you tomorrow," Michael said as he wished her goodnight and hung up the phone. Guilt swarmed around him like hornets looking for their nest. He washed his face, brushed his teeth, and left to meet Heather.

# # #

As Michael entered Harry's Bar he caught sight of Heather sitting at the bar, facing the doorway. She looked even more stunning than he had allowed himself to remember. Heather stood and moved toward him when she saw him enter. She wore a sleek, black silk dress that accentuated her voluptuousness; her auburn hair fell across her shoulders in soft, large curls. She reached out to hug Michael. He felt aroused by her touch.

"It's nice to see you again," Heather whispered.

Michael tightened his embrace. "It sure is."

They hugged a moment longer then walked to the bar where Heather had saved him a seat. She ordered a Cosmopolitan and Michael asked for a Heineken. They were silent for a moment as they looked at each other in amazement.

"I can't believe it," Heather said, breaking the spell of silence. "You're really here."

"Neither can I." Michael shifted on his bar stool. "It's strange, isn't it?"

"It's wonderful," Heather gazed at him, her violet eyes shimmering. She raised her glass, he raised his, they clinked, and took a celebratory sip.

Heather's beauty took Michael's breath away. He was at a loss for words. He felt guilty yet elated sitting by her side. Part of him wanted to politely excuse himself and run, the other part felt bolted to the bar stool beneath him.

"Michael, how did it go today? Please, tell me everything."

Michael recapped the day's events in vivid detail while Heather leaned toward him, seizing every word as it left his lips. After finishing he asked Heather about her day and she returned the exchange with equal detail. As Michael's nervousness eased, conversation flowed. Several hours and numerous drinks later, Michael glanced at his watch.

"Oh my God, Heather, it's after midnight!"

"It can't be that late," Heather said as she looked at her watch to confirm. "You're right. It seems like we just got here, doesn't it?"

"It sure does and I don't want to end this great night, Heather." Michael's eyes reflected as much disappointment as his tone. "But I'm afraid I'm going to have to. I have an early flight to San Diego." Michael stood up and reached in his pocket to pay the tab. "Let me walk you to your car to make sure you are safe."

"I walked here, Michael. It's only two blocks from my condo."

"Well then, I'll walk you back to your place and make sure you get home safely," Michael decided, leaving no room for discussion. He paid the bartender and they headed out the door.

It was a cool, California evening. The salt-water breeze prickled their skin. Stars peered down in abundance from the sky above. Michael put his suit jacket across Heather's shoulders. She slipped her arm through his as they walked quietly in the night air toward her condo.

"Well, this is it," Heather said as they arrived at her three-story light brick building with wrought iron balconies. "Do you want to come up for a cup of coffee before you leave?"

"Thanks, Heather, but I don't think that would be such a good idea," Michael said as he returned her gaze, gently placing his hands on her shoulders. Longing raged through his body but caution captured his libido. "It's been wonderful to see you again, Heather," he said as he pulled Heather toward him, kissed her forehead, and embraced her. She hung in his arms, memorizing the feeling, before pulling away and removing his jacket from her shoulders.

"Thanks," Heather whispered as she handed back his suit jacket. "Thanks for everything." She continued, looking into his eyes, "I can't remember a moment that I ever felt so happy."

Michael kissed her forehead again, turned quickly on his heels, and walked away.

Heather watched him move into the distance before reaching

for her keys and ambling up the stairs. Joy mixed with disappointment washed over her as she undressed and got ready for bed. She had waited for this evening for a long time and it was over. As she pulled down the comforter on her bed, the buzzer rang from downstairs.

"Who is it?" she asked into the intercom.

"It's Michael."

Without hesitation, Heather buzzed him into the complex. A few minutes later there was a gentle knock on her door. Heather opened it. Michael entered without a word, closing and locking the door behind him. He reached for her, pulled her toward him, and kissed her. Passion exploded. He picked her up and carried her to the bedroom. Love and sorrow swept through him as he made love to every inch of her. He ached for the woman he shouldn't be with, and the woman he couldn't be without.

They fell asleep as the sun poked its head above the horizon. The alarm jolted them awake within the hour. Facing Heather in the morning light was like staring into a hot, summer sun without sunglasses, blinding and overwhelming. Michael silently showered and dressed. He needed to hurry back to his hotel and change before his flight.

Heather understood. She watched every move that his muscular body made. She sat curled on her bed, her legs pulled up under her arms. She could still smell his scent on her naked skin. She reached for him as he headed for the door. "Michael," she whispered, "we didn't plan this. It just happened."

Michael embraced her, kissed her forehead, and left, without saying a word. He couldn't believe he had returned to her place last night. He'd been so strong, so righteous, so disciplined, only to see his resolve collapse in the end. Guilt twisted his gut like the nausea that accompanies a sudden bout of seasickness.

Heather slid back down on her bed. She stared at the ceiling and let her love for Michael rush over her. She knew Michael was struggling, deeply. She understood him in a way Christine didn't. She loved him in a way that Christine hadn't, and she knew she reached a part of him that Christine couldn't. Heather wondered whether this was the end or just the beginning for her and Michael. Heather thought about Michael all morning long. She knew that he had fallen in love with her. She also knew that for the first time in her life, she was vulnerable. Maybe she had allowed herself to get close to Michael because she knew she couldn't be with him. Maybe not. She had grown to need Michael as well as love him. Her life was fulfilling, but with Michael, it was complete. The more Heather thought the more confused she became. She didn't want to interfere with Michael's marriage but Christine didn't seem to love him the way he needed to be loved. Michael was in pain and had fallen in love with Heather because he felt alone.

Later that morning, Heather stopped by a drug store between two of her appointments. She wanted to find a card for Michael, something special. She browsed through racks and racks of cards until finding just the perfect one. The scene on the front was a lustrous sunset over the ocean, two birds silhouetted against the sky. It was blank inside. Heather paid for the card, put it in her purse and returned home to make her additions to it.

Dear Michael,

I sat on the bed this morning after you left, letting the scent of your skin, the taste of your mouth and the touch of your hands, fill my senses. When I finally showered, I let your love and passion wash over every inch of me. I feel you inside me – still. We're like two birds, meeting by chance but now bound in life's ever-changing flight. This isn't something we expected to happen and neither one of us want to hurt anyone. I want you to know that I love you and want to see you happy. I also want you to know that you have touched me in a way no one else ever has, or will.

Love and friendship forever,

Heather

Heather sealed the envelope, placed a stamp on it and walked outside to drop it in the mailbox. She was sending it to Michael's office and hoped it would reach him by Monday. She wrapped her arms around herself. A pensive and sad expression crept its way across her face as she slowly climbed the steps back to her condo entrance.

THIRTY-TWO

Christine awakened early Friday morning, excited for Michael's return that the evening. His flight arrived around ten and she promised the children they could accompany her to the airport to greet him. This was the longest business trip Michael had ever taken during their eight years of marriage. He occasionally traveled for two or three days at a time, but never for an entire week. She, Joseph, and Elizabeth missed him and could hardly wait for his return.

Christine lay in bed. Her mind drifted to thoughts of her parents. It had been over four months since the accident, but the daunting reality of their death still had to be re-digested at the beginning of each day. The waves of grief still found their way to her heart. She never knew when or where they would strike but she knew they'd return for a very long time, probably forever. She'd feel the moments deeply and completely, surrender to the sadness, then move on to the moment at hand, focusing on all the good that remained. This morning the tears rolled freely as memories of her childhood skated across her mind – the family rides for ice cream each Sunday, her mother's reaction when dad brought home a puppy without prior notice, the holidays, the birthdays, the weekend rides through the countryside, the dinner conversations – a panorama of events that had shaped her life. As each tear kissed her pillow, deeper acceptance of death's painful finality followed.

The largest tribute she could give her parents was to be the best parent she could be, to Joseph, Elizabeth, and any future children she and Michael would have. Like her parents, she and Michael had created a family of unconditional love and acceptance, an environment where their children would have the same solid foundation from which to grow and become healthy, independent, loving adults.

The tears subsided as she thought about Michael's arrival in the evening. Music blared from her clock radio. It was time to wake the children. She smiled, stretched, and placed her feet on the floor, ready for another day. She wrapped herself in her toasty fleece bathrobe and went to rouse them. As she stepped into the hallway, she grew dizzy. She reached for the wall to regain her steadiness. She took a deep breath and waited several moments for the feeling to pass before continuing to Joseph's room. Several people at the law office had come down with the flu the past two weeks. She quickly decided she was much too busy to succumb to it also.

"Good morning, honey," Christine whispered as she gently stroked Joseph's forehead. "It's Friday. Daddy gets home tonight."

"Daddy's home?" Elizabeth asked as she came tearing around the corner into Joseph's room.

"Daddy's coming home tonight, sweetie," Christine corrected. "His plane arrives at ten o'clock. After dinner, maybe you two can rest before we leave for the airport. It'll be a late night for both of you."

Suddenly Joseph's eyes opened wide as his mother's and sister's words registered. "Yeah!" Joseph exclaimed. "Daddy's coming home!"

Joseph reached to give his mom a hug while Elizabeth twirled in place. The two of them raced down the hallway to the kitchen, laughing. Christine followed behind, slightly unsteady, still not feeling quite like her normal self.

"I won!" Elizabeth squealed with delight.

"You did, indeed." Christine winked at Joseph who always allowed his younger sister the honor of winning at races that didn't count.

She made their favorite breakfast, banana nut pancakes with chocolate chips. It was a special day for them all. They finished their morning routine and were soon on their way out the door.

She arrived at the office early. David was entering the building as she approached.

"I'll start the coffee, get some things lined up, and then come down to your office," she said as they arrived on their floor.

Within ten minutes she was in David's doorway. "Is this a good time or would you like me to come back a little later to discuss the Courtney file?"

David was looking out his office window, lost in thought. Her voice startled him. He rebounded and looked in her direction. "This is fine, Christine." Pointing to a chair he said, "Please, have a seat."

She pulled a chair up to the end of his desk, laid her folder out, and sat down. David lingered at the window a moment longer, then walked to his desk and sat down to join her.

"What have you discovered, Christine?" he asked as he reached for the folder.

When she finished explaining every detail, David quietly digested the information. "Well done, Christine. You've accomplished quite a bit. This information gives us a solid foundation to prepare our line of questioning for the depositions." He sat at attention, rested his arms on his desk, and looked intently at her. "Would you like to take a stab at preparing them?"

"I'd love it!" This would be her first opportunity to participate in this part of the process. She leaned forward and spoke with unmistakable deliberation. "David, thank you. This will be great experience for me."

He leaned back in his chair, threaded his fingers, and rubbed the palms of his hands together. "Christine, you've earned every opportunity you've been given. The more experience you have before entering law school, the better. Just let me know when you have a rough draft of questions for me to review."

"Will do." She was aglow as she collected her file and prepared to leave. She paused as she reached his doorway, turned around, and said, "You really are something, David. I love working with you." Without waiting for a response, she turned, exited, and glided down the hallway to her office.

A subtle smile inched across David's face. The feeling was mutual.

Christine dove into her new assignment with vigor. Before she knew it, lunch had come and gone; the day was over. Anticipation of Michael's return rapidly replaced the thrill of her days' work. She stopped and leaned her head inside David's office.

"David, I should have the questions for you by the end of the day on Monday. Will that be enough time for you to review and edit them prior to Thursday?"

"That'll be plenty of time. We'll schedule a meeting for first thing Tuesday."

"Great. Have a nice weekend, David."

"You do the same," David replied. Then remembering, he added, "I'm sure you will with Michael returning."

"You bet I will!" She said goodnight and departed.

When she got home, she fixed the special dinner she'd

promised, grandma's meatloaf. It was Elizabeth's favorite meal from the moment she tasted it. Grandma's special recipe ranked high on Joseph's food chart as well. Christine remembered all the years her mother had fixed it for their family. To her surprise, the meatloaf and the memories didn't bring more sadness. Instead, she felt peaceful, loving, and complete. These were the moments she wished she could capture, or at least maintain longer.

"Mommy," Elizabeth said as she skipped into the kitchen, "I'm hungry. Will grandma's meatloaf be ready soon?"

"It's all made, sweetie. Now it just has to bake but that will take a little while. Do you want some carrots and dip to snack on while we wait?"

"Sure." Elizabeth's smile faded. "Mommy," she whispered, "I miss grandma and grandpa. I want them back." Tears began to well and trickle down her little cheeks.

Christine reached down and pulled her into her chest while Elizabeth wept. "I know, honey. I know." She continued holding Elizabeth, letting her share her sadness, not saying a word, just hugging her closely. Elizabeth wept for several minutes before her tears subsided. There were many times that Christine or Michael or both held Joseph and Elizabeth when grief overwhelmed them. It pained her to watch each of them suffer with their loss. Anger still tormented Joseph. Elizabeth continued to fight her sadness. She understood that both children needed to grieve in their own way, in their own time; grieving is as unique as the individual experiencing it.

Elizabeth pulled away from her, sniffled and said, "I need a tissue, mommy."

She kissed Elizabeth on her wet cheek and went to get a tissue. She bent down, handed the tissue to Elizabeth, then wiped her cherub face with a warm washcloth. "Do you feel better?"

"Yep," Elizabeth said as she threw the tissue out. "Now can I please have some carrots? I'm starving."

She marveled again at Elizabeth's ability to rebound from her emotional bouts. Elizabeth didn't dwell on things. Once the sadness or anger was expressed, it was gone. Christine wondered why as we grow older we clutter our minds and hearts with thoughts of the past or worrying about the future instead of just living fully in the present. She realized how conditioned she had become over the years. Her mind always had a million things running through it at any given moment - a million thoughts, a million things to do, a million things to think about. It took concentrated energy to really focus on the present, to quiet the internal chatter and fully engage in the moment at hand. When she was capable of doing it, the experience of living was qualitatively different, more connected, more complete.

After dinner, she read Elizabeth her favorite book, <u>Bread and Jam for Francis,</u> while Joseph built towers of Legos on the floor. Elizabeth dozed off to sleep but not before Christine reassured her that she'd awaken her for the airport. With Elizabeth fast asleep, and Joseph in the height of creativity, she reached for the mail. On the top of the stack was a letter from Max. She had not heard from him in months. The letter was dated late December. He must have held onto it all this time before sending it. Her hand trembled as she opened it. Tears gently cascaded down her cheeks as she read it.

Dear Christine,

Maybe in the past, or someday in the future, we stood, or shall stand, side by side. But for now, we stand on different sides of the same mountain, with different views.

Enjoy your view and live it well. Always remain true to

who you really are and be strong in the choices that you make. Be sure they are aligned with your soul. I shall do the same. The time has come to bid you farewell.

Max

She read it and reread it. She had touched Max's heart. She had reached his soul. He needed to say goodbye. He could never settle for a platonic relationship. It would weaken his spirit and destroy all the barriers that protected him. She had been forever changed, enriched, enlightened. She would return to her fulfilling life with Michael, her children, family, and friends. Max would return to his safe-haven of momentary, hedonistic existence. It was what it was – nothing more, nothing less. She folded up the letter and returned it to its envelope. She sat at her desk and put pen to paper one last time.

As she sealed her letter in an envelope, streaks of orange, red, and yellow reached through her bay window and made their final bow before slipping silently beneath the horizon. The moon took center stage and orchestrated the glistening band of stars surrounding it.

The hallway clock struck eight. It was time to wake Elizabeth from her nap and get the children ready to leave for the airport.

THIRTY-THREE

Michael stared out the plane window as they approached the DIA. He was physically, mentally, and emotionally exhausted. The day in San Diego had been a long one with less than two hours of sleep the night before. He had done his best to concentrate throughout the day but knew his business presentations had been less than stellar.

He realized that he had fallen in love with Heather over the last several months. Making love to her was something he didn't intend but couldn't resist. Part of him felt guilty, part of him fulfilled.

He still loved Christine. He loved Joseph. He loved Elizabeth. He loved Heather. He was confused and couldn't sort through the range of emotions swirling within him. How would he tell Christine what had happened? Could he? Should he? Over all these months he thought there would come a time to tell Christine about his friendship with Heather. But now, after this, how could he ever expect her to understand? The plane landed.

As he reached the end of the concourse he heard Joseph shout, "There he is. There's daddy!" He caught sight of Christine holding Elizabeth and all three of them waving wildly, grinning from ear to ear. When Michael reached them, Joseph was first to leap into his arms for a hug. Elizabeth was right behind him. To Joseph, this was a race that counted.

Christine stood back and let the children have their moment

before she walked up and kissed Michael on the lips. "Welcome home," she whispered in his ear.

"It's good to be home," Michael said as his throat constricted. "Let's get my luggage and go home."

"Michael, what's wrong?"

"Nothing, Christine, I'm just exhausted," Michael said, avoiding her eyes. "It feels like I've been gone longer than a week and I'm anxious to get home."

She knew there was something more, but let it pass for the time being. She'd talk to him after Joseph and Elizabeth went to bed. She took his arm and they walked to the baggage claim area.

Joseph drilled Michael with questions about California. Michael told them about each city before asking the children to recap their weeks. Joseph's synopsis was short and succinct with minimal detail. Elizabeth gladly shared every facet of her week that she could remember. The more recent the experience, the more she remembered. The banana nut, chocolate chip pancakes and meatloaf were definite highlights.

Once home, Michael read part of a book to each of them before tucking them into bed for the night.

"Thanks for meeting me at the airport, buddy," he said as he kissed Joseph's cheek goodnight.

"You're welcome, daddy." Joseph hugged Michael tightly around his neck. "I'm glad you're home. I missed you."

"I missed you too. You sleep well. Okay?"

Joseph nodded in agreement.

"I have to tuck your sister in now." Michael stood, pulled up Joseph's covers, and tucked them in before leaving his room.

Elizabeth clung to Michael longer than usual when he kissed her goodnight. "I love you, daddy." Her mouth widened in a big yawn. "Bunches," she added as she stretched under her covers.

"I love you, too, princess," Michael sighed as he kissed her forehead. He ached with love.

Christine was waiting for Michael in the den. She had opened a bottle of champagne and poured two glasses. Michael sat next to her on the sofa and said, "Christine, I appreciate the thought but I'm too tired to drink champagne tonight. I think I want to crawl in bed and get some solid sleep. I hope you don't mind."

She anticipated a romantic reunion but understood. She saw the exhaustion in his eyes and knew the week had been a demanding one for him.

"That's all right. You look absolutely drained." She kissed him on the cheek. "Is something bothering you, Michael? You seem troubled."

Michael knew he should tell her everything but just couldn't find the energy to begin. Without looking at her, he patted her arm, kissed her on the cheek, and rose from the couch. "I'm just exhausted. I'm going to bed before I'm down for the count on the sofa." He leaned down, kissed her forehead, and left for the bedroom.

She sat quietly for a few moments. She knew something was wrong. She also knew this wasn't the time to press the issue. She was sure he'd talk to her after a good night's sleep.

She stood up, corked the champagne bottle, poured the two glasses down the sink, and joined Michael in the bedroom. She found him fast asleep and snoring. She undressed, slid between the sheets, and snuggled up against his back. It felt so good to have him home.

THIRTY-FOUR

The sun lingered over the horizon, spraying rays of gold ingots through the bedroom window. Christine opened her eyes, sensing just the slightest hint of spring in the air. She stretched her arms, yawned, and rolled over to hug Michael. He was still sleeping soundly. Not wanting to disturb him, she snuck from the bed, reached for her bathrobe, and wrapped it around her. She bent down and placed her warm, moccasin slippers onto her feet. She slid out the bedroom door shutting it behind her without making a sound.

She pulled the bay patio door open that overlooked the woods behind their home and stepped onto the solid oak deck. The sun was still inching its way above the horizon. The air was crisp and clean. The faintest trace of newly formed buds dotted the trees as the melodious chirping of birds drifted through the air. It was the beginning of spring, her favorite time of year. She walked past their ensemble of wicker patio furniture to the deck railing, stretched her arms across the oak rail, resting her palms on its smooth, finished surface. She took a deep breath and let the cool sensation fill every inch of her lungs before exhaling. She closed her eyes and let each sound and smell of spring resonate within her. The birds fine-tuned each note as if singing in chorus while the frogs riveted in belching unison. She smelled the rich morning dew as it hung on the Blue Grama grass. She could picture earthworms creeping their way through the thawing terrain. It felt good to be alive. She opened her eyes in time to catch sight of a Lark Bunting taking flight. It was several weeks early in its return to the area, she thought. It was the male bird, black with snowy white wing patches and edgings. It wouldn't be long before she'd hear him singing his distinctive mating song, complete with warbles and trills. She stood at the railing several minutes, sensing, absorbing, and connecting to all that surrounded her. Her mind was silent as her thoughts and feelings rested in quiet harmony. She didn't hear Michael approach.

"You look lost in thought," Michael commented as he stepped onto the deck.

"Oh," Christine replied with a start, "good morning. You snuck up on me." She took a few steps to reach him and wrapped her arms around his neck. "God, how I love you, Michael. I'm standing here realizing what a lucky woman I am – for you, for the kids, for my health, for the sun, the birds, for everything." She stretched her arms upward and sighed. "It's amazing to me how life is such a gift, even the difficult parts."

Michael looked into her eyes and saw love and happiness sparkling back at him. He pulled her close and hugged her. "I know what you mean," he whispered.

She sensed his struggle and pulled away to look at him. "Michael, what is it? I've never seen you look so sad."

Michael held her with all his strength. She embraced him back, stroking his head, feeling his sadness. They stood there for what seemed an eternity to Michael, consumed with guilt, shame, sorrow, and love. Michael finally broke the silence. "Christine, I'm so sorry for everything. I'm sorry you needed to find someone else to grow. I'm sorry I haven't been a better husband. I..."

She interrupted. "Michael, you've nothing to be sorry about. You're the 'best' husband and a wonderful father." She pulled back and looked at him. "Everything happens for a reason. You're not to blame that Max was a catalyst in my life. It just happened, but it never changed my love for you. It only made it stronger, deeper, more conscious. Besides, he sent a goodbye letter and I did the same. So, please, please let it go." She took Michael's face in her hands. "Think about all that we have between us, all that lies ahead of us. I love you, Michael, and I've never wanted to be with anyone but you. You have to trust and believe that because it's the truth."

Her words poured over Michael. He felt her love, her belief in him, and her belief in them. Maybe she was right. Maybe everything does happen for a reason. Maybe his love for Heather was just a catalyst to bring him and Christine closer. If her relationship with Max was really over, then he could end it with Heather and move on from there. Maybe it would be better to tell Christine after he ended it. No. He couldn't live with this dark secret. How could he look Christine in the eyes? How could he make love to her? How could he carry this inside day after day without telling her? As each thought resonated through his brain, his decision hanging in the balance, he heard Elizabeth's little voice from behind them.

"Morning," she said with a stretch and a yawn. Michael's back was to her as she approached. "Please pick me up, daddy," she requested with a sleepy smile.

"Okay," Michael said as he took a deep breath. "Family hug." He lifted Elizabeth up with a twirl. She giggled and the three of them embraced. Michael felt relieved that Elizabeth had interrupted his confusion and indecisiveness. As they held one another, clarity returned. This is where he belonged – with Christine and his children. He would end it completely with Heather. He would tell Christine, but not now. He would tell her later when they were alone again. Michael's breathing eased, as if a hundred pound bag of sand had just been lifted from his chest. He hoped and trusted that somehow Christine would find a way to understand and forgive him.

"I believe I promised you and your brother a special day today." Michael kissed Elizabeth's cheek. "Let's wake him up and get the day moving." Michael swung Elizabeth in the air, her squeals of delight echoing through the woods.

"Can we go to the zoo?" Elizabeth asked as Michael returned her from flight to her feet.

"I think we'll check with your big brother before deciding," Michael replied as he squeezed Christine's hand.

"The zoo sounds fun," Joseph unexpectedly chimed in from the doorway. "Can we have banana nut pancakes with chocolate chips again for breakfast?"

THIRTY-FIVE

Heather awoke Saturday morning feeling both fulfilled and apprehensive from Thursday night with Michael. She laid in bed, gazing out her bedroom window at the blinding, mid-morning sun. She had slept later than usual. Last night, she'd fallen asleep early, exhausted from the activity and lack of sleep the night before.

Doubts gradually crept inside her. What if Michael decided not to see her again? What if he told Christine and she insisted the relationship end? What if Christine threatened divorce and child custody? What if this was just a passing romance for Michael – something he needed at the time but didn't need anymore? What if she never heard from him again at all?

Anxiety hit Heather like a deadly viral infection, rapidly spreading out of control. She wrapped her legs under her arms and pulled them close to her chest, rocking back and forth. What was she thinking? She knew Michael loved Christine and his children. Michael never misled her in any way. Michael never intended to fall in love with her. It just happened because of the situation he was in. He had a family to go back to. She had no one. Sure, she could start another relationship with someone but Michael had opened up a part of her that had been sealed away like a hidden treasure in a remote vault. There was no other man Heather wanted. She wanted Michael – only Michael.

She began to cry, her loneliness devouring her. It was the

dreaded feeling she had as a little girl, frightened, alone, and vulnerable. Why had she allowed Michael to penetrate her wall of protection? Could she return to who she was before knowing him? Each thought brought more emptiness, more aloneness.

Heather's sadness subsided as her survival instincts arose. She refused to allow her life to fall apart because of this. She was stronger than that. She knew she loved and understood Michael in a way that Christine didn't but she didn't want to destroy Michael's family that he held so dear. If Christine had given Michael all that he needed, this never would have happened. Christine may not have been sexually unfaithful to Michael, but she was emotionally unfaithful and Heather believed that was worse. Heather decided she would see this through, one way or another, and she would survive. She reached for her running clothes. A five-mile run was just what she needed to clear her head.

When Heather returned from her run, she showered and dressed in a bright yellow and blue sundress with matching sandals. She brushed her long, auburn mane and placed just the hint of makeup on her sparkling, violet eyes. She felt better already. Her first stop was Rodeo Drive. It was mid- afternoon by the time she made her way outdoors. It was an unseasonably, warm, spring day, even for Los Angeles. The sun had eradicated the usual smog. The hot air felt unbearable with the temperature pushing an unexpected eighty degrees. Shopping was a soothing pastime for Heather and today, an exceptionally successful one. Two and a half hours later, and fifteen hundred dollars spent, Heather headed back to her steel blue, Mercedes convertible. She had found three new interchangeable ensembles in a rainbow of colors from pastel pinks and greens to deep, rich violet.

Her next stop was the pet store. She held off buying a kitten or puppy for years because Matt had allergies. Today Heather was determined to purchase a companion. As she entered the pet store, the variety of animal smells peppered her nostrils, triggering childhood memories of the zoo. A friendly, pimply, teenage male clerk approached her with a smile.

"Hello, my name is John. Can I help you find something, Miss?" he asked. John learned that in LA every woman was referred to as Miss, regardless of age.

"Maybe you can, John," Heather said as she mulled over the aisles, pushing her sunglasses from her face to the top of her head. "I want to purchase a pet but I'm not sure exactly what I have in mind yet."

"Well, you've definitely come to the right place," the smiling, now almost drooling, clerk responded. Heather's beauty was an unexpected delight for him. "Are you home a lot or do you travel? It makes a difference, you know. Dogs need a lot of companionship while cats are more independent by nature. Now birds, they can be quite nice, especially the talking ones."

Birds, now that was something Heather hadn't considered. "Can you show me the birds that you have and tell me a little about them?" Heather inquired, her eyes and voice dancing with interest.

"Sure, please follow me." John led Heather to the middle of the store where there was a vast display of feathered creatures. The colors were as countless as the types of birds they decorated. Heather had never seen this many birds in one place other than the aviary at the zoo.

In the center, an exquisite, colorful parrot chattered away within his house of ornate, sculptured, brass. Only in Los Angeles, Heather thought.

Heather's eye caught a cage, behind the parrot that housed two smaller, parrot-like birds, gray in color with hints of green and white blended throughout. They were sharing a swing, with one of the birds rubbing its head gently against the other.

"What are those?" she asked pointing to the cozy pair in the nearby cage.

"This might sound silly," John replied with a sheepish grin. "But they are called lovebirds. They're named that because of the affection they show their mate."

"I'll take them," Heather said abruptly. "They're perfect."

John proceeded to give Heather all the necessary instructions for the birds' transition and care. He helped her carry the cage and additional bag of necessities to her car. It was a tight fit, but they were able to secure the cage for the birds' safe ride to their new home.

Heather shook John's hand. "Thank you, John. You were a tremendous help. I really appreciate it." She slipped him a ten-dollar bill for his extra help, gave him a quick kiss on the forehead, got into her car, started the engine, and drove off. John stood there shocked, blushing, and excited.

Heather's final stop was the video store. She hadn't watched a movie in months. She dashed in, aware of the birds in a smoldering death trap, rented Casablanca, and was back to her car in less than five minutes. Once home, she found the perfect table for her new friends. Hunger tugged at her stomach as she finished unloading her car, hanging up her new clothes, and chatting with the birds. As she broiled herself a salmon filet and tossed a salad, she pondered what she would name her lovebirds.

Dinner was ready. She opened a bottle of Sterling Merlot, poured herself a glass, popped the movie into the DVD, and curled up on her leather couch, with her new friends close beside her. Contentment wrapped around her as she settled in for the evening.

THIRTY-SIX

Michael, Christine, and the kids returned home late in the afternoon after a tiring but fun-filled day at the zoo. They had devoured their picnic lunch late morning and were now famished.

Elizabeth and Joseph finished setting the patio table while Christine brought out the side dishes. She went back to the kitchen and returned with last night's champagne, hoping it hadn't gone flat. She poured some in Michael's glass and was relieved to see bubbles swimming to the surface. She filled her and Michael's glasses with the champagne, and then poured sparkling grape juice for Joseph and Elizabeth.

"See, Elizabeth, you have bubbles too," Christine said as she leaned down and kissed the top of her head before taking her seat at the table.

"Who wants to lead grace tonight?" Michael asked. Grace before meals was a family ritual, not to be broken even by the heights of hunger.

"I will," Joseph offered. "God bless mommy and daddy and Elizabeth and all the animals at the zoo and the good food daddy grilled."

"Amen," the four of them said simultaneously.

"That was very nice, Joseph," Michael said, as he gave him a nod of approval and winked at Christine. Conversation succumbed to hunger as they devoured their meal. Too full for dessert, they cleaned off the table and returned to the patio to relax. No sooner had they settled into their chairs than Elizabeth's eyes began to droop and her head bobbed.

"Someone's tired," Michael said and pointed in Elizabeth's direction. "How about I get you ready for bed and read you a story?" he asked.

"I'm not tired," Elizabeth protested. "I want to stay up."

"Well, let's at least get you bathed and in your pajamas. Then we'll see," Michael coaxed.

Joseph's mouth stretched wide in a yawn. Surprisingly, he volunteered to join them. "I'm tired. I'm going too."

Without further argument, Elizabeth grabbed one of Michael's hands, Joseph took hold of the other, and they ambled into the house. Christine leaned back in her forest green, cushioned patio chair, took a sip of champagne, and closed her eyes. The smell of the lingering grill extravaganza hung in the air. The crickets had picked up in song where the birds and frogs had left off in the morning. The gentle evening air whispered through the trees as the sun slowly slid into slumber.

She couldn't remember a time she felt so peaceful. She reflected on the fullness of the day – breakfast on the patio, the fun-filled day at the zoo, the grilled feast for dinner. Even bedtime was accepted without the kid's usual resistance. It suddenly struck her that she'd spent other fulfilling days with Michael and the children but it was as if she'd been half asleep before - living, doing, experiencing - not fully aware of each moment's richness and purpose.

"Well, it looks like I have another sleepy one on my hands," Michael teased as he stepped back onto the deck and saw her eyes closed.

"That was quick," she replied as she slowly opened her eyes. "I'm just thinking what a perfect day it's been and how happy and content I feel." She pulled herself up in her chair and looked at him. "We are so lucky, aren't we?" Her eyes and voice mirrored the loving calm within her.

"We sure are." Any thought of telling Christine about Heather quickly vanished. Michael wouldn't ruin this perfect day for either one of them. He would call Heather on Monday and end the relationship. Then he would tell Christine everything. He walked over to the chair where she was sitting, reached down, and ran his fingers through her hair. "What do you say we make it an early night? I have a lot of making up to do since I've been gone for a week."

She lifted her glass and let the last sip of champagne slowly trickle down her throat. "You have yourself a deal." She stood up, wrapped her arms around him, and kissed him fiercely. They locked the patio door and walked arm and arm to the bedroom.

THIRTY-SEVEN

Michael awoke early Sunday morning. He reached over and pulled Christine close to him, gently kissing her forehead, cheeks, and lips. She glided her fingertips down his back. She knew every ripple of muscle and inch of his skin by heart. She loved the tactile differences on Michael's body from the hair on his chest, to the skin on his wrist, to the mass of muscle in his upper arms. They joined in spontaneous, rhythmic lovemaking – a perfect symphony – each movement graceful, responsive, and harmonious.

Dripping in sweat, she lay with her head against Michael's chest. "Wow, you sure must have missed me. Between last night and this morning, I consider myself quite loved." She ran her fingers through the matted hair on his chest. "You're a great lover, Michael."

"So are you. I love you so much, Christine." The depth and truth of his words exploded within him. He pulled her up to kiss her mouth and embrace her. How could he ever have been so weak? Christine satiated his every physical need, always had. Heather reached the part of him that felt alone and isolated. Heather knew his thoughts and feelings before he expressed them. Christine did not. At this moment, Michael was grateful that she didn't.

They heard a gentle knock on their bedroom door. "Mommy, daddy, are you up yet?" Elizabeth asked.

Christine smiled at Michael. "We're just getting up, sweetie," she responded. "Why don't you wait for us either in your room or in the den? We'll be there shortly, okay?"

"Okay. I guess." Elizabeth sighed. "I'm starving."

"We won't be long," Michael assured her.

Michael and Christine jumped in the shower together, toweled off, grabbed their robes, and went in search for their hungry little girl. Before leaving the bedroom, Michael pulled her close to him and whispered in her ear, "I love you more than you know and I hope you always remember that."

He opened the door and playfully shouted, "Here we come, ready or not."

Christine followed him toward the den, trying to shake the uncertainty Michael's words had imparted.

They found Elizabeth sitting on the couch in the den with her favorite book sprawled between her legs. She was reciting it from memory, the best she could. She glanced up. A grin stretched from one ear to the other, leaving her remaining petite features barely visible.

"We told you we wouldn't be long." Michael tossed her up in the air, letting the book sail to the floor.

"Ooops. You should be careful with books, daddy," Elizabeth informed him as she watched her favorite book take flight.

"You're right." Michael reached down, still holding Elizabeth and retrieved her prized possession. He placed it on the coffee table. "There. Is that better?"

"Yes, thanks, daddy." Elizabeth hugged his neck. "Are we doing something special again today?"

"I hadn't given it much thought." The three of them were on autopilot toward the kitchen with their appetites raging. "What do you think, hon?" Michael asked Christine.

"I think I will think better after some breakfast. I'm going to make everyone's favorite pancakes, along with scrambled eggs and bacon. How does that sound?" She was already gathering the necessary ingredients for their breakfast feast.

"Great!" Michael and Elizabeth cheered simultaneously.

Within minutes the sizzling smell of bacon wafted through the hallway into Joseph's bedroom. His eyes popped open as the aroma reached his nostrils. He raced to the kitchen to join them.

When breakfast was ready, Joseph again led grace before the four of them attacked their meals as if they hadn't eaten in weeks. They decided to spend time at the playground, and picnic in the park. It was still chilly, mid-fifties, but forecasted to warm up to the low sixties by mid-afternoon, perfect weather to spend a day outdoors.

Michael chuckled as Elizabeth squealed, "Higher daddy, higher." He was pushing her on her favorite swing at the park. Christine's legs were pumping away on the swing beside Elizabeth, soaring further upward with each motion. Joseph was busy mastering the nearby monkey bars. It was getting late but Joseph and Elizabeth had convinced both Christine and Michael to stay 'just fifteen more minutes' in the park before going home.

Michael felt happier than he'd felt in months. He knew with each giggle, squeal, and sound of delight, that this is where he belonged. Thoughts of Heather evaporated in the warmth and comfort of his family.

THIRTY-EIGHT

Max locked his office door and walked briskly toward the elevator. He was ready for some fresh air after working several hours on this Sunday afternoon. An unseasonably cold breeze spiced the spring air as Max greeted the streets of London. The heat of the sun through his office window had been deceiving. With each step he took, his muscles relaxed, adjusting to the change in temperature. Within moments he was enjoying the cold air rushing over his body, heightening his senses. Shafts of sunlight skipped across the Thames River. The azure sky enveloped the city, silhouetting each building with precision and clarity. All of London resonated as if captured on high speed film, perfect in every detail – river flickering, people walking, vehicles winding their way through cobblestone streets, stone buildings standing guard around each intersection. London's heartbeat pulsated through Max as he slowly walked toward his favorite pub. This was the first time in weeks he'd been to his familiar place of relaxation. As of late, Max had focused on work with little interest in other pleasures. He'd attempted to drown Christine's memory in his ongoing stream of consciousness. So far, he only managed to mentally place her on a boat, sending her afloat downstream, moving further and further out of sight with each passing day.

As Max entered the pub, his pupils dilated, momentarily blinded, struggling to adjust from sunlight to the dimly lit softness of the pub. He slipped into his favorite booth. The pub was full for a late Sunday afternoon. Max inventoried the faces, recognizing many of the regular weekend clientele, and finding unfamiliarity in others. Angela immediately noticed his presence and made her way through the crowd to his booth.

"Would you like the usual?"

Max looked up and stared at her for a moment. "Yes, thank you. You know, Angela, your eyes are as cerulean as a summer's eve sky." He was matter of fact with his off handed compliment.

"Thanks, Max." A smile emerged across her face, raising her cheekbones even higher. She turned and walked to the bar, returning with his Grey Goose vodka and dash of cranberry juice. As she placed the drink on Max's table, he reached for her hand.

"What time do you get off work today?"

"It's an early day for me, Max. I should be finished by six." Angela let her hand linger within his.

"Would you like to have dinner with me?"

"I would like that very much," Angela said, never breaking the gaze between them. It had been over eight months since she last spent time with Max and she welcomed the opportunity to be with him again.

"Then it's settled. I'll wait for you and we'll make an evening of it." The hint of a smile was struggling to find a place on Max's somber face.

"That will be fine." Angela continued to hold his eyes within hers. "You know, Max, it would only hurt for a minute if you let that smile escape onto your face. It looks fairly determined to succeed." She chuckled, withdrew her hand, turned, and returned to her other customers.

Max laughed, releasing the imprisoned grin and watched her walk away.

Several drinks and several hours later, he closed out his tab and waited for Angela by the front door. Her Calvin Klein jeans highlighted her long legs and graceful stride. Her cashmere sweater matched her blue eyes.

Once outside, he reached for her hand, and they walked silently toward a nearby café. It was too cold to sit outdoors so Max arranged for a window table, that faced Oxford street.

"I'm glad you could join me." Max pulled out Angela's chair for her to be seated.

"It's my pleasure." She slithered into her seat. "Max, you haven't been in the pub for weeks. Even today, you don't seem as energetic as usual. Is something wrong?"

Max took his seat and waited several minutes before responding. Angela hung within the silence and within his steady gaze.

"I never realized how much you see through those eyes of yours," Max finally said as he cocked his head, never moving his eyes from hers. "You are wise beyond your years."

Silence dangled in the air a moment longer before Angela replied. "I don't know if its wisdom or intuition. Maybe it's both. Maybe they're one in the same." She smiled. "I've never thought that chronological age was the measure of wisdom. There are many people that live to a ripe old age but never learn much about themselves or life in general. There are some children I've met that are wiser than many adults. I don't know what makes the difference, why some people never really think or feel much, and why others seemingly think and feel everything." She paused for a moment. "Max, you never did answer my question."

"No, Angela, I did not and I don't intend to. Let it suffice to say that your observations are correct and leave it at that." He withdrew his gaze and handed her a glass of Chateau Mouton Rothschild that the waiter had just finished pouring.

The Unexpected Awakening

They clinked glasses and took a sip of the rich, red, Bordeaux. They silently enjoyed the pleasure of the wine as it slipped past their lips, tantalizing their taste buds. Their dinner arrived. They savored every bite of their steak and lobster, finished their wine, and relaxed. They left the café, arm in arm, strolling slowly, quietly absorbing the cold night air and clear, starlit sky. They headed to Max's flat, to complete their evening of unspoken, knowing pleasure.

THIRTY-NINE

Michael reached for the alarm as it buzzed Monday morning's arrival. It was five-thirty. He decided to get in early after traveling for a week. There would be volumes of work that awaited him.

Christine turned over and snuggled up against his back. "Good morning," she whispered in his ear.

Michael rolled over to face her. He peeked in her barely open eyes and said, "Good morning." He pulled her close to him, embracing her tightly. "I wish I had more time this morning," he said as he rubbed his hand gently across her face and down her side.

"I do too," she sighed, "but, it would be noon before either one of us had our fill of each other. And, besides, you'll need your strength for work today."

"I know," Michael agreed as he began kissing her lips and stroking her breasts. "To hell with it. Work will wait." He pulled the sheet up over their heads.

When they finished, she reached up, nibbled on Michael's ear and said, "I love the animal in you." Michael gave her a huge kiss, and the two of them quickly showered, dressed, and finished getting ready for the day. It was rapidly approaching six forty-five.

"What can I fix you for breakfast?" Christine asked as they walked toward the kitchen.

"It's too late for that. Don't worry, I'll just grab something at the cafeteria and take it to my office." Michael gave her another hug, reached for his briefcase, and made his way to the door. He stopped, turned around, and walked towards the children's rooms. Glancing over his shoulder at her he said, "I almost forgot to give them a good morning kiss."

She listened as Michael roused them, kissed them both good morning and goodbye, then returned down the hall to leave. He gave Christine another squeeze and was on his way.

Elizabeth came wandering down the hall, rubbing her sleepy eyes. "It's time to get up already?" she asked rather than stated.

"Yes, it is, sweetheart." Christine reached down and picked her up. "Let's go get your sleepyhead brother and make us all some breakfast. I'm starving. How about you?"

Elizabeth nodded yes, rested her tired head on Christine's shoulder, and the two of them meandered toward Joseph's room.

# # #

Michael whistled as he made his way down the bank corridors to the cafeteria. Gary Hudson approached him en route.

"Welcome back, Michael," Gary said with a warm handshake. "Successful trip, I hear."

"Thanks, Gary. Yes, the trip went well. I'll be anxious to track the results and success of the programs," Michael stated.

"I'm glad to see that you're in better spirits than before this trip. You had me concerned," Gary said, not wanting to be overheard.

"I know I must have, Gary. But I'm fine now. Everything is fine again," Michael said, still glowing from the weekend.

The change in Michael's demeanor left Gary wondering as he walked back to his office.

"Good morning, Michael, and welcome back," Evelyn said with a welcoming smile. "We missed you."

"It's good to be back. Or maybe I should reserve judgment

until I see the stack of things you have waiting for me," Michael teased as he juggled his cup of coffee and set his plate of eggs, bacon, and pancakes on his desk.

"There's quite a bit, I'm afraid," Evelyn acknowledged.

"Then let's get started." Michael reached for his food. They worked solidly until it was time for his meeting with Gary. The meeting lasted an hour and Michael requested that Susan Richmond be included. She had worked long and hard hours on short notice to help Michael meet the deadlines and pull it all together before his trip. Gary couldn't have been more pleased with the final product and the recap of the rollout. Initial results were positive and trending upward each day. It was decided that Susan would stay involved with the project. She'd assist in tracking results and enjoy the rewards of her outstanding effort.

As Susan and Michael walked back to their offices, Michael turned to her and said, "Susan, I really couldn't have pulled this off without you. You're a tremendous help and I want you to know that."

"Thanks, Michael. I enjoyed it." She shook Michael's hand, turned and walked down the hall.

When Michael returned to his office he asked Evelyn to purchase a gift certificate to Susan's favorite restaurant as a small token of appreciation for the effort and contribution she had made.

Michael brought lunch in so that he could continue making a dent in his workload. His energy was focused and clear. His passion for his work was rekindled. He took a bite of his Reuben sandwich and reached for the pile of mail that Evelyn left on his desk. He thumbed through it until he reached the bright blue envelope with a California postmark, no return address. A bead of sweat formed on his forehead as he withdrew the card from its envelope. He knew the moment he saw the birds on the front, that card was from Heather. He held the card unopened as his fingers began to tremble. He had somehow managed to push the events of last Thursday far into the recesses of his brain, like a squirrel burying a precious nut for later retrieval. Now, reality stared boldly at him from the face of a greeting card. He opened the card and read it, slowly, numbly.

He pictured Heather's face. Echoes of her laughter and love played through him like the melodious sounds of an Itzhak Perlman violin concerto.

His pensiveness was interrupted when Evelyn returned to his office, ready to continue their work.

"Now, where were we?" He regained his focus and the two of them delved into the slowly shrinking stack of work before them.

The hours flew as Michael responded to messages, sent memos, and scheduled meetings. It was after six before either one of them realized the office building had emptied out over an hour before.

"Evelyn, it's late. Why don't you go home? We made solid headway today. We can pick up where we left off tomorrow," Michael said, closing the folder in front of him.

"Are you sure?" Evelyn asked. "I don't mind staying longer if you need me."

"I'm sure. Thanks for having everything so organized and manageable. It made it much easier to tackle. I'll see you tomorrow," he said, indicating it was time for her to leave.

Michael waited several minutes after Evelyn's departure and then retrieved Heather's card from his desk drawer. He read it again, realizing the long reaching consequences of the choices he had made. Now was as good a time as any to call Heather and tell her it was over. There would never be a good time. The sooner it was behind him the better. As he reached for the telephone, his private line rang. Michael jumped with a start from the unexpected sound.

"Michael Amory speaking," he stated as he pressed the flashing button.

"Michael, I thought this might be the best time to catch you." It was Heather. "I wanted to see if you received my card today."

Heather was greeted with silence.

"Michael?" Heather asked. "Are you there?"

His mouth felt as if it was filled with cotton, soft but tightly packed, making it impossible to speak.

"Michael?" Heather repeated with concern in her voice. "I can hear you breathing. Are you all right?"

Finally, Michael gained control and softly replied, "Yes, Heather. I'm here."

"Michael, look." Heather spoke quickly. "I didn't call to upset you and I hope the card didn't either. I just want you to know how much I still value our friendship. We lost control last Thursday but neither one of us meant any harm to anyone. We can't and won't let it happen again but we can remain friends, as long as we keep our distance. Don't you agree?"

"Heather," Michael groped to find the words to convey both his love and his decision. "This isn't easy for me so please hear me out." Silence. "I love you, Heather. I can't deny that. I can't deny the positive things your friendship and support have done for me." A pain began to stretch from behind Michael's eyes to his temples. "I also can't deny that I love Christine and my children. I belong with my family and as much as I don't want to end our friendship, I think that's what I need to do." Michael wrestled with his spinning emotions as he leaned forward, pressing his elbows into his desktop. "The last thing on earth I ever wanted was to hurt you, Heather." Michael's voice began to falter as the pain in his head increased.

Heather knew Michael well enough to know that upon his return to Christine, guilt and remorse would lunge upon him like a hawk on wounded fowl. She also knew that she loved Michael enough to still befriend him. "I understand Michael. This must be so hard for you. Please don't worry about me. You haven't hurt me." Heather remained consoling and concerned. "I'm more worried about you and how you're handling all of this. Did you tell Christine about us when you returned home?" Heather curled her legs up underneath her on the sofa.

The tension in Michael's head and shoulders slowly dissipated. His determination waned, like a spinning top that loses momentum and begins to teeter. "No, Heather. It just wasn't the right time. I figure it'll be easier once I can tell her our relationship has ended."

"Didn't she sense something was wrong?"

"Yes, she asked me several times what was bothering me but I just didn't have the heart to tell her. We had such a wonderful weekend together – the four of us." He stretched his neck in a circle. "It just wasn't the time or place, Heather. I do intend to tell her but I'll know when the time is right." Michael stood up and walked over to his office window and paused before words began to flow unrestrained. He told Heather everything – his struggle, his decision, his renewed commitment to his marriage and family – everything.

Heather listened. Michael unloaded for a while longer, before catching himself.

"Heather, this is crazy!"

"No. Michael. That's what I was trying to tell you. We can still be friends. But, we can never cross the line again. That would tear you apart and your family apart. Friends, we'll always be forever friends," Heather insisted. "I have to run, Michael. I have a dinner meeting with a client. Don't worry. Things will be fine." She said goodbye and hung up.

Michael sat at his desk with the receiver still in his hand. He never expected Heather to understand. He expected her to be upset and hurt, even angry. Instead, she was caring and loving. He knew the relationship wasn't completely over but he thought if he gradually diminished contact, it would fade away, with time. Michael looked at the clock on his computer. It was seven-fifteen. He quickly pressed the button to regain a dial tone and called home. He told Christine he was on his way and would see them shortly. He would make it home before the kid's bedtime.

As Michael prepared to leave, he took Heather's card and placed it in the top pocket of his briefcase, not wanting to leave it in his office. He locked his office door and left for home.

Christine had Michael's dinner waiting for him when he arrived. She'd eaten earlier with Joseph and Elizabeth.

"I'm finally home," Michael said as he came through the door.

"Daddy!" Elizabeth squealed, jumped off the couch, and raced to embrace him.

"Hi daddy," Joseph chimed in as he joined in Michael's home coming.

Michael ate then took turns reading to Joseph and Elizabeth before tucking them both in bed. He returned shortly to join Christine in the den.

"That was quick," Christine commented.

"They were exhausted. Elizabeth fell asleep halfway through the first book so I carried her to her room and Joseph was right behind her." Michael yawned and sat next to Christine on the couch. He pulled her close. "Tell me about your day," he said as they both eased into the couch.

"It was a busy one," she replied, "but they all are. I'm really looking forward to starting law school in the fall." She snuggled into Michael's side. "I'm sure your day was a lot more hectic than mine. How did it go?"

"Actually, I made a pretty good dent in the stacks of messages and work that Evelyn gave me. She's incredible. I don't know what I'd do without her," Michael said. He turned his head so that he was facing Christine and added, "I don't know what I'd do without you." He kissed her.

"There's no need to worry about that." She returned the kiss. "You're stuck with me forever."

FORTY

Max began spending many evenings with Angela. He found her confident, intuitive nature refreshing. She was mature and independent. She made no demands. She had no expectations. They enjoyed their time together fully and then returned to their separate lives.

It was Friday evening. Max and Angela returned to Max's flat after an evening of dining and dancing. He perused his mail while Angela rummaged through his music selection, deciding what to play. He reached for the letter he recognized as Christine's. He hesitated but decided to open and read it.

Dear Max,

I received your letter and I understand. I will not write to you after tonight. I will respect your wishes but please know this:

I will never be able to thank you for all that I have learned through knowing you.

I will always love you – not flesh to flesh, but soul-to-soul - forever.

I wish the following for you:

I wish that someday – you will stand on the mountain and feel the sun again.

That someday – you will dance in the Light – feeling its warmth and letting it heal your wounded heart and soul.

That someday – you will once again embrace your feelings as deeply as your thoughts – and be able to enjoy the beauty of them both.

That someday – you will be free from the past to make choices that will bring you true peace.

It is this that I wish for you – now and always.

Love,

Christine

Max could visualize Christine's face and raven eyes as if she were standing in front of him. He wanted to hold her, to touch, and embrace her.

"What is it Max?" Angela asked as she approached, noticing his distant stare.

"It's everything and nothing," he replied as he folded Christine's letter back in its envelope and placed it in his middle desk drawer. As he shut the drawer, he erased the image of Christine from his consciousness. He turned to face Angela. "I'm thinking of taking a long weekend in Paris. Would you like to join me?"

Angela rested her forefinger on her lips as she thought a moment. "When are you thinking of going? I'd have to see about arranging time off from the pub and finals are in two weeks. So, I guess it depends on when."

"I finish a major project in three weeks. I'll leave the following Thursday and return late Sunday." Max remained matter-of-fact and detached, as if discussing a bus schedule with a stranger. "Just let me know if that will work for you. If not, there might be another time you can join me."

"I'll look into it and let you know," Angela replied with a

mirroring voice. Sensing Max's distance, she added, "I think I'll head back to my flat. I'll let you know about the trip the next time I see you in the pub." Angela leaned up and kissed him on the cheek before departing.

FORTY-ONE

The next couple of weeks were extremely busy for both Michael and Christine. Michael was fully engaged in tracking and reporting the bank's successful new marketing program and Christine was excitedly buried in depositions, follow up, and trial preparation for the Courtney case. Michael had resisted his urges to call Heather as Heather waited patiently for their next interaction, believing it was only a matter of time.

# # #

The following Friday, May 30th, Michael awakened at five. He wanted to arrive at the office early to prepare for a meeting that was scheduled for nine o'clock with Gary, the key people in marketing, and the executives of the bank. The purpose of the meeting was to review the details of the marketing rollout, the first month's results, and the projections of longer-term impact and success of the program. Michael quietly showered, dressed, and left after kissing Christine on the cheek. He didn't want to disturb her since she didn't need to get moving for another hour.

Michael felt prepared for the meeting but as he arrived in the parking lot, he realized he left his briefcase in the bedroom. It contained his notes and comments for his presentation. He called Christine when he reached his office. She'd just finished showering. Despite his best efforts, she'd awakened shortly after his departure.

"Christine, I can't believe it but I left my briefcase at home this morning. Would you mind faxing me the few pages that I need for my presentation from our home office?"

"Sure. I'll be glad to." She reached down and grabbed his briefcase from the floor. "Which ones do you need?" she asked as she placed the briefcase on the edge of the bed and opened it.

"Do you see the top manila folder?"

"Yes."

"If you open it up, there should be four pages of information with my notations in the margins. That's what I need," Michael finished.

"I've got them." Christine took the small stack of papers. "I'll fax them to you right now."

"You're a godsend. I can't remember the last time I forgot my briefcase." Michael shook his head.

"It's probably because you were being so thoughtful, dressing in the dark this morning," Christine said as she tucked the receiver under her chin and headed down the hallway toward their office. "I'll fax them right away. Just let me know if they don't come through for some reason." She paused, then added, "And, Michael, knock 'em dead this morning."

"Thanks. I feel good about it but the notes will make a difference. By the way," Michael added, "good luck with the final preparations for the Courtney trial."

"Thanks. Well, let me get this faxed to you."

"Great. I'll catch up with you later in the day," Michael replied before they both said goodbye and hung up.

She entered their office and faxed the pages to Michael. She returned to the bedroom to replace them in the folder. As she reached to place the folder back inside the briefcase, her hand caught the edge of the briefcase and sent it tumbling to the bedroom floor, spilling its contents across the carpet. As she gathered the array of strewn papers, she noticed the greeting card. The birds on the front caught her attention. She thought it might be a sympathy card Michael had received and saved after her parents' death. She opened it. At first, the words didn't make any sense to her. The card must belong to someone else. Then she reread each word. 'The scent of your skin, the taste of your mouth.' She remembered Heather from the cruise. Could it be her? She stopped analyzing as the words crystallized into nuggets of truth. 'I let the feeling of your love and passion wash over every inch of me.' She doubled over. 'I feel you inside me – still.' The wind was knocked out of her, as if a three hundred pound wrestler had driven his boot up into her gut. She was gasping for air. She ran to the bathroom and vomited. Tears streamed down her face as her stomach retched in the truth of Michael's actions. Her head was swirling, stomach spewing, and heart breaking. She didn't know how long she was crouched on her knees, holding the toilet, before she heard a knock on the bathroom door.

"Mommy, is that you? Are you sick, mommy?" Joseph asked with near panic in his voice. He'd been awakened by the noise.

She raised her head. *"Oh my God, the kids!"*

"Is mommy okay?" Elizabeth asked Joseph as she joined him in the hallway.

Christine mustered every ounce of her energy as she choked back the tears. "I'm fine, kids. My tummy was upset but I'm okay now." She took a long, deep breath. "I'll be out in just a minute. Okay?" Her mind started racing. She could not and would not hurt the children. She had to gain control, at least enough control to make it through the next thirty or forty minutes. She would feed them, make sure they were dressed, and get them to school safely. Then she could fall apart, but not now. As her mind began to clear, another wave of pain overtook her. She retched again but there was nothing left in her stomach, nothing but the deep, aching, bile of reality.

"Mommy, I'm worried," Joseph said, sounding anxious and unnerved.

"I'm sorry. I promise I'll be out in just a minute." She tried to reassure him. Her inner voice quietly whispered, "*You can do this. You must do this. You must. You can. Just think about the children and you can do it.*" She stood up, walked to the sink, and doused her face with water. She brushed her teeth and gargled with mouthwash. She refused to look in the mirror. She knew one glance at her face would eradicate the minute-by-minute survival she was achieving. She had thrown herself on autopilot and needed to maintain altitude as long as she could. She opened the bathroom door and leaned down to embrace her frightened, teary-eyed, children.

"I'm sorry. I didn't mean to frighten you two," she said as she hugged them tightly. Seeing their trusting faces reinforced her strength. If she could continue to focus on the two of them, she could make it through the next minute, and hopefully long enough to get them dropped off at school before crumbling.

She lifted both their chins, looked back and forth between them and asked, "Now that I'm feeling better, what can I make you two for breakfast this morning?"

She could see the tension ease from Joseph's frown and Elizabeth's limbs. A smile began to reappear on Joseph's face as he studied Christine. "Are you sure you're okay, mommy?"

"I'm sure, honey." She gave him a kiss, stood up, and took both their hands to walk to the kitchen. "Should we have our favorite pancakes again?" She felt as if she had stepped completely outside herself and now robotically functioned forward.

"Yes!" they shouted in unison.

"I'm glad you're okay, mommy," Joseph said as he tightened his grip on her hand.

"I'm fine, honey. Don't you worry, I'm just fine," she murmured as she clasped Joseph's hand in return.

She suddenly remembered that it was Friday. She would check with Melanie and see if she and her husband, James, could keep Joseph and Elizabeth for the weekend. It would give her the opportunity to confront Michael without the presence of the children. The couples often took turns having the kids stay over at the other's house for a weekend. It gave each couple occasional time alone and all the kids loved the change in routine. Usually, Christine and Michael would join them Sunday afternoon, spend the rest of the day, have dinner, and then return with the kids. All four of the children seemed to benefit from the additional playtime with one another as they gradually adjusted to the loss of their grandparents.

After breakfast, while Joseph and Elizabeth were dressing, she made the arrangements with her sister. Melanie would pick the kids up from school and bring them back late Sunday. Christine asked if it would be too much trouble for Melanie to drive the children back after dinner on Sunday. Melanie knew something was terribly wrong but respected Christine's privacy. She knew Christine would talk about whatever was troubling her, if and when she wanted to.

"How would you like to stay the weekend at your cousins Chet and Hannah's house?" Christine asked as the three of them piled into the car.

"Really?" Elizabeth's face lit up like a pumpkin on Halloween.

"Yes, really," Christine confirmed.

"Cool!" Joseph added.

"Aunt Melanie will pick you up from school today and bring

you back Sunday after dinner." She was glad to see both Joseph's and Elizabeth's enthusiasm. It reconfirmed that she was thinking clearly, even under the circumstances. As they headed out the back door to the garage, the telephone began to ring. She decided whoever it was, could wait. She couldn't and wouldn't talk to anyone right now.

When they arrived at the school, Joseph and Elizabeth were still glowing with the news of their weekend visit with their favorite cousins. As they hugged and said goodbye, Joseph turned to her and said, "Mommy, I didn't get to say goodbye to daddy this morning and now I won't see him all weekend. Will you give him a hug for me?"

"Me too," added Elizabeth.

Christine's strength began to wane. "Sure. I'll also have him give you both a call at Aunt Melanie's house. Okay?" She struggled to get the words out. She gave them each another quick kiss on the cheek, waited for them to join the other children, then dashed for the door as she burst into tears.

FORTY-TWO

Max and Angela were on their second day of holiday in Paris. Angela felt transported through time as she entered the luxurious grey marble foyer of the Four Seasons Hotel George V., complete with breath-taking chandelier and restored 17th century tapestries. Their suite was a blend of soft blue, mauve and green fabrics, with Louis XIV antique furniture, and impressive artwork from the same era. The bathroom dripped in pink marble. It was elegance and indulgence at its finest. Angela soaked in the sights, sounds, and scents of Paris and the River Seine as if she were a dehydrated flower being watered.

On Thursday, Max had taken Angela to the Eiffel Tower and Notre Dame. Today he would show her Napoleon's tomb and the Louvre Museum. Then tonight it was off to the opera.

They were finishing an early and light lunch at Le Café Marly in the Richelieu wing of the Louvre Palace. As they sipped on their Laurent Perrier Grand Siecle Champagne, Max was suddenly overtaken by a sensation of angst. His body tightened and his brow furrowed. He placed his wine glass on the table, waiting for the sensation to pass but it grew stronger rather than diminish. His shoulders continued constricting.

"What is it Max?" Angela asked, noticing his body stiffen.

Max was silent for a moment while he let the sensation wash through him, trying to identify its source. After an extended silence he said, "It's Christine. Something's wrong." Max spoke as though speaking to himself, oblivious to Angela's presence.

"Who's Christine? What's happened?"

Ignoring her question, Max checked his pockets for his cell phone before realizing he'd left it in the hotel. Without explanation, Max paid the bill and headed back toward their hotel. It was a solid fifteen-minute walk but with traffic, Max knew he'd make better time on foot than in a taxi. Angela followed silently.

Max headed to their suite and reached for the telephone while Angela grabbed a book and sat on the sofa in the adjoining sitting room, knowing not to interfere. Calculating the time difference, Max tried Christine's home number first. He let it ring several times. The answering machine picked up. He hung up without leaving a message and immediately called the law firm.

"Montgomery, McCarthy and Steinberg, may I help you?" David answered the telephone. It was early and no one else had arrived yet.

"Christine Amory, please," Max demanded.

David recognized the voice, the accent, and the abrupt tone. "Mr. Fairchild, Christine has not arrived yet this morning. Would you like to leave her a message?"

"Is she all right?"

David was surprised by the question and the alarm in Max's voice. "I assume she's fine. I haven't heard otherwise." David paused for a moment. "Is there some reason for your concern, Mr. Fairchild?"

Max thought a moment before responding. "Please have her call me as soon as she arrives. I'm traveling but I'll wait in my hotel suite until I hear from her." Max gave David the number for his hotel and cell phone, then hung up without further explanation. Max began to pace back and forth in the room, his hands clasped behind his back.

# # #

David placed the receiver back in its cradle. He glanced at his watch. Christine wasn't late. Nonetheless, he began to worry as he awaited her arrival.

Finally, he saw her as she passed his doorway and headed for her desk.

"Christine, can you come in here for a moment, please?"

She hoped to slip by David's office, unnoticed, until she could get to the restroom and fix her makeup. She knew her eyes were red and puffy and had tried her best to wipe off the streaks of mascara before entering the law office building. She had managed to steal past Tom in the main lobby.

"David, can it wait just a few minutes?" She inquired from the hallway, maintaining the distance between them. "I'd like to put my things down on my desk and stop by the restroom if you don't mind."

"Sure, Christine. Just stop by when you're finished." Max was right. There was definitely something wrong.

She set her briefcase on her desk and walked to the restroom. She looked in the mirror and hardly recognized the face staring back at her. She looked swollen, exhausted, and defeated, as if she'd just finished four rounds in the ring with a world champion boxer. She wanted to cry again but refused. She stared into her own dark eyes. At that moment, her survival instinct awakened within her. Nothing and no one would destroy her. Not now – not ever.

This was different than the death of her parents. She couldn't wrap this reality up in a nice little package labeled 'Accidental Death – Out of My Control – No Responsibility Attached – Only Acceptance and Integration Required.' No, this was different. This was a box that had unanswered questions written all over it. Why?

How? When? Who? Heather from the cruise? How could he? Why didn't she know? Why? Why? Why? This pain had the familiarity of grief's clutching grip, but it was deeper. It ripped her to the bone. It was a black hole, a dark, spiked vortex. This wasn't just a wave of grief to ride out, accept, and integrate. This needed to be understood. She was an integral part of it – somehow responsible and accountable for its existence. The feeling of inner peace that once filled her now seemed a mirage, a distant memory from another life. Anger, slow rising but steady, made its entrance, meshing wildly with the pain, churning a chaotic pattern of emotion within her.

She washed her face, touched up her makeup, brushed her hair, and straightened her business suit. She glared at her reflection. Her face had been transformed from devastation to determination, from reaction to resolution. She walked briskly to David's office.

"I'm sorry to keep you waiting, David. What can I help you with?" She was pleasant but very matter-of-fact.

"Please, shut the door, Christine."

She reached behind her and closed his office door. David motioned for her to sit down. He leaned forward, his chin resting on his wrapped fists. He studied her carefully. The only telltale signs of her earlier demeanor were her puffy, bloodshot eyes.

"Christine, Maximilian Fairchild called here around twenty minutes ago. He was concerned about you. He's in Paris and waiting in his hotel suite for you to call him back," David continued, studying her every motion.

She looked past David to the window behind him. She bit her lower lip and twisted her neck to one side as if struggling to hear something in the distance. She sat in that posture, without moving, for several moments before answering.

"He never ceases to amaze me," she mumbled and then turned back to face David. "I'll be fine, David. It will take time, but I *will* be fine."

David was at a loss. "What is it, Christine? What has happened?"

"I wish I knew," she said softly as she looked down at her folded hands on her lap.

"Christine, I don't want to intrude but whatever it is obviously has you upset." David tried to regain eye contact but she kept her head down, her eyes lowered.

David's private line buzzed. He ignored it. Christine remained silent, struggling to find a way to communicate without surrendering to her emotions. There was a gentle knock on David's door.

"I'm busy right now," David said through the closed door.

"I'm terribly sorry, sir," Tina Ludlow responded without opening the door. "Is Christine in there with you? I have Mr. Fairchild on the line and he's quite determined to speak with her."

David waited for Christine's response.

"I'll take it," she said without hesitation, rising from the chair. Remembering David, she turned to him and asked, "Is that all right, David? I won't be long. I promise. I just don't want him to worry needlessly."

"It's fine Christine. Why don't you take it in here? I'll get some coffee and make the rounds. Take your time." David grabbed his coffee mug, walked around the desk, and put his hand on her shoulder. "Whatever it is, Christine. I hope it works out the way you need it to." David didn't wait for her response. He went out the door and closed it behind him. He directed Tina to put the call through to his office.

"Hello," Christine said into the receiver as she maneuvered her way around David's desk.

"Christine, why didn't you call me? I left word with---."

She interrupted. "Max, I just got in and David was giving me your message when you called again. I was going to call you as soon as he gave me your number." She paused a moment and continued, "Max, how - how in the world did you know something was wrong? I - I - just don't understand how you--- "

It was Max's turn to interrupt. "I sense when something happens to you. It was the same with Rachel. For whatever reason, I just know." Max's tone switched from disturbed to caring. "So tell me, Christine. What is it?"

She didn't know how or where to begin. Max waited, sensing her struggle. "Max, it has to do with Michael."

"Is he all right? Don't tell me..." Max thought that death in double doses was overwhelming enough, but a triple dose?

"No, he's fine," she interjected. "Max," her voice faltered, "Michael is having an affair. I-I..." That was all she could manage.

"Ahh," Max sighed, understanding the magnitude of her desolation. He closed his eyes and visualized her face, grief-stricken, swollen eyed, Christine. "I understand," he said as he focused on her image. "Christine, you'll be all right. You are strong. You will find a way to make it through this." Max grew silent as his visualization grew stronger. He was mentally connecting to her, feeling her pain.

Christine remained silent, sensing his strength, and compassion. Finally, she murmured, "Max, thank you."

"No thanks necessary. I'm sure you'd rather not talk at work, so I'll let you go for now. Call me later when you can. I'll be in and out but will call you back when I receive your message and you can also try my cell."

"I don't know when that will be, Max. I made arrangements

for the kids to stay at my sister's for the weekend so I can confront Michael alone. I can't even begin to think what this weekend..." Her voice faded as reality crashed in on her again.

"He doesn't know that you know?"

"No, I found a card this morning. It - was..." She couldn't bring herself to relive the details.

"Shhh. save your strength, Christine. You'll need it for other things, not for explaining details to me." Tenderness cuddled every word that Max spoke as if he had reached through the telephone, pulled her close, and embraced her.

They were comfortably silent with one another before saying goodbye.

# # #

Max slowly hung up the telephone and stood for several moments before walking to the window.

Realizing he'd finished talking, Angela closed her book, got up from the sofa, and walked into the master suite. Max was staring out the window, his back to her. "Max, is everything all right?"

Max replied without turning to face her. "No, Angela, it isn't, but in time, it will be."

"Max, this woman, Christine, who is she?"

Max was silent for several moments before answering. Still gazing out the window, he replied, "She is a rare and precious flower. She is a constant amidst the chaos."

Angela grappled with the meaning conveyed by Max's strange choice of words. "You're in love with her, aren't you Max?" Angela's tone was curious not accusatory.

Max turned away from the window and looked directly at Angela. He spoke softly, with conviction. "I don't choose to be 'in love' with anyone, Angela. 'In love' is self-centered and narcissistic. 'In love' lasts only as long as people's expectations of another are placated."

"So you don't believe real love exists?" Angela questioned as she sat down on the bed.

Max turned back toward the window. "Real love is when we love and understand someone for who 'they' are, not for what we want, need or expect them to be for 'us'."

Max began pacing again. Beams of light streamed through the window and surrounded him as he proselytized. "True love isn't needy, demanding, and selfish. It is an appreciation and respect for the differences as well as the commonalities."

He stopped, turned, and seated himself next to Angela on the bed. "You see, Angela, most people want someone else to fulfill something they lack in themselves. As a result, most people that are 'in love' have unfair and unreasonable expectations of a partner. Over time, they find themselves blaming the other person for their unhappiness rather than learning to be happy within themselves. So, in answer to your questions, no I am not 'in love' with Christine."

"Wow," Angela chuckled, "that was the longest and most philosophical 'no' I've ever heard." She smiled then took a serious tone. "Okay, Max. You're not 'in love' with her but you do love her, don't you?"

Silence hung in the air.

Max glanced up from the bed and looked out the window again. "I suppose I do."

"Then why aren't you with her?" Angela wasn't threatened or disappointed. She had no expectations of Max other than to enjoy her time with him. She knew there wasn't a future with him, only moments in time.

Without hesitation, Max replied, "Because, Angela, she doesn't belong with me. She belongs with her husband and children. Her life is across the ocean and mine is here. It's as simple as that." Max stood up and pulled Angela up beside him. "Now, let's go. Paris awaits us."

# # #

After Christine hung up the phone with Max, she found David down the hall, reviewing some information with one of the law clerks. She approached them and said, "Thanks, David. I'm through in your office. When would you like to meet to discuss the final issues on the Courtney trial?"

Surprise skipped across David's face. She was noticeably more composed. "You're welcome, Christine. We can meet now if you have everything ready. If not, we can meet this afternoon when I return from my luncheon appointment."

"Now will be fine." She managed a tiny smile. It was a first since placing herself on autopilot earlier in the morning. "I'll get my files and meet you back in your office." She turned, headed to her desk, grabbed her briefcase, and returned to David's office.

As she walked away, David mused that her phone call with Max must have helped in some way. What had devastated her so deeply? How did Max know? What did Michael think about Max? Questions whizzed through David's mind like cars buzzing on a busy freeway as he excused himself from the law clerk and walked down the hallway to join Christine in his office.

David closed the door behind him.

"Christine, we were interrupted when you were about to tell me what happened." David's concern and curiosity had won the war against his usual lack of intrusiveness.

"David, it's very personal and I'd rather not discuss it, if that's okay." Christine avoided eye contact as she spoke.

"Christine, we've known each other almost seven years and I consider us friends as well as colleagues. You've been through a lot these last few months. Whatever has happened, you can confide in me."

Confusion blanketed her face, as she looked David in the eyes. "David, I - I don't know how to talk about it without getting emotionally upset. I appreciate your concern but I just can't talk now – maybe later." Her voice was soft but strong. "I think it will help, David, if I get back to work. I'll have the weekend to deal with my personal life."

"I'm sorry, Christine, I didn't mean to intrude." He stood up, walked to his office door, opened it, and returned to his desk. "Now, what do you have there?" David asked pointing to the folders.

They worked through the morning and resumed again after David's luncheon meeting. Preparing for next week's trial was a welcomed escape for Christine. They finished around four. She returned to her desk to finish revisions and check messages. Her direct line rang while she was editing one of her documents.

"This is Christine," she answered, placing the receiver on her shoulder, holding it with her chin, and stretching her neck, so she could continue blazing away on the computer.

"Hi hon. I wanted to see how your day is going and check on when you might be leaving. The weather is so nice that I thought we might have a picnic dinner with the kids to kick off the weekend." Michael paused, waiting for a response. "If you have to work late don't worry about it. It was just a thought." Silence. "Christine, are you there?"

"I'm here," she said through tight lips. Her throat constricted as she tried to contain her looming rage.

"What's wrong?"

She battled the urge to detonate on the telephone and replied coolly, "Just having a hectic day. I should be home by six or so. I really have to finish this up, Michael. Trial starts Monday so I'll see you at home later." She hung up before Michael could probe any further. She knew this was not the time or place for her to let loose on him.

Christine's shortness shocked Michael. Even on the craziest of days, she was never this abrupt. Michael was surprised he hadn't heard from her throughout the day since she would normally have managed a call over lunch to see how his presentation went. The pressure of her upcoming trial must be building. Michael wondered what life would be like once she finished law school and became an attorney.

FORTY-THREE

When Michael walked in the back door of his home from the garage, Christine was waiting for him. She was sitting on the couch in the den, crying, with Heather's card in hand. Michael took one look at her face. "Christine! What is it? What's wrong?" A chill ran down his spine when he saw the card in her hand. "Oh," he said with a reserved, sarcastic tone, "another love letter from Max?"

"How dare you?" She stood up and faced Michael, seething anger boiling to the surface. "You son of a bitch! How dare you open your mouth in judgment of me after sleeping with someone else? How could you? It's Heather from the cruise, isn't it?"

Michael was dumbfounded. He caught a glimpse of the card that she was waving wildly. He nodded yes.

Her anger turned to rage. "And all this time I've been trying to explain how innocent my relationship is with Max. I wrote him several letters - and you - you had the nerve - the unbelievable nerve - to be upset with '*me*'?" She was screaming now and could not stop the words spewing from her mouth. Filled with hurt and consumed with fury, she threw Heather's card at him. "And all this time – not a word – not a hint – not one iota mentioned about your relationship with '*her*'? How could you do this, Michael? How? Why?" Tears began tracing patterns down her enraged face.

Michael bowed his head and stared at the floor. Heather's card seemed like a mountain size boulder that just crashed down on his home, his happy family, loving wife, and innocent children crushed beneath its weight. "Oh, God, Christine. It's not what you think. We were just friends. It just happened - only once. That's all. It was a mistake. It's over. I'm so sorry." Michael reached to embrace her.

"Don't you touch me!" She shouted as she jerked away. "It wasn't what I think? Like sleeping with someone just happens?" she yelled as she stepped back further out of Michael's reach. Her head was spinning, and her ears ringing from the sound of her own screaming. She fell back onto the couch, staring at the floor, her feelings writhing within her.

"Where are the kids?" Michael asked looking down the hallway.

"There at Melanie's house for the weekend," she snapped.

Michael bent down on one knee, trying to gain eye contact. "Christine, I don't blame you for being angry and upset. I feel awful. I love you. I love Joseph and Elizabeth. I can't picture my life without all of you. You have to believe me, Christine. It's the truth," he pleaded.

She was silent a moment, then whispered, "Truth - what a joke! Like you really know what the word means." She continued as if talking to herself, "What a fool I've been - always trusting - always believing - never questioning anything. Unbelievable! I've been such an idiot. Heather must have gotten a good laugh over that one. How absurd! This is all so absurd."

Michael stood up, reached down and pulled her off the couch. He gently held her arms and looked into her distant gaze. "Christine, please look at me." He waited a moment. "Please." She glanced up to meet his eyes. "Christine, I love you. I made a tremendous mistake - one that I don't know if you'll ever be able to forgive but there's no doubt in my mind or heart of how much I love you and want to be with you."

"Let me see," she said in a mocking tone, "you love me so much that you slept with someone else. Umm." Then she glared at Michael and said, "That kind of love, I can live without." She pulled away from him, marched out of the den, grabbed her purse, and stormed out of the house slamming the door behind her.

She got into her car, pulled out of the driveway, and drove away. Within a block, the deluge of pain, tears, and anguish gripped her insides. She drove to her favorite spot in the nearby park, doing her best to control the emotional whirlwind gaining force within her. She pulled into the parking lot, turned off the engine, and put her head on the steering wheel, letting the irrepressible tornado of emotions rip through her, turning her upside down, pulling her inside out, and leaving her in pieces. She sobbed until she had no tears left. Darkness had replaced dusk when she raised her head and looked outside. She decided to walk. The evening air was cool with a gentle, spring breeze blowing.

With each step that she took, her ability to think returned. She couldn't believe that within a span of several months, she had lost her parents and Michael had an affair. How? Why? How was she going to survive all of this? She was learning to manage the grieving process for her parents' death. It was slow and painful but she was making progress. She had developed the ability to grieve each of them separately and together. She had learned to accept the pain of their loss as well as the joy for all the well-lived memories.

How could she accept the situation with Michael in the same way? Her parents' death was an accident. She had no part in it. It was out of her control. She had no responsibility or accountability to consider. But this? This was an event that involved the living, which demanded understanding and action. The death of her parents was an unforeseen calamity. The outcome was determined and unchangeable. Michael's infidelity was voluntary. It destroyed the blind trust she had in him and initiated a painful process of redefining her relationship with him. This outcome was unknown and uncertain.

She began to slowly realize the similarities between her parents' sudden death and Michael's infidelity. Both life events created consuming emotions of pain and emptiness, both involved loss, and both would take time to process. Above all, both required a response. The more she thought, the more she realized once again, that she was free - free to choose her response. She was free to remain angry, accusatory, and distant. She was also free to understand and forgive. She knew, deep in her soul, that in the long run, the first path would leave her empty and unfulfilled; the latter would eventually bring her inner peace and wholeness. The more she thought, the more her choices and their potential consequences loomed before her. She realized whatever her choices, they would have far reaching effects, not just for herself and Michael, but also for Joseph and Elizabeth. The choice that would be best for all must be best for her.

She couldn't consciously walk away from her marriage, blaming Michael and never looking deep inside for the reason "why". She knew the 'right' path to take but it was far from the easiest. The 'right' path meant dealing with her emotions but not being consumed or ruled by them. It meant being open to Michael's thoughts and feelings, facing her own shortcomings, and accepting the reality that faced her. It would be so much easier to lay blame rather than to seek understanding, so much easier to be angry rather than to forgive, so much easier to cease caring rather than to continue loving.

Her mind started spinning. Was her friendship with Max the final straw for Michael? Had Michael grown tired of her constant exploration of other men even if they were just friends? She now realized how naïve and emotionally immature she'd been for so many years. Why hadn't she seen what she was doing? How could she have been so blind? Why didn't Michael understand the recent changes in her? Why didn't he understand that she was finally aware of what their marriage could be? Why now? Of all the times over the last eight years, why now? And why did he make love to Heather? Christine could understand if he was a friend to her. Maybe Heather had awakened things in Michael the way that Max had in herself. But how could Michael take the monumental leap from friendship into Heather's bed?

Her racing mind suddenly ceased as another physical wave of reality roiled in her stomach. This was real. Michael had touched Heather, kissed her, made love to her. She dropped to her knees, buried her face in her hands and rocked back and forth. She couldn't bear the thought of his intimacy with another woman. She vomited.

# # #

After Christine walked out of the house, Michael fell onto the couch. He laid his head back, and closed his eyes. How did his life become so unraveled? A year ago everything was fine or at least recognizable. Christine had gradually changed over the last few years but since the cruise she had nearly become a stranger. So had he. He thought about the comfort and solace he found in Heather's friendship. The relationship he shared with Heather was special and different from anything he ever shared with Christine. If only he hadn't crossed the line. If only he hadn't made love to Heather. He hadn't planned to. It just happened. It seemed so right at the time. Besides, if Christine hadn't been involved with Max, he never would have pursued the friendship with Heather. He didn't want to hurt Christine. He didn't want to hurt Heather either. Michaels' mind replayed scene after scene over the last several months – moments with Christine – the death of her parents – moments with Joseph – moments with Elizabeth – moments with Heather. Exhaustion overcame him. Michael shifted from drifting thoughts to fitful sleep.

It was close to midnight when Michael was awakened by the sound of the back door opening. He stood up and went to meet Christine. Her pale face greeted him, her eyes almost swollen shut from crying.

"Oh, Christine," Michael said as he reached for her. This time, she welcomed his embrace.

Michael held her tightly while she whispered in his ear, "Why, Michael? I need to understand why. Please, just tell me why."

"Christine, you've changed so much. I felt so alone. She is – was – a friend that just listened to the things I was struggling with. It just helped to talk." Michael found it difficult to articulate and defend his actions.

"But, Michael. Why didn't you talk to me? Why didn't you tell me that you were talking with her? I understand friendship, but why did you make love to her? That's what I don't understand. I've had male friends but I never in a million years would consider sleeping with them. I thought, I really thought..." Her voice trailed off as emotion swelled within her.

"Let's sit down and talk," Michael said as he led her by the arm back to the couch in the den. "It wasn't about the sex, Christine. It was about the friendship. I didn't anticipate it or plan it. It just happened. It was a mistake and I regret it. My god, do I regret it."

She looked straight at Michael and asked, "Do you love her, Michael?"

Michael blanched. He wasn't prepared for that question. He knew he should be, but he wasn't. She read the look on his face and answered for him. "You do love her. I can see it in your eyes. Oh, my god!" She was equally unprepared for the truth.

Michael's back stiffened. "Well, you love Max, don't you?"

"That's different. I never slept with him. Don't bring him into this," she retorted.

"If you hadn't let him into our lives, this never would have happened. You cheated too," Michael snapped. "You may not have gotten into his bed but you got into his heart and let him into yours."

Anger was slowly creeping into both their voices. Christine closed her eyes, composed herself and thought, 'Take the high road, Christine. Find a way to get at the truth and deal with it. You can do this. You can do this.'

Then to Michael she said, "Look, Michael, this is painful for both of us. We need to deal with the truth. No more lies, just truth. I'll start. Yes, I love Max, but I don't love him like a lover or spouse. I love him as another human being, period, end of statement. I've told you before that he could be a seventy-year-old woman and I would still love him the same way. I never wanted him as a lover. Don't you understand the difference?" She stood up and began pacing. "If anything, I'm grateful for all that I've learned from knowing Max because it opened my eyes to so many things."

Michael stared at her as she spoke. Her words echoed through him but did not take hold. She paused, took a few steps and then looked at Michael. "I learned that I don't need you in the same way I once did when I was insecure and frightened of life but I love you all the more as my partner in life." She took a few more steps, then stopped, turned, and returned to Michael on the couch. She sat down next to him and took his hands in hers. "Michael, don't you see? All of this has happened for a reason. It's meant to make us stronger and better." Her eyes began to sparkle with hope.

Michael was stunned. He could understand the ranting, raging woman from hours before, but this one? Who the hell was she? Where were her words coming from?

Before he could say anything, Christine continued, "Oh, Michael, I'm sorry for all that I haven't been to you over the years." She reached toward Michael and embraced him. He sat motionless, remaining silent.

Loneliness filled him. Noticing Michael's distance, she asked, "Michael, what is it? You seem unhappy rather than relieved." She implored, "Please, talk to me; tell me the truth, no more lies, Michael. Just talk to me."

Michael hesitated then unloaded. "All right, Christine, I'll talk to you. Are you listening to yourself? Here you are with all the answers again. You have it all figured out and now we can just move forward as if everything will be all right because of your 'big awakening' – your new ability to see and understand things." Michael spoke softly and deliberately, amazed at the total honesty rolling off his tongue. "Christine, from the moment I first saw you on campus, I loved you. I believed you were the one for me and I was the one for you. I've given you all of me over all these years. I believed in you and I believed in us."

Michael stood up. It was his turn to pace. "Now, I question that belief." Michael looked at the floor as he walked, hands clasped behind his back. "I knew back then that you didn't love me the same way that I loved you but I was patient because I knew the insecurities that drove you. I was patient because I loved you and believed that in time, we would be on the same page." Michael sat down next to her and took her face in his hands. "But,

Christine, instead of ending up on the same page, we've ended up in different books and in separate libraries." Michael swallowed hard and continued, "When we just live each day, sharing things with the kids, I think everything will be all right but then there are moments like this, when I realize I've grown more distant by the day. I just don't know if we'll ever be close again, if I'll ever really understand you again."

Each word that Michael spoke, brought clarity and validation to the internal struggle he'd endured for so long. He had shared these thoughts and feelings with Heather but never dreamed of telling Christine.

She listened as each word pierced her like a dagger, penetrating her heart with each truthful hit. She wanted truth, painful as it was. She reached out to Michael and they held each other.

"I agree with you Michael that we want to be close and walk a shared path. We just can't expect to be taking the exact same steps or walking at the same pace all the time." Christine tried desperately to reach him. "We need to understand and appreciate the differences between us. Michael, you are the one I want to share life with – you – only you."

Michael held her gaze. "Christine, what you're saying is true but please, please, tell me this." Michael groped for an answer that would change the reality staring him in the face. "How can you share life with someone that you don't understand? How do you share life when your partner has found a road that you can't seem to get on?"

"Michael, I believe we can grow close again. It will just take time. Please, promise me you'll give it time," she pleaded as she reached to embrace him again.

Michael ached for the wife he lost and the inadequacy he felt for the woman she'd become. Christine wept for the pain she had caused Michael in the past, for his confusion and transgression, and for the uncertainty that lie ahead.

It was late. They were both exhausted. Michael had his arm around her shoulder as they walked to the bedroom. She curled up on Michael's chest and they fell asleep.

FORTY-FOUR

Christine awoke to sunlight peering through the bedroom window. She stretched, smiled, still half asleep, and then realized her eyes were nearly swollen shut. She rolled over to see if Michael was still sleeping. His side of the bed was empty. The memory of yesterday's discovery rattled her like the aftershock of an earthquake, leaving her shaken and disoriented. Life as she knew it was gone. Nothing was the same. Her parents were dead and Michael had slept with another woman. How could they put the pieces of their marriage back together again? She was tired and the road ahead seemed unbearably long. The strength and courage she displayed the night before seemed to evaporate like the morning mist in the light of the new day. She felt sad, angry, and overwhelmed.

She couldn't and wouldn't, deny or ignore the pain and anger, but she refused to wallow in them. Her feelings were vital to the core of life itself. Internalizing and integrating those feelings were up to her. No one else could help her. It still came back to choice.

She glanced out her bedroom window at the blue sky and bright morning sun. It was another day. The sun was shining. She was alive, and someday all of this would be a past memory, rather than a present, painful reality.

She showered, snuggled into her bathrobe, and went looking for Michael. The house was quiet. She checked on the patio but he wasn't there either. As she walked into the kitchen, she noticed a note lying on the kitchen table. She picked it up.

Dear Christine,

I woke up early and couldn't fall back to sleep. I had breakfast and decided to take a walk to clear my head. I'll be back before noon.

Love,

Michael

Michael walked for hours, slowly, deliberately, trying to sort through his thoughts and feelings. The sun began to warm the crisp, morning air. The scent of spring surrounded him and filled his senses. Buds poked their tiny heads out from winter slumber, like green polka dots on a white backdrop. Michael's mind drifted from thoughts of Christine to thoughts of Heather. There was no question in his mind that Christine was a wonderful woman but he didn't understand her anymore. The last couple of weeks he had deluded himself into believing that the old Christine had returned. Last night had pummeled Michael with the reality of Christine's changes. Christine's mind went places that he'd never been. She handled her feelings in ways he didn't recognize. The new Christine was a stranger to him and she was here to stay. Maybe Christine was right. Maybe it would just take time for him to feel close to her again. He grew tired when he thought of the energy and effort it would take. He loved her deeply and treasured the life they had with Joseph and Elizabeth. Even so, he wasn't sure he was capable of being her true partner again.

Michael thought about Heather and how comfortable and natural he felt with her. There was no strain or effort to understand her. Heather had grown to know Michael inside and out. He decided to call Heather from his cell phone before returning home. He needed to tell her that everything was finally out in the open, that their friendship needed to come to a complete halt, rather than coast to a gradual conclusion.

It was getting late. Reluctantly, Michael made his way back towards his car. He got into his car and rested his head against the back of his seat. He dreaded saying goodbye to Heather. She made him feel so alive and complete. He reached for his cell phone and dialed her number. Michael knew it was early in California. He didn't care.

"Hello," Heather answered sounding wide-awake.

"Heather, it's Michael."

"Michael, what is it?"

"Christine found your card. Everything hit the fan last night."

"Oh my God, Michael. How did she take it?"

"At first she was enraged and crushed. She left the house for hours. When she returned, she was totally different. She was calm and forgiving." Michael relived the moments in his head as he spoke, never changing his tone.

"Well, that's good, isn't it? I mean you wouldn't want her to stay angry would you?"

"No, but Heather, it's just that. Well, I..." Michael paused, knowing he shouldn't continue.

"What is it, Michael?"

"I know that I have to end my friendship with you if my marriage is going to work but it hurts like hell to do it."

Heather thought a moment before responding. "Michael, I truly just want to see you happy. I understand."

"I wish it were that simple." Michael's stomach knotted. "Heather, I don't want to drag this out." His stomach knotted tighter. "I'll never be able to thank you and I'll never forget you or your friendship and love."

"Michael, please just remember that I'm here for you. If things get tough and you just need to talk, I'm only a phone call away. Promise me you'll remember that."

Michael was quiet for a moment before he replied, "I promise."

"Well, I guess this is it," Heather whispered.

"Yes." Michael paused for several moments longer. "I love you, Heather."

"I love you too, Michael," Heather said as she hung up the receiver.

As he said goodbye, Michael felt the gaping hole Heather's absence would create.

Heather sat quietly, letting her conversation with Michael slowly sink in. All she wanted was for Michael to be truly happy – wherever that may lie. She reached for her running shoes before sadness devoured her.

# # #

Michael returned home depressed and withdrawn. Christine was sitting on the patio. She was trying to understand things from Michael's perspective. She understood the emotional abandonment Michael felt. She understood the confusion it had created. She didn't understand how he found someone else and never mentioned it. She also didn't understand Michael's jump from emotional need to Heather's bed. She never anticipated Michael's lack of honesty and openness.

"I'm back," Michael said as he opened the patio door and interrupted her train of thought.

"Oh," she said, startled as she turned to face him. "You look exhausted."

"I guess I am," he replied after a moment of silence. "I didn't sleep much last night. I think I'll try to nap for a little while if you don't mind."

"I don't mind."

Michael turned and headed for the bedroom, closing the patio door behind him.

She continued to sit with her head back, feet propped up, facing the sun. She felt Michael's depression and assumed it was a result of his remorse and guilt. That it was the outcome of his longing for Heather never crossed her mind or heart.

As Michael lay down on the bed, sorrow swept through him. Life without Heather would be empty. Life with Christine would be exhausting. He quickly succumbed to sleep's welcomed escape.

While Christine sat thinking, she suddenly remembered she'd promised to call Max. She slowly rose from the patio and walked inside to the den. She searched for the number Max had given her for his hotel in Paris. She dialed, planning to leave a message, and was surprised when Max answered.

"Maximilian Fairchild," he said as he picked up the receiver.

"Max?"

"Christine?"

"Yes, hi. I...I didn't expect you to be in," she fumbled.

"Christine, I'm glad that you called. How are you?"

"I'm okay. That's what I called to tell you. I remembered that I promised to let you know how things went." She didn't know how to explain all that had transpired. She heard a woman's voice in the background speaking to Max. Embarrassed, Christine said, "Oh, Max, I didn't mean to interrupt you. I just wanted you to know that everything is all right here so you don't need to worry about me."

Angela had returned from a shopping spree and didn't realize Max was on the telephone when she came striding into the hotel suite, sporting her Paris bargains. Max pointed to the telephone and returned to his conversation with Christine.

"You're not interrupting me, Christine." Max paused, sensing her anguish and uncertainty. "I hear the words dripping from your lips but they do not match the feelings pouring from your heart."

Christine remained silent. Max's presence emerged before her as if he was looking straight into her eyes and taking her hand in his. "You may be right," she responded. "I thought the death of my parents was the toughest thing I'd ever face. It was – until now. But this, this is so much harder in different ways." She grew quiet. He waited for her to continue. "Max, it's not easy to be honest with myself but I have to be. I understand why Michael felt alone and turned to someone else. What I still don't understand is why he made love to her. I…." Her voice softened as flashes of Michael and Heather sprung upon her.

"Shhh," Max soothed. "It's all right. I understand. Christine, as I said before, you will come through this just fine. The journey will be long and painful but you will find the strength and answers you need to make it through. Live the way you need to live, and make the choices you feel are right for you to make."

Christine waited for Max to go on.

"Christine, others may not understand, but you do not answer to others. You answer to life itself." Max's voice faded as his mind reached further and further into the abstract.

"Max," Christine interjected, "I won't be calling or writing you anymore." She paused. "It's the right thing to do for me, and for you." She sighed. "I know you understand."

"Indeed." Max hesitated a moment before continuing. "I do understand."

"Thank you, Max. I can never…," she started.

Max interrupted. "Further words are not necessary. It is what it is. Take care of yourself, Christine."

"You do the same Max."

As Angela finished getting dressed for dinner Max walked to the hotel window. Paris looked magnificent at sundown. The sun marinated the Paris skyline in purples and pinks, and seasoned the Seine River with gold. The Eiffel Tower sprayed shades of platinum and silver, while tints of blue and grey rippled around the Arch de Triumph. Peacefulness slowly spread across Max's regal face. He understood the energy and butterflies he felt all those months ago on the cruise. Christine was someone capable of touching his abandoned soul. She would remain a part of him – forever.

# # #

Michael didn't rouse until late afternoon. When he opened his eyes it took him several moments to get his bearings. Within minutes, the cloud of depression returned and cast its shadow across him. He slowly rose. He struggled to make his way to the bathroom. Each step felt heavier than the one before. He showered, hoping to wash away the darkness that clung to him. Though lessened, depression still draped around him as he toweled, dressed, and walked to the patio.

Christine was lying on her back on the chaise lounge, legs extended, arms resting by her sides, eyes closed. She had returned to the patio after her conversation with Max. She felt sad and peaceful, sad that she would never speak to Max again, peaceful because it was the right thing to do for the right reasons. Max had served an incredible purpose in her life, whether he ever realized it or not. She could never repay him. He would always be a part of her. Now she must live her life, each moment of each day, actualizing all she had come to know, the best she could. She heard the sliding motion of the patio door and turned to face

Michael.

"Feel better?" Christine asked.

"A little, I guess," Michael replied. "I was thinking," he said, staring downward, "maybe it would be good for us to go to your sister's tomorrow and have dinner with everyone like we usually do. I miss having the kids around."

"Michael, don't you think it would be better if we took this time alone to talk about everything? I miss the kids too, but we can't talk openly about this when they're around. It wouldn't be fair to them." She watched Michael as she spoke, hoping he'd agree.

Michael sat down on the chair next to her, eyes downward, shoulders slumped. "Christine, I really don't know what else there is to talk about. Last night we pretty much covered it all, don't you think?" He glanced up to meet her eyes. "I told you how sorry I am, Christine. There's nothing else I can say."

"Michael, I'm not looking for more apologies. I'm just trying desperately to understand *how* this all happened. I just want to listen and understand the best that I can."

"Christine, I'm exhausted. I just don't have the energy to talk about this anymore right now. Can you understand that?"

Christine knew Michael well enough to know that pressing him for further conversation was futile. She could see the strain in his eyes and the tiredness in his movements. "Okay, Michael," she replied. Internalizing her decision, she added, "Why don't we just order a pizza tonight. I'll give Melanie a call and let her know that we'll be coming over tomorrow. I'm sure the kids will be thrilled." She reached for Michael's hand.

He tightened his hand around hers and said, "Thanks."

# # #

The next day Michael was sociable and pleasant with everyone at Melanie's house, but remained distant from Christine. Joseph and Elizabeth received most of his attention. Christine understood. She realized it would take time for them to work through all of this and regain their closeness. She was willing to give it all the time and energy it would take.

She surprised herself by not telling Melanie what had transpired. She was used to sharing everything with her siblings, especially Melanie and John. Since the death of her parents she had become noticeably self-contained and decided this was something she needed to work through on her own – at least for now.

FORTY-FIVE

It had been almost a month since Christine discovered Michael's infidelity. The weeks since had passed slowly for them both as they groped their way through each day. They agreed they needed counseling and after researching their options, had decided on someone that had been highly recommended in the area. Their first appointment had been two weeks ago.

David and Christine worked industriously to finalize preparations for the Courtney trial. The day finally arrived when it began.

# # #

Michael struggled through the morning at work. His head ached. Late morning, he took a break from analyzing the market data delivered to his office several hours earlier. He walked to his office window. Denver's skyline shimmered in the morning sunlight.

Michael's mind wandered through the last few weeks since Christine discovered his infidelity. He felt renewed being with his children, but longed for closeness to Christine. How could she forgive him so easily after discovering what he had done? He wished she were still angry or at least still struggling. Instead, she was acting like some superhuman or saint, not a martyr, just a saint. That was tough enough. He didn't know how to find the feelings he once had for her. The more he thought, the more his head began to throb.

"Michael." The voice from Michael's office doorway startled him. He turned back from the window. Gary entered Michael's office and pulled both chairs out from in front of his desk. He sat in one and pointed to the other for Michael to join him.

"What is it, Gary?"

"It seems that we have a problem in Los Angeles concerning our marketing promotion. We have two branches that started out strong but reported unusual decreases this past week."

"I've been analyzing the latest reports all morning and haven't gotten to the LA market yet." Michael reached across his desk for his reports. "The others seem to be gaining momentum, not losing ground."

"That's what concerns me. Something's going on and I don't like it. The sudden trend downward doesn't make sense, especially when the other three branches in Los Angeles are going gangbusters. I wondered if you'd mind taking a quick trip out there. I wouldn't normally ask you to travel again on such short notice but since you were insistent on handling the rollout, I thought you'd be the best person to get on top of this, and fast, before it escalates." Gary stood up and walked to the window. "I'd like you to leave tomorrow morning if you can work it out. If not, then Wednesday will be fine. You can spend Wednesday and Thursday at the Rodeo Drive branch, spend Friday at the Century City location, and if need be, spend the weekend and finish up early the following week. Just take the time you need to get to the root cause of this."

Michael was speechless. Flashes of Heather, his last visit, Christine's reaction, ripped through his mind like a bolt of lightning.

"Michael?" Gary probed noticing Michaels' apprehension.

"Yes, I – uh- this is so unexpected," Michael equivocated, but recovered. "I'm thinking of the various aspects we'll need to look at in order to determine the source of the problem. I'll give Christine a call and let you know if I'll leave tomorrow or Wednesday." Michael stood up and turned toward Gary. "Gary, I just realized Christine will be in court all day. I'll speak with her this evening and leave you a voice mail. Will that work for you?"

"Why don't you give me a call at home? I'll be in all evening. That will give us both some time to think about strategy. We can talk further then." Gary looked at his watch, stood up, and walked toward the door. "I have to leave for a meeting with our Finance Department." Glancing back he added, "Thanks, Michael. I appreciate your flexibility with this. There's no one else I feel comfortable sending. I'll look forward to your call this evening."

Michael said goodbye then returned to his office window. Anxiety clawed at him as thoughts of Heather swept through his mind.

FORTY-SIX

Christine and the children anxiously awaited Michael's entrance. She cooked his favorite, pork roast, scalloped potatoes, and French green bean casserole to perfection. Joseph and Elizabeth helped set the table. Candles stood at attention in the center, guarding the centerpiece of white roses.

"This is fun, mommy," Elizabeth stated as she put the final touch on the table.

Christine turned from the sink to face them. "Great job you two. Thanks for the help." A sense of awe overcame her as she focused her attention fully on her children. She stood in silence, letting the sensation fill her. It was the same feeling of connectedness that she first experienced months ago as she listened to Dulcie Taylor's music, observing the fall scenery. It was a sensation of completeness, wholeness. She experienced more of these moments, in varying degrees since. Whenever she stopped, focused her attention, and appreciated the moment at hand, the sensation would return. This morning on her way to court, she felt it as the sun poured over her. She felt it now with Joseph and Elizabeth. She realized that it was love - pure, simple love - a reaching out, a movement toward and into, someone or something outside oneself that created the feeling. It was stopping long enough to appreciate and love the person, place, situation, or moment - just as it is.

"Mommy," Joseph interjected, "daddy's home!" Joseph and

Elizabeth scrambled to the door to greet him.

Michael greeted each of them with a hug and kiss. He walked into the kitchen with Elizabeth hanging around his neck and Joseph by his side. Michael made his way to Christine and kissed her.

"Something smells good," he said as the scent of the roast teased his nose.

"All your favorites," she replied, surprised at Michael's good spirits. "Everything's ready when you are."

Michael and the kids scurried to the bathroom to wash their hands and returned to a table full of steaming delights. Elizabeth said grace and dinner began.

Michael asked Joseph and Elizabeth about their day.

Joseph scrunched up his face and thought a moment. "We read a lot about animals today." His lip turned up in further thought. "Oh, yeah, and no one fought on the playground today either." Joseph smiled at his parents, picked up his fork, and resumed eating. Then he looked at Michael and asked, "What about your day, daddy?"

"Well," Michael began, "it was very busy. And, I have to go out of town again." Looking at Christine, he tried to explain. "Gary didn't give me a choice on this one. Apparently, we have some serious problems in two of the Los Angeles branches. He wants me to leave either tomorrow or Wednesday and come back sometime early next week, allowing enough time to analyze the issues and correct them."

Her stomach twisted. Her appetite disappeared. Her clenched jaw struggled to stretch wide enough to speak. "Isn't there someone else who can go instead of you?"

"No, Gary insisted I'm the only one for the job. He expects a call from me this evening to finalize details." Michael apologized.

"I'm sorry, Christine. I really don't have a choice."

She nodded curtly, not wanting to discuss it further in the children's presence. "Well, I guess you have to do what you have to do," she added. Each word snapped at Michael like the jaws of a piranha.

Michael reached across the table and took her hand. "I really am sorry, but we can talk more about it later, okay?"

"That's fine," she murmured without looking at him.

"I'll miss you too, daddy," Elizabeth said, noticing her mother's drastic change in demeanor.

"We'll keep you company mommy," Joseph added trying to diffuse the tugging tension that filled the room.

Realizing her impact, Christine looked, first at Elizabeth, then at Joseph. "That's right. We'll think of all kinds of fun things to do together. Now, let's finish dinner so we have time to read before bedtime."

Elizabeth's shoulders relaxed. Joseph lessened the choking grip on his fork and continued eating. Michael squeezed Christine's hand and said, "Thanks." She felt like a shaken bottle of champagne that was ready to explode.

Later that evening, after the children were fast asleep and Michael had finished his call with Gary, Christine coldly questioned, "Are you going to see Heather while you're there?"

Michael joined her on the couch. "I don't plan on it."

"Let me ask the question a different way. Do you *want* to see her?" Before Michael could answer, she added, "Remember, no more lies."

Michael hesitated a moment, then replied, "Yes, I would like to see her." He shifted on the couch. "As I said before, Christine, she is, was, a friend more than anything else. I will miss her friendship but I know I have to give it up if you and I are going to make our marriage work." He looked directly at her. "Yes, I would like to see her but no, I don't intend to."

She thought she would have more questions or want more discussion but instead she turned to him and said, "Thanks for being honest. I'm going to bed." Tears kissed her cheeks as she undressed and slipped under the covers. Michael loved Heather more than she had imagined. She saw it in his eyes. She felt it in his words. She knew it in her heart. She quietly cried herself to sleep.

They woke early the next morning. Michael had an early-morning flight to Los Angeles and she was expected to meet David early at the courthouse prior to the second day of trial. They spoke little as they showered, dressed, awakened the children, ate, and prepared to leave.

As the taxi horn beeped, announcing its arrival, Michael hugged and kissed Joseph and Elizabeth, then turned to face Christine. He reached out and pulled her into his chest. He whispered into her ear, "Christine, I do love you. I always have. I always will." He released his embrace, kissed her on the lips, and headed out the door.

She watched his every movement as he walked to the taxi and waved goodbye before the driver pulled away. Her heart felt anchored to the hallway floor. She stood motionless, engulfed in the distance between herself and the only man she had ever truly loved.

FORTY-SEVEN

As Michael's plane soared toward Los Angeles, he reviewed the recent market data. Thoughts of Christine and Heather intermittently interrupted his concentration. He refused to call Heather while in town. He would resist the urge to see her again. He loved Christine and the kids enough to give his marriage all that he could. Maybe the marriage counseling would help. Barraged by endless numbers and conflicting feelings, Michael surrendered to sleep.

Upon arrival, Michael checked into his hotel, unpacked, and went directly to the Rodeo Drive branch of the bank. When he arrived, Lisa, the branch manager, approached him. She was nearly six feet tall and lanky with chestnut hair that hung down the middle of her back like brown silk drapes.

"Hello, Mr. Amory. Welcome to our Rodeo Drive branch. We've been expecting you," Lisa said as she tossed her mane. "I'll be happy to assist you in any way that I can during your visit."

"Thank you, Lisa, but please call me Michael," he said as he greeted her with a handshake. "Do you have the detailed list of transactions that I requested before leaving Colorado?"

"Yes, sir, I do. If you'd please follow me, we set up Karen's office for you to use while you're in town. She's on vacation this week." Lisa led Michael to a small office set behind the teller area with full view of the branch. "The documents you need are on the desk in labeled folders. I hope this will be satisfactory for you,"

Lisa said indicating Michael's temporary office space.

Michael inspected the area and smiled. "This will be just fine. Thank you again, Lisa." Michael started removing his suit jacket to place it on the back of the desk chair but reconsidered. "Lisa, I'm going to grab an espresso at the corner coffee shop before getting started. Can I bring something back for you?"

Lisa hesitated, surprised by his thoughtfulness. She smiled and replied, "A white chocolate mocha with skim milk would be great. Thanks."

"You got it," Michael said over his shoulder as he headed for the door.

The breeze and early morning sun felt refreshing to Michael as he joined the other people walking and jogging down Rodeo Drive. Suddenly he stopped dead in his tracks as he recognized Heather heading in his direction, out for a morning run.

"Oh my God, Michael!" Heather exclaimed. She was as surprised to see him, as he was to see her. "What are you doing in town?"

"I was asked to look into a few things in our Rodeo Drive branch," Michael explained. He couldn't help but notice how sensational Heather looked without any makeup and with her hair in a ponytail. "Uh," he fumbled, "how have you been?"

"I've been fine Michael." She looked into his eyes as sweat trickled down her face. "More importantly, how have *you* been?"

Michael glanced away as he shifted his weight from one foot to the other. "I'm getting by okay. Some days are tougher than others but overall I'm hanging in there." He looked back to catch her eye. "Heather, it is so good to see you but I really need to get going."

"Me too," Heather replied without hesitating, feeling the awkwardness of the moment for them both. "Take care of yourself

Michael," she added with a soft smile before turning and resuming her run.

"You too," Michael said as he watched her take one stride after another away from him.

When he returned to the office he had difficulty concentrating. He had much to accomplish in a short period of time. He would think about his chance encounter with Heather later. He immersed himself in the folders, analyzing one account after another, identifying trends and evaluating possible threads that bound them together. The hours flew by. Michael was energized by the discoveries he made and actions to be taken.

Lisa poked her head into the office. "Michael, Heather Smithstone is on line one for you. Would you like me to take a message or do you have time to speak with her?" Lisa stood tall, straight backed and at attention.

Michael glanced at his watch. It was four fifty. The branch closed at five. "I'll take the call." He glanced up at Lisa and added, "Thank you, Lisa. Today's been very productive and I appreciate your assistance. You pulled every document I needed. It helped not having to chase down information.

Lisa's posture heightened further at Michael's compliment. "I'm glad you found what you needed. When would you like to discuss your findings?"

"Will you be available at ten o'clock tomorrow morning? I'd like to analyze a few more things before we meet."

"That will be fine," Lisa said before gliding away.

Michael reached for the telephone. A knot of apprehension curled his gut.

"This is Michael," he said as he pushed line one.

"Michael, it's Heather." She sounded tentative. "I was so surprised to run into you this morning." She hesitated. "I wish we could talk."

Michael pressed his elbows firmly on the desk. "I would love to see you Heather but I don't think that's a very good idea for either one of us."

Silence.

"I understand," Heather said fighting back the tears. "Well, please take care of yourself Michael."

"Wait, Heather," he said before she hung up. "Maybe we can see each other one last time to say goodbye in person."

"Oh Michael," Heather sighed. "I really would like that." She took a deep breath. "Where would you like to meet?"

"Any suggestions?" Michael asked.

"There's a little Italian place just around the corner from the hotel you stayed at before. Their food is terrific. How does that sound?"

"That sounds fine. I'm staying at the same place." Adrenaline surged throughout Michael's body drowning out the caution that screamed inside of him.

"I'll meet you in the lobby of your hotel at six. Will that work?"

"That will work. I'll want to go to my room, drop off my briefcase and call home before we go. I'm going to tell Christine that we're having dinner." Michael almost believed the sound of determination in his own voice.

"That's fine, Michael. I'll see you then," Heather stated before hanging up, hoping Michael wouldn't change his mind.

Lisa poked her head around the corner to Michael's temporary office. "Michael, I'm just about finished for the day. Would you like me to show you how to lock up?"

Michael managed a slight smile as he hung up the phone. "No, Lisa, I'll leave with you. I have some information to review tonight in my hotel room and I'll be back here bright and early tomorrow."

They gathered their belongings and walked out the front door together. Lisa turned, set the alarm and locked the door behind them. "Michael, do you need a ride to your hotel? It would save you waiting for a taxi."

Michael thought for a moment. "No. Thanks anyway, Lisa. I prefer to walk. Several blocks of exercise will feel good after sitting most of the day."

"Well, if you're sure," Lisa confirmed.

Michael nodded.

Michael watched as she sashayed down the sidewalk. The sun coiled through her coffee colored locks as they swung in the light breeze. Michael turned and began his walk back to his hotel. The sun was hot, the breeze limited, but the fresh air felt as sweet and refreshing as a mint julep. Michael surveyed his surroundings, the hurrying faces, the honking horns, impatient traffic and storeowners locking up their expensive merchandise. Walking down Rodeo Drive was like stepping into a contemporary painting, each person, place, and thing, painted to perfection with exacting detail. Men and women alike periodically checked their reflections in store windows as they made their way down the busy street. Michael wondered how many body parts of the passerby's were original, not implanted, sucked, tucked, or lifted. Gorgeous was a prerequisite, he thought, to live in this city and walk this street. He amused himself with observations and found himself at the front of his hotel in what seemed like two minutes rather than thirty.

Michael entered the hotel lobby and moved toward the elevator when he noticed another gorgeous face approaching him. It took him a moment to recognize that it belonged to Heather.

"Hi, buddy," Heather said sheepishly. Her peach, silk dress clung to her deeply tanned body revealing every curve. Her long auburn hair was pulled up loosely in a clip, accentuating her exquisite facial features. "I'm a little early but hoped you wouldn't mind."

Michael grinned. "I don't mind. Let me run up to my room and give Christine a call before we go."

"Okay. I'll wait right here." Heather walked to the circular bench that surrounded a center of small tropical trees and flowers. She smiled and waved him away, anxious for his return.

Michael shook his head from side to side, the left corner of his mouth tilted up just slightly. "I'll be back shortly." The sound of his heart pounding almost deafened him by the time he reached his room.

He unlocked his door, entered his room, turned, locked the door and leaned his back against it with a sigh. Desire soared within him. He felt as if he just entered an emotional Indy 500 – excitement, fear, thrill, angst, all fighting for the lead in the race. One emotion would gain momentum until another would rally its energy and burst past the first, his gut clinging to each twist and turn. And so it went, for two, three, maybe five minutes. Michael stood with his back to his hotel door, immobilized, overwhelmed, unsure.

He finally took a deep breath, laid his briefcase on the desk and reached for the telephone before he lost courage. First one ring, then another, then a third, the answering machine picked up. Michael realized that Christine and the children must have gone out for dinner. He left a brief message, "Hi. I'm finished for the day and going out to grab some dinner. I'll call you when I return. It won't be late. Love you." Click. He hung up, grateful for the momentary escape from confrontation. Michael walked to the bathroom, doused his face with cold water, put on a fresh shirt, grabbed his suit coat, and headed back downstairs.

As he exited the elevator, he beamed at the site of Heather. It felt so good, so right, to be with her, here, now.

Heather took his arm and they exited the hotel lobby.

"It's just a block up the street." Heather pointed to the right. They walked arm in arm toward the restaurant, feeling natural, at ease, at home, as if they'd been together for years and this was just another evening out.

They entered the restaurant and Michael digested the inviting ambiance that surrounded them. The place was small but impressive. Red linen tablecloths, matching napkins and floating candles amidst a bed of fresh rose petals adorned each table. This family owned Italian restaurant had just celebrated its seventy-fifth anniversary. Gold framed pictures hung throughout the restaurant, exhibiting past and current stars that had dined within these same walls.

The current owner sported hawk-like features and coal black hair with just a hint of gray. He wore a crisp, black tuxedo with a red shirt that matched the linens. He bowed, smiled and walked them to a cozy booth in the back corner. He stood back, waved his arm for Heather to enter, then gave the same gesture for Michael. As he handed them their menus, he looked from one to the other and politely asked, "Are the two of you celebrating any special occasion this evening?"

They blushed. Michael answered, "Yes, friendship."

The owner nodded in understanding, handed Michael the extensive wine list, and departed. Heather and Michael looked at each other, raised their empty wine glasses, and toasted one another. "To friendship!"

They dined in delight with Ruffino Classic Chianti wine, fresh oyster appetizers, veal parmesan for Michael, eggplant for Heather, and homemade Italian bread piping hot from the oven accompanied by fluffy whipped honey butter. They ate slowly, savoring every bite. They talked, sharing every thought. Music by Andrea Bocelli played in the background as they immersed themselves in the soft candlelight and succulent feast.

Michael came alive with every wanton look, every word spoken, every sip of wine taken. He watched as Heather sensually wrapped her lips around every forkful of food, becoming more aroused with each bite. They were finishing their second bottle of wine and examining desert menus when Michael noticed the time. It was eight-thirty. The hours had passed like milliseconds.

"Heather, I didn't realize it was getting so late. I promised I would call home before the kids went to bed. We'll have to pass on dessert. I need to get back." He reached across the table and gently pulled Heather's hand into his. "This has been one of the most enjoyable evenings of my entire life. Thank you." He inched her hand toward his mouth and kissed it.

Heather smiled. "It's been 'the best' evening of my life." She gently blew him a kiss across the table. "Back at'ya, buddy." Sensuality dripped from her pores like hot fudge, inching its way over ice cream, melting everything in its path.

Michael motioned for the waiter, handed him his American Express card, left a handsome tip, and turned to Heather. "Shall we?" He tilted his head in a motion for them to leave.

"Regretfully," she paused, "we shall."

Michael stood first, took Heather's hand as she gracefully exited the booth. He wrapped his arm around her waist as they walked through the restaurant toward the door. The owner bowed and inquired, "Was everything to your satisfaction?"

"Everything was delicious," Heather replied.

"Perfect," Michael added.

"I'm very pleased that you enjoyed yourselves." He winked and bowed again as they departed.

They squinted as they opened the door and reentered the street. The sun, though setting, temporarily blinded them as they emerged from the sensuous cave.

Michael faced Heather. "Heather, would you like me to get a taxi for you?"

"No thanks, Michael. I drove to your hotel so I'll just walk back with you and drive home from there."

When they arrived at the hotel parking lot, they lingered, enjoying each other's presence. Heather leaned into Michael, slowly raised her violet eyes to meet his and kissed him on the lips. "Thank you, Michael, for a wonderful evening." She turned and began to get into her car. She stopped and turned back. "I love you, Michael." Heather slid into her Mercedes and drove off.

Michael stood in place. Between the wine, dinner, sunlight and Heather, he felt dizzy and lightheaded. He looked at his watch - almost nine-thirty. He turned and walked into the hotel, onto the elevator and up to his room.

Michael reached for the telephone and noticed his message light was blinking. He dialed the automated voice mail and found three messages, one from his boss, Gary, inquiring about his day and two from Christine, one from an hour ago and one within the last fifteen minutes. He quickly dialed home first.

"Hello?" Christine answered.

"Hi, Christine. It's me. Sorry it's so late but dinner went longer than expected." He tried to pronounce his words clearly, as if sober.

She heard the alcohol in his lack of articulation. She bit her lower lip. "Oh." She knew. "Did Heather come back to your room with you?"

"No!" Michael exclaimed, insulted, as if even the hint of such a transgression was inconceivable. He calmed his voice. "We just had dinner. I ran into her by chance when she was out running this morning and we decided to have dinner, as friends. Just dinner, Christine." Michael was defensive and obstinate.

She thought to herself, "*He doth protest too much*," but refrained from verbalizing it.

"Are the kids still awake?" Michael asked, changing the subject.

"No, I'm sorry, Michael, you missed them. You know they're usually in bed by eight." She was cool and detached, trying to refrain from over reacting.

"Look, Christine. I'm sorry. What do you want from me?" Michael lashed out. "What the hell do you want from me?" He hated the situation he was in. He hated himself for creating it. Recognizing his unfair backlash, Michael whispered, "I'm sorry, Christine. I shouldn't be barking at you. This is my issue and I have to deal with it. I'm just..." He took a long pause. "I'm just so damned confused."

She remained silent, waiting for him to continue, knowing alcohol usually produced honesty when it involved Michael.

"Christine, it's not that I don't love you anymore. It's just that, well, it's just that I don't love you like I once did. You were my everything, Christine. I mean everything! But then I lost you. You changed. You became someone different. I just don't know." Michael's words and feelings flowed unrestrained. "I don't know how to feel close to you again."

Michael paused, his thoughts and emotions whirling within him like a twirly ride at a museum park that's gone out of control. Christine waited.

"Christine, I love Joseph and Elizabeth and I love what you and

I have with them. I can't picture my life without the three of you. And yet..." His voice trailed off.

She finished his sentence. "And yet, there's Heather and you love her and you want to be with her."

"Yes," Michael admitted without thinking. He continued talking, as if he, rather than Christine, had filled in the blanks. "Christine, I never felt this way before. I mean I felt this way with you, but it was one sided. I waited for the day that you'd love me the way I loved you. But Heather really loves me, Christine. Being with her is effortless. I'm so ha..." Michael suddenly realized that words were pouring from his mouth like water from an opened spigot.

"Happy with her." She finished his sentence again.

Michael remained silent.

"I finally understand," she whispered as the truth tore her heart to shreds.

Sadness swept through them both, leaving them silent and still.

"I am so sorry, Christine," Michael finally managed to mutter.

"So am I," she whispered. After several more minutes of agonizing silence, she added, "I guess it all comes back to choice."

"What?" Michael asked, not able to hear her mumble.

She took a moment, still reeling and numb from truth's brutality. She spoke deliberately, as if in a trance. "Life is choice, Michael. And you have a choice to make. I can't make it for you." She wasn't angry, just honest. "I love you. Michael. I want you to be happy. Only you can decide where that lies."

Michael listened, without response.

"I'm tired, Michael. I'm sure you are too. Let's say goodnight for now." Her voice was frail but loving.

"I love you too, Christine. Goodnight," Michael murmured and hung up the receiver.

FORTY-EIGHT

Michael plopped down on the edge of the bed and put his head in his hands. Nothing made sense to him anymore. His life seemed like a reflection in a shattered mirror - all just pieces and parts - nothing whole. All that he believed growing up had evaporated over the last several months. None of the rules he learned and followed in his youth applied. Where would he go from here? How would he find his way? Why was Christine so understanding? Why now instead of years before? Why, even with her love, did he feel so removed from her? So many questions and no place to look for the answers. Michael sat with his head spinning, oblivious to the knock at his hotel door. The knock grew louder.

Michael lifted his head and strained to identify the unexpected sound. Someone was knocking at his hotel room door. Still in a mild stupor, Michael shuffled toward the door. He opened it a crack and peered out. It was Heather. He opened the door the rest of the way and just looked at her, as if he had never seen her before.

"Michael, you look awful," Heather said as she kissed him on the cheek and ducked under his arm to enter the room.

Michael looked at her and noticed the overnight bag she placed on a chair near the bed.

"You might want to close the door." Heather waived her index finger toward the open door behind him.

Michael reached behind him and closed the door.

Heather walked up to him, put her arms around his neck, and looked into his eyes. "I had a feeling you might need a friend tonight so I packed a few things and came over to keep you company."

Michael stood motionless, unresponsive.

Heather pulled back and looked more closely. "Michael, what is it?"

Michael returned to the bed and sat down on the side. Heather sat next to him. "It's insane," Michael murmured. "I just can't believe my life has become so incredibly insane." His head was in his hands, looking downward at the floor.

"Talk to me, Michael. Tell me what happened."

Michael continued. "Life shouldn't be like this. I never should have met you. I never should have grown so close to you. I never should have fallen in love with you. I never should have hurt Christine. And Joseph, Elizabeth – oh God – the kids."

Heather listened, careful not to interrupt.

"I've tried to be a good husband and loving father. I've always tried to live by the rules. And yet – look at me." Michael paused. "It was all a lie. I'm a fraud." Michael was silent for several minutes. He lifted his head and looked at Heather, his eyes filled with confusion and guilt. "Do you believe in God, Heather?"

Without hesitation, Heather answered. "Yes, Michael, I do. I always have. I believe in a God that's loving and forgiving and a God that wants us to be happy, not guilt ridden, miserable, and full of self-hate." She spoke rapidly. "God created us to happy. He created us to be kind to others but to take care of ourselves. He didn't create us to kill, steal, hurt, or violate others." She rested her hand on his shoulder. "But Michael, you didn't intentionally hurt Christine."

Heather took hold of Michaels' hands and slowed her words, just a bit before continuing. "Michael, you've changed my life in a way that no one else ever has, or could." Heather moved closer to Michael on the bed. "I can't believe God wants you to feel guilty and awful about bringing happiness to someone else's life. It's sad that Christine was hurt and I don't want your children to be hurt but that isn't your intention, or mine."

Michael looked away.

"Michael, did something happen when you called home?"

He remained silent before he lifted his head and turned to face her. "Christine knew we had dinner together even before I could tell her. She just knew. The kids tried waiting up for me but fell asleep before I finally called." Michael's tone was despondent. "Heather, this is all too much for me right now. I'm exhausted and want to sleep."

He stood up, walked to the bathroom, and closed the door behind him. He stripped down to his boxers, splashed water in his face, brushed his teeth, and caught his reflection in the mirror. An unrecognizable image stared back at him. He returned to the bedroom, hung up his suit, walked around the other side of the bed, crawled in, turned his back on Heather, pulled up the sheet, and over his shoulder said, "Goodnight, Heather." He fell fast asleep within minutes.

Heather undressed, climbed into her side of the bed, and curled her naked body up behind Michael, rubbing his back until she also fell asleep.

# # #

Christine hung up the telephone and lay down on the couch. Deep inside she feared this was the beginning of the end but her heart and mind refused to acknowledge the gut-wrenching possibility. Things would work out between her and Michael, she thought. They had to. They loved each other. Their marriage had endured other difficult times. This was an unforeseen obstacle for their love and commitment to overcome. After all, marriage was for keeps, for better or worse, till death do we part. She was determined to remain steadfast. She would overcome her anger and pain. She would find a way. She had to. Any other path would negate all that she believed. She slipped softly into slumber.

# # #

Max awoke from a sound sleep and glimpsed at the clock on his bed stand, two-thirty in the morning. He rolled onto his back and stared at the ceiling. Angela stirred next to him, slightly wakened, then rolled over and fell back to sleep. In the darkness, across the ocean, Max felt Christine's sadness. Her pain swept through him like a ruthless, wintry wind, leaving him alert and concerned. Her gentle spirit and loving face floated within him as he tried to recapture sleep. Hours passed. Max lay awake and resolute - not to interfere.

FORTY-NINE

Several hours later Christine wakened and rubbed her stiff neck. She'd fallen asleep on the couch. Streaks of gold and white flickered into the den through the patio window, signaling the first hint of daylight.

She sat up and checked the grandfather clock in the corner. It was only five o'clock in the morning. She walked over to the desk and pulled out the chair. She switched on the desk lamp, reached in the drawer for some paper, grabbed the nearest pen, and began to write:

Dear Max,

These past few weeks have been the most difficult in my life, even more challenging than accepting the death of my parents. I'm sure it pales by comparison to all that you have endured.

I have come to realize that when life brings us to our knees in pain, when taking one more step seems impossible; it is with the next step taken that we can truly learn to walk. For it is within those darkest moments that our deepest and most defining choices lie. It is in those moments that we can find an inner strength and higher purpose that we never knew existed.

For me, loss as a result of death is easier to accept than loss as a result of living. For you, I am sure it is just the opposite. I find it amazing that acceptance is easier for me when something can't be changed but becomes seemingly impossible when it can. Again, this is probably an absurd statement from your perspective. Loving someone – unconditionally – is, in my opinion, the most daunting challenge we face as human beings. Actually, loving life unconditionally is the ultimate challenge but, within that lies the ability to truly embrace others as "others" rather than reflections of our imposed expectations and judgments. Maybe for you it was not a struggle because you and Rachel were truly soul mates.

I'm rambling because I'm struggling. I know deep in my heart that I should accept and love Michael as he is rather than what I want or expect him to be. At this moment, it is the most difficult choice I have ever had to make. I believe that I must do so not because of anyone's expectations but because it is the right thing to do for the right reasons. I must take the loving route. I realize this path may appear naïve and desperate to many but what others think will never guide my choices again. This is the most conscious choice I have ever made in my life. I do not make it out of fear but rather out of faith in what I believe to be true.

Each of us answers to our own beliefs, to life, or to God, whatever we perceive that to be. For me, I cannot make choices without thinking about the "whole" and my relationship to it. I have come to realize that everyone must reflect upon their personal growth and individual journey to find their own inner meaning and purpose in life.

I want my marriage to heal and become all that I believe it is meant to be. Michael's relationship with Heather might be a necessary part of the process, just as my growth has been *so intertwined with knowing you. I cannot demand that Michael love me or that he choose me over Heather. He must make his choice for his reasons, within his belief system. I know that deep in my heart he loves me and wants to make our marriage work. With understanding and love, I hope he will find his way back home.*

I will close for now, enough reflections for an early morning. I hope your days are filled with the moments that matter most to you.

Forever indebted,

Christine

As she reread her letter, she knew she would never send it. She promised Michael to end her friendship with Max and she intended to keep her word. She realized that writing helped her sort through her thoughts and feelings. It didn't matter if the words were ever read. The act of writing them had served its purpose. She folded the letter, placed it in an envelope, and set it in her personal file. Someday, she thought, she would reread this letter and remember back to this time of incredible challenge. But today, it was time to wake Elizabeth and Joseph and begin a new day.

She stood up, stretched and yawned. Her head grew dizzy and her feet unsteady. She grabbed onto the desk to balance herself and held on tightly until her wooziness passed. She had been pushing herself too hard lately and she knew it.

# # #

Michael woke up to a throbbing headache from too much wine the night before. He was disoriented in the unfamiliar bed, even more unsettled by the naked body next to him.

Heather, being a very light sleeper, opened her eyes at Michael's movement next to her. Michael looked bewildered. "Good morning," Heather whispered.

Michael forced a smile in return while the events of last evening slowly drifted across his foggy consciousness. "I didn't realize you stayed the night," he mumbled.

"I didn't think you'd mind. You fell right to sleep and I was too tired to head back home."

Michael couldn't fight it any longer. He grabbed her in his arms and repressed passion exploded between them. After lovemaking, they wordlessly showered, dressed, and prepared for the day. They moved in perfect harmony, naturally and effortlessly. It was understood that they would spend the rest of Michael's free time in Los Angeles, together.

They breakfasted at a nearby deli before kissing goodbye, wishing each other a good day, and agreeing to meet back at the room after work. That evening they dined early, less wine, more conversation. They returned to the hotel room with plenty of time for Michael to call home before the children's bedtime. Michael reached for the telephone.

"Hello," Christine answered.

"Hello, Christine." Michael's voice resonated with detached confidence. "Are the children there?"

Her stomach buckled. "Is Heather with you?"

"Yes, Christine, she is. Now, are they still awake and can I please speak with them?" he asked with cool insistence.

"Yes, they're in their bedrooms picking out books." Christine's voice grew cold. "Michael, we need to talk."

"I know, Christine." Michael's voice softened. "We'll talk about it when I get home." He hesitated. "We'll talk about everything when I return."

Elizabeth came skipping down the hallway with book in hand. "I picked one, mommy. It's the one with George, the monkey!" she squealed. Michael could hear his little princess in the background.

Christine extended her hand to Elizabeth and handed her the receiver. "It's your father," she said, trying to hide her anger and disgust, but Elizabeth's puzzled face told her she'd not succeeded.

Elizabeth took hold of the receiver. "Hi daddy! How are you? How was your day? When will you be home?" Elizabeth fired questions without waiting for responses.

"Hi princess." A soothing flutter rippled through Michael as he heard her little voice on the line's other end. "I'm just fine. My day was good and I will be home late on Friday. That's two more days." Before Elizabeth could continue her enthusiastic inquisition, Michael asked, "How about you? I called to see how you're doing and to hear about your day."

Elizabeth recited every ounce of minutia that comprised her day. Michael took delight in her storytelling.

"Here's Joseph." Elizabeth handed the receiver to her brother anxiously waiting his turn.

"Hi daddy," Joseph echoed.

"Hey little man, how 'ya doing?"

"Fine." Joseph held the phone tightly to his ear, clenching the receiver in his little hand.

"Anything new?" Michael probed.

"No, not really," Joseph replied. "How about you?"

Michael groped. "No, uh, no, nothing new. Work is going well. I think I'm beginning to solve the problem for the bank so that's good."

"That 'is' good," Joseph agreed. "You want to talk to mommy?"

Michael hesitated. "Sure. You enjoy your book, little man and I love you."

"Okay," Joseph answered. "Here's mommy." He began handing over the receiver, then abruptly pulled it back. "Oh, daddy, I love you, too."

"Me too!" Elizabeth shouted over Joseph's shoulder.

"Thanks, Joseph, and please tell Elizabeth the same for me." Michael sighed and braced himself for Christine.

She took the phone. "We'll talk again soon."

"Look, Christine, I...," Michael began, but she quickly cut him off.

"I love you too, Michael, talk to you later." She gingerly placed the receiver back in its carriage, resisting the urge to hurl it across the room. She took a deep breath, drew a smile from somewhere deep inside, patted the couch with her hand, and said to Elizabeth and Joseph, "Come on you two. Up on the couch, so we can read all about George the monkey."

Elizabeth didn't notice the strain in Christine's smile or voice. She was too excited about George. Joseph noticed but didn't ask. Christine switched gears into autopilot. She would not allow her pain to permeate the children. She would do her best to shelter them from every facet of her struggle. She felt slightly schizophrenic, reading with enthusiasm and laughter while silently boiling and seething with mounting rage.

She read to Joseph and Elizabeth for an hour, each moment an eternity of suppressed fury. She helped them prepare for bedtime, pajamas, brushing teeth, and nightly prayers. Joseph fell asleep quickly. As Elizabeth climbed into bed she turned to Christine. "Mommy, will you rub my back tonight?" Back rubs were Elizabeth's favorite treat next to banana nut pancakes with chocolate chips for breakfast.

"You bet, sweetie."

Elizabeth rolled onto her stomach and pulled up the back of her pajamas, ensuring every inch of her tiny back would feel the calming delight of Christine's nails gliding lightly across her skin. Christine watched Elizabeth as her fingers delicately danced patterns across her petite back. Elizabeth's vulnerability, blind trust, and total dependence poured over Christine, leaving her doused and drenched in reality. Anger swelled within her and rallied its troops to attack. She covered Elizabeth's back, pulled the comforter across her shoulders, kissed her forehead, and walked out of her room, shutting the door behind her.

She leaned the back of her head against the bedroom door, her hand still on the knob, trying frantically to buffer herself from the rage that ambushed her. The battle was on and she wondered if she had the internal ammunition to handle the combat with Michael, much less fight the war.

She envisioned running through the streets, screaming at the top of her lungs, her hands pulling at her hair. A pleasing fantasy, but she knew she couldn't leave the children alone in the house to indulge in such behavior. She began pacing fervidly, frenetically. She strode from one room to the next, out to the patio and back again, circling, circling, unable to think, as fury unleashed its vehemence. The more she circled the more enraged she became.

She pounded toward the desk, fumbled through some papers until she found the name and number for the hotel where Michael was staying. She stomped down the stairs to the basement, picked up the telephone in the laundry room, and dialed the number.

The pleasant speaking receptionist at the hotel was greeted by an incensed voice on the other end of the line, demanding to be connected to Michael Amory's room.

Michael and Heather were lying naked in each other's arms,

watching television and relaxing. When the phone rang, Michael decided he better answer it. It could be his boss, Gary, calling to ask some additional questions.

"Hello," Michael answered with his best professional voice.

"You bastard!" Christine seethed. "How dare you? Where in the hell do you get off dismissing me on the phone like I'm some child that will be dealt with later?" She mimicked Michael's earlier words with vicious sarcasm. "'We'll talk about it when I get home, Christine. We'll talk about everything when I return.'" She continued, barely breathing, rage running rampant. Her voice moved quickly from low and controlled to loud and violent. "What are you thinking? Who the hell do you think you are to unilaterally screw your brains out in LA while the kids and I play house back here in Colorado? Nice wife, nice son, nice daughter. I'll call home when I come up for air. I might be too busy with my whore to make sure I call at a reasonable time. But don't worry, 'We'll talk about it when I get home.'" She was a raving, screaming maniac, unrecognizable to herself and Michael alike. She could hear the gibbering, frenzied words pouring out of her mouth, but was unable to acknowledge them as her own. Who was this bizarre fanatic that possessed her?

Shock and uncertainty swept over Michael as Christine unleashed her verbal assault. This unexpected battle caught him ill equipped and defenseless. He listened without uttering a sound. Heather lay quietly, overhearing every word Christine shouted through the telephone.

"How dare she?" Christine continued. "How dare Heather have the nerve to intrude on our marriage, our family? What a selfish, self-absorbed, uncaring bitch!!"

Michael interrupted her before she could continue her ranting attack on Heather's character. "Now you wait a minute, Christine.

I can understand if you need to vent your anger and frustration on me but I won't stand by and let you attack Heather. You don't even know her."

Michael's protectiveness fueled her rage. "Isn't that touching? You're defending the little tramp. Fine, Michael, have it your way. To hell with you both. You deserve each other." She slammed down the receiver before she could verbalize one more, vile, hateful, contemptible, thought. She slumped down onto the basement steps, stunned and horrified at her display of behavior, mortified at her loss of control, terrified of the demon within her.

Michael stared at the silent receiver in his hand. He slowly reached toward the end table to replace it in its carriage. Without a word, he stood up and began getting dressed.

Heather sat up in bed and watched Michael move through his silent paces.

"Michael, what are you doing?"

"I'm taking a walk."

"Would you like me to join you?"

"I need to be alone." Michael put on his shoes and headed for the door. "I'll be back later." He didn't look back, just closed the door behind him and walked toward the elevator.

#

Christine awoke with her face pressed against the tile on the basement steps. The stiff muscles in her neck and back snapped her to attention. She was momentarily confused at her surroundings until visions of the raging demon flashed within her stirring memory. She clasped her hand to her mouth in disbelief. Maybe it was just a bad dream, a terrifying nightmare. Was she truly capable of such behavior? Where was all the unconditional love that she professed? Where was her belief in choosing to understand and forgive? Her head throbbed; her heart ached.

Shame devoured her. She looked at her watch. It was six o'clock, Thursday morning. She couldn't fathom enduring the day at work and maintaining a positive attitude with the children. She longed to curl up in a tight ball like a pill bug, bury herself under her covers, and stay there until all of this somehow miraculously disappeared and returned to normal. Normal, what a joke.

She jumped as the telephone rang. She stood up and reached to answer it.

"Hello."

"Christine, it's Michael. I owe you an apology," Michael said. "I understand why you are so angry and I don't blame you."

She remained speechless and listened, relieved that Michael was reaching out to her after her outrageous behavior hours earlier.

Michael paused, waiting for her response. Respecting her chosen silence, he added, "Christine, I'm so damned confused. I don't want to lose you and the kids but I also don't know how to end it with Heather. I love her, Christine. She makes me feel that I can one day grow strong enough to be the man I need to be, for you. I know that must sound crazy but it's true. It's so hard to explain but I'm trying, Christine. I'm really trying."

As she listened, she again understood Michael's struggle. Her anger, released, was now subdued, giving rise to remorse. "Michael, I'm sorry, too. I'm entitled to be angry, but I'm not entitled to say hateful things." Her voice faltered. "This is so hard." She couldn't continue.

"I know," Michael whispered. "I know."

Unspoken understanding bound them in silence for several minutes before they said goodbye and hung up. Michael promised to call again early in the evening. She assured Michael that she and the kids would be home.

Michael showered, dressed, and left for his office.

Christine refused to speculate what the rest of Michael's time in California would entail. Whatever it was, it was. She couldn't change it. All she could do was find a way to deal with it, the best that she could. She needed to survive, one minute at a time. She hoped that somehow, someway, Michael would return to her and their marriage would endure. It would be a slow, painful journey, one baby step at a time, one foot in front of the other, but their marriage could survive. She believed they loved each other too much for it not to.

FIFTY

It was Friday morning. The alarm clock beckoned its third summons to awaken Christine, but she resisted its invitation to salute the new day. She rolled onto her back; eyes still closed and reached her right arm to punch relief on the snooze button. She couldn't remember a time she felt this fatigued. It must be the stress, she thought. Then she remembered that both the children had the flu the prior week and she hoped the same bug wouldn't bite her. She extended her legs, opened her eyes, and thought about what lie ahead of her. Michael's plane was due around nine this evening. Her stomach tightened at the thought. How would they even begin to start over after this week? She shook her head. Slowly, she swung her legs to the side of the bed, placed one, then the other on the floor and shakily stood up. Dizziness overcame her. She plopped back onto the bed, trying to regain her equilibrium. A wave of nausea swept through her stomach. It passed as she rested her head back down onto the pillow. She waited several minutes until she felt steady enough to try again. This time, she was successful, still a bit tenuous in her movements, but able to shower, dress, and get the children up and ready for school.

When she arrived at the office, David noticed she seemed pale, almost fragile in appearance. Yesterday, when she showed up at court, she'd looked as though she'd been crying, today, as if she was tangling with a bout of the flu.

"Good morning, Christine. Although by the looks of you, I wouldn't say it's as good as most mornings for you, even though we won the Courtney case yesterday." He looked at her with concern. "Christine, do you feel all right? You are as pale as a ghost and seem a little green around the edges. Maybe you should turn around, head home, and spend the day in bed."

"Don't be silly," she replied. "I'll be fine. Maybe I have a light touch of something, or maybe the trial took more out of me than I thought, but I promise to keep my distance and I won't consider missing the day just because I feel a little off. You should know me better than that, David."

David was somewhat reassured by her good humor. "I know, Christine. You'd have to be on your deathbed to miss work. I'm only trying to point out that sometimes it's better to give your body the rest it needs, when you need it."

Her eyes widened. "Now look who is calling the kettle black, 'Mr. in the office before seven every day and never leave before nine or ten at night', not to mention weekends. As I recall," she paused and placed her index finger on her cheek, as if pondering, "last year you never missed a day of work, even with bronchitis." She cocked her head. "Uhm - uhm."

David cheerfully conceded. "Well, Christine," he said with an exaggerated 'attorney" tone, "I was just giving you solid advice. I never said that I followed it myself."

They both laughed. She turned to go to her office and looked back over her shoulder. "Have a great day, David."

"You too, Christine."

She buried herself in the mounds of follow up work after the quick but victorious Courtney trial. It was midmorning before she decided to stretch and get some coffee. As she began to stand, dizziness again overcame her, pain suddenly pierced her abdomen, and sweat beaded on her forehead. She doubled over her desk, tried to summon Tina, then crumpled into a heap on the floor. Tina heard the unexpected thud and raced to Christine's office, finding her lying on the floor, surrounded by blood.

Tina gasped, grabbed the telephone, and dialed 911, before calling out to David. "David, it's Christine! She's passed out and seems to be hemorrhaging. I've already called 911 and they're on their way."

David dashed down the hallway to Christine's office. Shock and horror hit him as he gazed upon her limp, bloodied body. "Is she breathing?"

"She was a moment ago," Tina replied as she knelt down by Christine's side, again checking for normal signs of breathing. "Her breathing sounds more labored now. Damn it! Where is the ambulance?"

David was momentarily immobilized. He felt suspended in time and space as he helplessly watched Christine slowly lose color as the pool of blood grew around her. "If they're not here in two minutes, I'm taking her myself," David shouted angrily.

"Oh, God, David, she stopped breathing!" Tina screamed. She tilted Christine's head back and began blowing rhythmically into her mouth, pressing on her chest, trying to revive her. No reaction. David pushed Tina aside and began working on Christine.

# # #

Christine watched Tina and David huddled on the floor. She wondered what they were doing. She tried to speak out and get their attention but to no avail. Their backs were to her, as she hovered overhead. How strange, she thought. Warmth and light surrounded her. She could hear her father's voice say, "No, Christine, no. Not yet. Not now." She looked around trying to find the source of the voice but without success. She heard sirens blaring, closer and closer. Now David was screaming, "Please! Breathe – damn it – breathe!"

# # #

Restlessness distracted Max most of the morning and into the early afternoon. Thoughts of Christine pounded his mind with increasing intensity. By mid-morning, he left his office for a brisk, and hopefully, mind-altering walk. He returned frustrated and annoyed. Max had contained his distracting thoughts of Christine for several weeks. Yet now, today, these intrusive thoughts increased in both frequency and force. As Max continued his incessant pacing throughout his office, he looked at his watch, relieved that three o'clock was rapidly approaching. The company's quarterly meeting would begin shortly. He intended to ensure brevity before heading for the nearest pub to obliterate his obnoxious consciousness.

Jane knocked gently on Max's door.

"What is it?"

She opened the door a sliver and peered inside. "I want to let you know that everyone has arrived for the company meeting, sir. They are approximately ten minutes early and wondered if you wanted to start immediately or wait until the scheduled time to begin."

"We'll start right away, I'll be right in." As Jane began to withdraw her head from the office he added, "Thank you, Jane." In spite of his efforts to remain detached, Max found himself expressing more appreciation for all of his employees, especially Jane over the last few months.

Within two minutes, Max initiated the meeting. Harold Trumpeter, the company's Chief Financial Officer, began with a financial overview before each department recapped their efforts over the last quarter. The meeting was short and as it was concluding, visions of Christine assaulted Max's mind. He stood up and excused himself abruptly. "Harold, I'm sure you can wrap things up here."

Max walked quickly from the room with neither apology nor explanation. His pace quickened as he reached his office, slammed the door behind him, and grabbed for the telephone before landing behind his desk. The receiver slipped from his fumbling left hand as the trembling fingers on his right hand began dialing Christine's office.

"Answer the phone, damn it," he shouted into the receiver that continued to ring, one ring, then another, then another. No one racing to answer it, to tell him he was insane. "Answer, damn it, answer!" Max demanded with his hand clenching the receiver and his heart pounding loudly, completely oblivious to Jane's entrance and her shocked, observing silence.

Finally, a faint and tenuous voice answered the line. "Montgomery, McCarthy and Steinberg."

"It's about time!" Max shouted at the unsuspecting female. "Christine Amory, please. Let me speak with her this instant." Max's tone was severe and overbearing, ignoring all protocol.

The barely audible voice on the other end of the line faltered, sputtered, and finally replied, "I'm sorry, she's - uh - she's - uh - not - avail - uh…"

"Put her on the line - now!" Max commanded.

The feminine voice, rattled and intimidated, grew temporarily bold. "I'm sorry, sir, but that's impossible. She's on her way to the hospital." Click - the anonymous voice hung up before more bullying threats lurched at her through the phone line.

Max slammed down the receiver.

Concerned and frightened, Jane asked, "Mr. Fairchild, is there anything I can do?"

Max raised his head and glimpsed Jane's silhouette across the room. "Yes," he said standing upright and pounding his fist on his desk. "Call my pilot. Tell him I need my plane ready to leave for the United States, for Colorado, immediately."

"At once, sir. I'll get right on it." Jane spun on her heels and raced to her office to make the necessary arrangements.

# # #

Tina stood up to let the paramedics through. Christine saw David pumping desperately, breathing continuously on someone lying in a pool of blood. As the medical workers moved David aside, Christine saw that it was she. Visions of Joseph and Elizabeth catapulted through her mind. She began coughing, gasping for air, breathing.

# # #

Hours later, she awoke to a room full of machines, tubes, and lights.

"She's awake," a shadowed face with an unfamiliar voice stated.

She tried to speak but the tube down her throat thwarted her effort.

Her mind was groggy and confused. She must be in a hospital but why? She was at work, felt dizzy. Oh, the incredible pain in her abdomen. She vaguely remembered the sensation of floating in her office while David and Tina worked on her body. How strange it all was. Maybe this was all a dream. She closed her eyes and drifted back to sleep.

The surgeon, Dr. Koster, made his way down the hallway, through the double doors, and to the corner of the waiting room where Tina and David waited anxiously.

"It looks like she's going to be all right," he said cautiously. "We'll have to watch her closely for infection. She's very weak, but

I think she'll be all right, given time." He turned to David. "Any luck in reaching her husband yet?"

"Yes, Michael just received his messages and returned my call. I shared with him what you told us. That Christine had a tubal or ectopic pregnancy that burst. You were doing emergency surgery and I promised to call him back as soon as you gave us an update. He's at LAX waiting for the first flight home. I've made arrangements for Christine's sister to pick up their children at school." David formally recited the information to the surgeon like a soldier following up with his commander. Only focused, purposeful action could combat David's feelings of shock and helplessness.

"I'll call him directly," Dr. Koster stated. "May I please have his cell phone number?"

"Oh - uh - of course." David delivered the number to the surgeon.

"Thank you," Dr. Koster said politely. "I will have someone keep you both apprised of Mrs. Amory's condition. If there are any changes, you will be directly notified. Now, if you will excuse me, I need to call Mr. Amory before I prepare for another surgery." He turned sharply, with military precision, and walked away without further discussion.

David and Tina silently sat back down onto the cushioned chairs they had occupied for the last few hours in the waiting room. After several reflective moments, David turned to Tina and suggested she give the office a call and let them know Christine was out of surgery and doing well. He would call Melanie, Christine's sister.

"Oh, thank God," Melanie sighed with relief. "Thank you. David, for calling and letting me know."

"How are the kids doing?"

"Pretty well, I didn't tell them Christine is in the hospital. I just told them she was busy and asked if I could pick them up from school today." Melanie let out another sigh of relief. "Christine's going to be all right isn't she David?"

"The surgeon seems to think so. They'll need to monitor her closely but she seems to be through the worst of it." David reassured her while doubts of the ultimate outcome hovered over him like a guillotine. David couldn't shake the vivid memory of holding Christine's lifeless body in his arms, trying to revive her, until the ambulance came. This day had changed him forever.

# # #

The surgeon's voice reverberated in Michael's ear as he numbly boarded his long awaited flight home. Each word bounced off his eardrum, heard but not believed. Michael had hung in a state of suspended animation for the past three hours, each minute, taking a day's length, to pass onto the next. "It looks like she'll make it. She's one tough little fighter. It's amazing she made it to the hospital. Her two co-workers, saved her life, kept her breathing until the ambulance arrived. She apparently had few, if any warning signs before her tube burst."

Dr. Koster waited to see if Michael had any questions. "When the tube ruptured, it caused severe hemorrhaging. It also ruptured her uterus. We operated immediately and removed the affected area. Her ovaries are intact." Dr. Koster paused for a moment. "Unfortunately, Mr. Amory, we were not able to save her uterus. I wanted to share all of this with you personally. Her co-workers only know she has made it through surgery and is holding her own, nothing more. We've not shared this news with your wife yet either. She hasn't become fully conscious, plus I feel it would be better to have you by her side when she hears the news." Again, Dr. Koster paused, anticipating questions from Michael, but only stunned silence met the surgeon's patient ears. "Mr. Amory, I understand. This is a lot to take in, especially miles away in an airport. I'll be here when you arrive. Just ask for me at the desk in the west wing of the third floor. We can talk more then."

FIFTY-ONE

Michael bolted past David and Tina as he raced down the hospital hallway to the third floor desk. "Dr. Koster, please," Michael demanded of the attending nurse. "Tell him Michael Amory is here."

"Michael," David said.

Michael spun around. "Oh - David - I - I - didn't see you."

David noticed Michael's glassy, bloodshot eyes, baffled and confused like those of a shell- shocked, wounded warrior returning from battle.

"She's going to be all right, Michael," David reassured him.

"Yes - that's uh - that's what the surgeon said on the telephone," Michael murmured as he stared blankly at the tile floor beneath him.

The inner door swung open and Dr. Koster approached them, extending his hand toward Michael. "You must be Michael Amory." Michael concurred with a nod of his head. "I'm Dr. Koster. Please, come with me." He led Michael back through the double doors and out of sight as David wandered back to the waiting room.

#

The words slammed her. She had lost an unborn child, and her womb, all without warning. She turned her head away from both Michael and the doctor as the reality of their news ripped through her like a scythe, shredding her dreams of more children, annihilating her vision of the future family she envisioned. "Please leave me alone," she whispered through a throat still raw from the tubes they had recently removed.

Michael gently took her hand and squeezed it. "Are you sure? I'll just sit here quietly if you like."

She pulled her hand away. "I'm sure." Her eyes remained cast downward, in the opposite direction. "Please."

Dr. Koster nodded at Michael, urging him toward the door.

"All right, Christine," Michael said as he reached over the edge of the bed to kiss her on the cheek.

She turned away, rebuffing his attentiveness and affection.

"I'll be right down the hall if you need me," Michael whispered before turning to leave the room.

As the door closed behind them, a ruthless wave of grief detonated within her, leaving her gasping and drowning in its tide.

# # #

"It's a natural reaction," Dr. Koster told Michael as they walked down the hallway. "She's been through quite a trauma. You'll need to be patient with her. It may take her a while to adjust. She'll need every ounce of understanding and support you can give her."

Michael kept pace as they walked, his head lowered, eyes glued to the white speckled tiles underfoot. He nodded as the doctor's words registered somewhere in his spongy consciousness. He wished the last week of his life had all been a dream, a reversible reality that would disappear when he awakened and shook his head. He wished he could rewind his life to a time before the cruise and change it all. Michael shook the doctor's hand when they reached the waiting room. He walked blindly past David and Tina to a nearby chair. He curled up in it, closed his eyes, and fell asleep.

David stared at Tina's worn face. "Tina, why don't you go home? I'll stay with Michael for a while and then head home myself. I'm fairly certain we won't be able to see Christine this evening." David checked the time. It was only four in the afternoon but it felt well past midnight. "There's really nothing more we can do here. Maybe tomorrow she'll be up for visitors."

Tina stared blankly at David, too tired to argue, too exhausted to budge.

"I'll call a cab for you."

Tina bobbed her head in agreement.

When Tina was safely on her way home, David returned to the waiting room where Michael snored softly. He began to pace. He longed to see Christine, to watch her breathe, to know she was really alive, still alive, still breathing. He stole past the nurse's station, through the double doors and down the hallway.

With the hallway empty, David slipped into her room. His chest pounded loudly as he entered. He peered across the room at the unmoving, almost lifeless body in the bed, and the unobservable face pointed in the opposite direction. He moved quietly toward the bedside, anxiety climbing with each step taken. Was this Christine? Was she breathing? He felt obsessed, consumed, crazed by the need to ensure she was still alive.

As he reached her bedside, she suddenly awoke and turned, aware of someone's presence. Her puffy, tear-stricken eyes searched to focus on the uninvited intruder.

"Oh – David," she mumbled, still groggy and weak.

"Shh - Christine. Please, don't try to talk. I didn't mean to disturb you. I just had to see for myself that you're okay." He unconsciously stroked the hair away from her face. "Please, go back to sleep." He began to pull his hand away, ready to depart, when she grasped it tightly.

"David, you saved my life," she uttered, the best she was able. Tears tugged at her cheeks as she relived the day's events. She pulled his hand up to her tear-stained cheek and held it closely. "Thank you."

"You gave us quite a scare, Christine," David murmured. "Thank God you're all right." He squeezed her clinging hand.

No further words were necessary. They remained intertwined, hand in hand, for several somber moments.

David rose and gently removed his hand from hers. "You get some sleep, Christine."

She nodded.

David turned and made his way out of her room.

He returned to the waiting area, unnoticed. Michael remained sleeping, uninterrupted as David settled into a nearby chair and welcomed the reprieve of a nap.

# # #

Several hours later, loud voices awakened David. He stretched his cramped legs, neck and back, then turned in the direction of the noisy tumult. Michael stood at the nurse's station next to a stately man David had never seen before.

"Gentlemen," the nurse reprimanded, "this is a hospital. You will need to go outside if you continue talking this loudly. This is no place for arguments."

The stranger in his dark Armani suit and bold yellow tie turned to Michael and said, "She's right. This is neither the time nor place to discuss our differences. Christine is all that matters. Just let her know that I'm here. If she chooses not to see me then I'll leave immediately. Just give her the choice."

David recognized the voice, the British accent, and the unmistakable demanding tone of the stranger.

Michael held his ground. "She's exhausted. She's been

through a lot. Why don't you come back in the morning?"

"Because," Max answered, his patience wearing thin, "I've just flown across the bloody ocean to see that she is all right and I will not wait until morning to do so." Max's voice was beginning to rise again.

"Who called you anyway?" Michael snapped.

Max peered into Michael's tenuous eyes. "No one. I just knew. Now," Max said turning his attention to the nurse, "what room is she in?"

The nurse deferred to Michael.

"Room three twenty-two," Michael retorted. "But I'm coming with you."

Ignoring Michael's proclamation, Max turned and marched through the double doors and down the hallway towards Christine's room. Michael rushed to follow him. David yearned to join the procession but thought Christine would have more than enough to handle when the entourage of two arrived in her room.

"Christine," Max murmured, looking over the edge of the bed at her frail and ghostlike figure. His hands gripped the bed railing.

She stirred, opened her eyes, then blinked several times, convinced she was either hallucinating or dreaming.

"Christine," Max repeated.

Her eyes focused on his. "Max?"

"Yes, Christine, it is I."

"But how..," she began.

Michael interrupted. "Christine, don't strain yourself. I tried to explain to Max that you are weak and exhausted but..."

She glanced at Michael. "That's okay, Michael. Really, it's okay." Looking back at Max she began to ask, "Max, how-?"

Max interrupted this time, saving her from further

verbalization. "I was in a meeting and suddenly knew you were in physical danger. I felt it in every fiber of my being. I called your office; someone said you were on the way to the hospital." Max shifted his stance and took a deep breath. "I arranged for my pilot to bring me here as soon as he could make proper preparations. I had to see with my own eyes that you are all right." His grip lessened on the railing as he softened his tone. "I am relieved to see you are going to be fine."

She reached up to touch his hand. He took her hand in his and held it tightly. He glanced first at Michael, then back at Christine. His voice grew factual and determined. "I didn't come here to intrude or disrupt your lives in any way. I simply had to see for myself, face to face, that you were all right, Christine." Looking back at Michael, he added, "She deserves total happiness and if you don't see to it, I will. Now, my pilot is on standby at the airport. I will be returning to London without further delay." Max took a step back, bowed slightly toward Christine, pivoted, and walked out of her room before they could respond. He disappeared as quickly as he had arrived.

FIFTY-TWO

Two years later:

Christine buttoned her coat, bracing herself for the bitter cold outside. "Come on sweetie," she urged Elizabeth. "We're going to be late getting you two to school unless we get moving."

"I'm all ready," Joseph said proudly as he stood at attention in the hallway, gloves and hat in place.

Elizabeth stepped around the corner from the kitchen, grinning. "Ok, I'm ready, mommy."

"Great, then we're on our way." She shuffled them both out the back door and into the garage.

Christine's stomach twisted with angst. Today was one year since she and Michael had separated and that was after a year of intensive counseling. Both Christine and Michael struggled to face the insecurities within themselves and the devastating events that had impacted their marriage. They loved each other deeply but it was brutal working through the pain of all that had transpired between them.

The children had slowly adjusted to the change when Michael found a three-bedroom apartment closer to work. Christine and Michael handled their separation in a way that ensured the children's protection from guilt and blame. They agreed that Joseph and Elizabeth would spend every weekend with Michael unless he was out of town.

As she dropped the children off at school, she reminded them,

"Don't forget. Daddy will pick you up after school for the long weekend and he has all sorts of fun things planned for you."

They both grinned with delight.

As she drove to her office, her mind wandered through the caverns of change she had endured these past several years. The cave was deep, carved with unrecognizable twists and turns. Her heart and soul had been transformed, forever. There were still many days that she woke up and expected to see Michael lying next to her. There were so many times she would reach for the telephone, longing to hear the reassuring voice of her parents. There were moments she wanted to reach out to Max but she never did. She knew their relationship was meant to vanish, like Max, when he walked out of her hospital room. Everything had its time and purpose.

As she pulled into her office parking lot, she took a deep breath and glanced out her car window at the scene around her. The trees glistened like prisms spraying rays of sunlight throughout the landscape. She took another deep breath and let the feeling of peace rise within her. She reflected on all that she had learned over the last few years and realized how grateful she was, irrespective of her challenges. Her awakening had left her with an unshakable belief in life itself with all that it entailed: joy and pain, laughter and tears, turmoil and peace. She frequently reminded herself that life was a divine process that she needed to trust - it had inherent meaning and purpose - even if understanding the specifics eluded her. She knew it sometimes wasn't what she wanted, needed, or expected it to be, but she always remembered – even in her darkest moments – that she was free choose how she would respond and what she would make of it - each minute of every day.

She checked her makeup in the rear view mirror, added a

touch of lip-gloss, grabbed her briefcase, and exited the car. She looked up at the sky and let the rays of the sun soak deep within her. A soft smile etched its way across her face as the winter wind whipped through her hair.

"Good morning Tom," she greeted as she entered the foyer, brushing the snow from her coat.

"Good morning, Christine," Tom replied with a welcoming tip of his hat. "Have a good day," he added as she reached the elevator.

She paused and turned to face him. "Thanks Tom. I'll do my best." She turned and stepped onto the elevator with the door closing behind her.

David greeted her with an unusual grin as she passed him in the hallway.

When she opened her office door, her heart skipped a beat.

There Michael stood, staring out her window. He turned to face her. "Hello Christine."

"Michael. What -?" Christine began. Her stomach fluttered as Michael walked toward her.

"Christine," Michael pulled her close. "I love you." He leaned his head back and looked into her dark eyes. "I've come to realize that no matter how hard the road ahead might be, I want to share it with you."

"But," Christine interjected.

"Please let me finish, Christine." He kissed her. "I know we still have a lot to work through and probably will for a very long time," Michael continued. "At the end of the day we take ourselves and our issues with us wherever we go and whoever we are with." He kissed her again. "I'm willing to step to the plate, completely and do my part if you can find it in your heart to do the same. I've also come to realize that we must know, understand, and love ourselves before we can ever have a true partnership. We cannot look to someone else to give us meaning and purpose. We must find that within ourselves and accept our partner for who they are, in their own process, with both the similarities and differences."

Christine closed her eyes and soaked in the moment. As she hugged him she thought of everything that lied ahead of them. "Michael, we have both grown and changed so much with all that has transpired. I always believed that if you could just accept me in my difference, we could make it. I also feel that for us to work, we will need to begin from where and who we are today, and not look back to who we once were." She paused, then held his face in her hands so she could look into his eyes. "But above all, I have never stopped believing that we can do it together, and I want nothing more in this entire world."

They kissed. They felt electrified, connected, and at home for the first time in years.

In Fond Memory

I would like to honor my Hospice patients and thank them for touching my life and teaching me priceless lessons. Part of the proceeds from the sale of this book will be donated to Hospice of the Western Reserve in Cleveland, Ohio where little miracles of love happen each moment of every day.

My loving thanks to:

Frank - You taught me to be a quiet and peaceful gardener of the soul. Thank you for sharing with me the secret of grafting, of creating one tree with four different fruits.

Mary - You could speak volumes with your silence. You knew how to hold your own and be strong even though you were physically weak. I will never forget your speaking eyes.

Ethel - Thank you for teaching me that all communication obstacles are overcome by speaking from the heart. Your cherub face, wide eyes, and toothless smile are forever a part of me.

Mack - You showed us all that being charming, charismatic, and spirited is not a function of age but rather a state of being that age and illness cannot diminish.

Florence - Thank you for reminding me of the dignity that always accompanies choice. You closed your eyes and several days later, you were gone.

KJ - You taught me that seventeen months on this earth is long enough to touch many lives and make a difference to all those who you encountered. The soul lives irrespective of brain capacity.

Thank you for your gentle spirit.

Seth - I was honored to be able to read to you in your final hours. Though you were sleeping, I could feel your peacefulness. Your mother taught me that a mother's love and devotion can surpass all boundaries and at times, even keep death at bay.

Jessie - Thank you for showing me that blindness is not so much what people don't see with their eyes, but more what they cannot see with their souls.

Sophie - What a loving and tender spirit you were. Your kind eyes, warm smile, and frail grasp taught me the power of nonverbal affection, the power of love from the tiniest and frailest of flowers.

Willis - There is rarely a day that I don't think of you and smile. Thank you for making me laugh and for bringing such joy to my life. I doubt I will ever meet another person that can swear with such gusto. I love you man…and I miss you…still.

Christine - I will always treasure the parties we planned together and will hold dear the look on your face as you sang along with the guitarist, munching on chocolate chip cookies. You were so refined and dignified; your passion for conversation and company never faded.

James - Though cancer took you quickly, not quickly enough to avoid your suffering. Your courage and bravery were exemplary and left my soul in awe. I will never forget your knowing eyes.

Sarah - It is amazing you held on for several years when others pass so quickly. I am relieved to know that your weary soul is finally at peace.

Roberta – Thank you for your golden smile and positive attitude. You lit up the room more than the fresh flowers you loved to be surrounded by. Your appreciative demeanor never waned.

Dorothy - You were so very tiny. Your son told me how you were born prematurely and you were carried in a cigar box because you were so little. Though small in body, you were feisty in spirit and you carried yourself with such mighty wings of strength.

Georgia - I shall hold you close in my heart and deep in my soul for so very many reasons – your honesty, your passion for food (especially Pepsi, peanut butter cookies and vanilla milkshakes), being known as "granny" to the staff that absolutely adored you, and for teaching me how to make black-eyed peas. I shall be forever grateful to have been blessed with knowing you.

Booker - Thank you for having a smile and laugh that were contagious! You never complained even when the pain was more than we ever could have imagined. You truly had a joyful spirit - even when facing death. I smile every day at the thought of you.

Sadie - Very few of us will ever make it to 107 years old, but you did! Listening to your stories was like stepping back in time, complete with vivid details of sights, sounds and smells of places long ago. Your presence was so dignified and gave such insight to your perseverance and grace.

Jenne - I only had the chance to visit with you several weeks before you were taken off Hospice but I loved reading to you. It was a delight to watch your eyes follow the words that I spoke and your smile when you enjoyed something. I hope beyond hope that you are still doing well.

Nora – My dear, sweet, Nora -it has been over a year since you passed away and it has taken me this long to be able to write about you. I do believe you were an angel on earth. I have never met someone with the depth of emotional capacity that you displayed. I loved how you sang to the movie Mulan, your passion for chocolate chip cookies, your princess dresses and trip to Disney, playing catch with the ball you made of paper and masking tape, reading to you, listening to books on tape with you, and your reference to death as "graduating". Above all, I will never forget your pure and loving spirit, your total love for your mom, dad, siblings, nieces and nephews, your statement of "what kind of daughter acts like that?" when you did nothing more than walk away disappointed that you couldn't have more cookies. You touched so many lives so deeply. We will love and remember you forever.

Ian - Though I only had the chance to visit you several times and never even could hold your eight month old little body because of the tubes for your tracheotomy, your gentleness and warmth shined through with each and every smile. You loved being read to, talked to and sung to. You were so calm and so easily soothed. I loved you the moment I saw you and trust your little soul is resting peacefully.

Malieak - Though I will miss visiting you, I am thrilled that you are no longer part of Hospice! I shall always remember your saucer-size beautiful brown eyes and loving smile. You melt my heart. Grow, be happy, be healthy, be loved.

Michael - I only visited you twice but your sky blue eyes and precious smile will remain in my heart forever.

8057186R0

Made in the USA
Charleston, SC
04 May 2011